PRAISE FOR WINTER RENSHAW

"Winter Renshaw crafts the best romances! She always delivers it all—angst, emotion, and humor. Her books are a true delight."

—Adriana Locke, *USA Today* bestselling author

"Passion. Drama. Angst. Renshaw nails the romance trifecta with her perfectly paced office love affair."

—Deanna Roy, *USA Today* bestselling romance author of the Forever series

"If you're looking for stories that are thought provoking, wildly sexy, and unputdownable, you'll never be disappointed with Winter Renshaw!"

—Jenika Snow, *USA Today* bestselling author

"The queen of contemporary angst knows how to curl toes while breaking hearts! A perfect romance for two imperfect lovers!"

—Sosie Frost, *Wall Street Journal* bestselling author

"Winter Renshaw is the queen of being unpredictable in the best way possible! Angst, chemistry, and all the feels will have you glued to your Kindle."

—Ava Harrison, *USA Today* bestselling author

"Winter Renshaw makes my little dark-romance-loving heart pitter-patter with her fast-paced, sultry, intense thrill rides. Her books are addicting, drawing you in with nail-biting suspense and intimacy so hot I usually devour them in one sitting."

Shameless Book Club

"Winter Renshaw is my go-to author when I'm looking for a book with a sexy alpha male and a strong heroine."

—Claire Contreras, *New York Times* bestselling author

THE *dirty* TRUTH

OTHER TITLES BY WINTER RENSHAW

THE NEVER SERIES

Never Kiss a Stranger

Never Is a Promise

Never Say Never

Bitter Rivals

THE ARROGANT SERIES

Arrogant Bastard

Arrogant Master

Arrogant Playboy

THE RIXTON FALLS SERIES

Royal

Bachelor

Filthy

Priceless (an Amato Brothers crossover)

THE AMATO BROTHERS SERIES

Heartless

Reckless

Priceless

THE PS SERIES

P.S. I Hate You

P.S. I Miss You

P.S. I Dare You

THE MONTGOMERY BROTHERS DUET

Dark Paradise

Dark Promises

STAND-ALONES

Single Dad Next Door

Cold Hearted

The Perfect Illusion

Country Nights

Absinthe

The Rebound

THE *dirty* TRUTH

winter renshaw

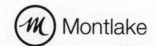 Montlake

Text copyright © 2022 by Nom de Plume LLC

Published by Montlake, Seattle

www.apub.com

Amazon, the Amazon logo, and Montlake are trademarks of Amazon.com, Inc., or its affiliates.

33614082972026

ISBN-13: 9781542038270
ISBN-10: 1542038278

Cover design by Elizabeth Turner Stokes

Printed in the United States of America

For my one and only and our three little everythings

CHAPTER ONE

ELLE

I didn't see God when I died. I didn't meet the Dalai Lama, the Buddha, Mother Teresa, or my beloved grandmother who passed unexpectedly when I was twelve. There was no parade of loved ones lining up to greet me. No bright light or radiant euphoria. Fortunately, no blazing hellscape. Just a simple, no-frills black void.

While the team of doctors who attended to me post–brain aneurysm assured me I was clinically dead for three minutes, not one of them can tell me where I went.

"Why aren't you in the meeting?" My assistant, Leah, perches outside my office door, mouth agape as she double-checks her watch. "It started fifteen minutes ago . . ."

Blinking out of my trance, I close out of my hundredth "near-death experience" Google search of the week, close my laptop lid, grab my files, phone, and keys in one impressive swoop—and promptly spill my lukewarm coffee down the front of my ivory wool pencil skirt.

This is not me. But in all fairness, I haven't been "me" since two months ago, when my life came to a screeching halt—literally—on the floor of my ex's apartment.

Rushing to my aid, Leah plucks a handful of tissues from a nearby Kleenex box before falling to her knees and dabbing the burnt-umber stain in vain.

"It's fine, Leah. You don't have to do that." I take a step back, arms still crammed with meeting materials.

I've been back to work exactly one week, and every time I turn around, I'm met with sympathetic regards and notoriously self-consumed colleagues suddenly jumping at the chance to grab a door for me, refill my coffee, or invite me to lunch like we're old friends due for a catch-up.

That's the thing about death. Or in my case—near death. Not only does it change you, but it changes everyone around you. At least that's what I'm learning so far.

I'm still new at this . . .

Still finding my bearings . . .

Still trying to make sense of everything because the die-hard journalist in me demands all the answers and then some.

Leah rises, examining me with unblinking intensity as she motions toward the door. "I'll phone the conference room and tell them you're stuck on a call . . ."

"That won't be necessary." I straighten my shoulders, drag in a long breath, and gather my composure, because I'm going to need it once I throw myself to the judge-eyed wolves in the conference room.

"You're just going to go in there?" Her confused hazel stare flicks to my coffee-stained skirt. "Like that?"

"As opposed to no-showing?" They're not going to fire me for spilling my coffee. They can, however, fire me on the spot for not doing my job. They've fired people for lesser offenses, and for every sad sap they send packing, there are a hundred more lining the Manhattan sidewalk outside waiting to take their place.

"They'll understand . . ." She worries the inner corner of her pillowy lips. "I mean, after what happened—"

"Leah." I offer a tepid smile and move for the door. "I'm *just* a little late, and it's *just* a stain . . . it's not the end of the world."

"I know, but . . ." She trails after me. *"Maxwell's here."*

I stop hard, my blood cracking like ice in my veins.

For five years I've typed my fingers to the bone for *Made Man* magazine, but the number of times I've been in the same room as our infamous editor in chief I can count on six of them. While the general public knows West Maxwell for his jaw-dropping good looks and larger-than-life persona, those who work for him know him for his rare presence and a reputation that sends most of his drones hiding behind cabinets, files, and laptop screens at the mere sound of his Italian loafers stepping off the elevator.

"You didn't tell me he was going to be in today." I tamp the disappointment in my tone. Leah's nothing like my last assistant, a charismatic type A Columbia grad student who married some Rothschild she met in the Hamptons and peaced out before the ink was dry on their marriage certificate. "A heads-up would've been nice, hon."

She bites her lip. "There was a company email that went out this morning."

"Oh."

It probably pinged my inbox when I was thirty-nine pages deep on some near-death message board thread on this nineties-looking website that was crammed with all kinds of fascinating experiences. Experiences that were nothing like mine.

Exhaling, I pinch my nose. "I'm sorry, Leah. I didn't mean to—"

"I have some yoga leggings in my bag," she says, voice pitched higher, hopeful. "If you pull your blouse over them, maybe they'll think they're just regular leggings?"

It's a thought.

And it wouldn't be the worst option.

I tug one corner of my silk blouse from my skirt—only to stop when I realize it's a crepey mess beyond fixing in this current scenario.

3

I'd need a steamer, at minimum, and even then, those things take time to heat up and—no. There's no time.

Two months ago, I kept a change of clothes in my desk for these kinds of mishaps—not that they ever happened. I was a bit more pulled together preaneurysm. And I was nothing if not prepared. But at some point during my stint in the hospital, they utilized my office as a makeshift space for temps and interns, and the dry-cleaned blouse and slacks I'd always kept on hand miraculously disappeared.

"It's okay," I say to her but also to myself, because it never hurts to hear those words. "It'll be fine."

Stopping at the little mirror by my door, I check my reflection, tucking one rain-frizzed chocolate wave behind my left ear before giving my cheeks a pinch for color. The old me would've had smooth, glossy curls, pristinely lined lips, and a creaseless, fresh-off-the-rack dress. I gather a hard breath and silently wish the hot mess staring back at me all the luck in the world, because she's going to need it.

With my heart in my stomach and the burn of nausea rising up to take its place, I march to the end of the hall, push through the double doors emblazoned with *Made Man*'s masculine-meets-modern logo, and plaster the easiest, breeziest of smiles across my face.

The room turns silent, and one by one mahogany chairs creak as various colleagues twist to take a look at the woman of the hour—she who dared show up late for a meeting with our feared and respected commander in chief. Chin up and shoulders back, I stride toward the only available spot—which happens to be next to none other than Maxwell himself.

"Rough morning?" he asks with an unnerving aquamarine gaze so intense it almost distracts me from the blatant condescension in his tone. In this moment, I silently take back every Photoshop accusation I've ever lodged against this infuriating Adonis. The man is flawless. Truly. Not a single dark circle. Not a square millimeter of texture on his bronzed skin. Not a tooth out of place or a wrinkle on his white dress shirt. Sex appeal wafting off him like a fine cologne. But he could be the most perfect specimen of man ever to walk this earth, and it wouldn't change the fact that he's a bona fide asshole.

Someone chuckles from the far side of the table.

Papers shuffle.

A pen clicks.

My cheeks flush ten degrees hotter, graciously disguised under a conservative layer of filter-effect foundation.

"Something like that," I fire back with an unfazed smile as I get settled.

His stare drifts to my stained skirt, which is half-obscured by the table. *Made Man* has an impeccable dress code, one necessitated by the fact that at any given moment world-famous photographers and A-list celebrities could walk through our halls in preparation for a shoot, interview, or highly anticipated promotional piece. West Maxwell would sooner die than have his prestigious staff appear less than perfect at all times. Not that I fault him for it. This company is his baby, his life, his world, and his soul mate all wrapped into one glossy eight-by-eleven magazine.

He's the Oprah of influencers—if Oprah were a thirty-seven-year-old dark-haired, teal-eyed titan of industry with the kind of broad shoulders and chiseled features that would give Khal Drogo stans a run for their money.

The suffocating weight of his stare lingers on me as I flip my notebook to a clean page and ready my pen.

In all my years working for this self-made gazillionaire, this marks the closest I've ever been to him physically. I've been copied on emails (likely sent by his assistant), and I've been in the same room as him at all of *Made Man*'s holiday parties. Once I almost passed him in the hallway—until he took a sharp left and disappeared into my supervising editor's office. It happened so quickly and unexpectedly I thought it was a mirage. And then I spent the rest of the afternoon convinced my supervisor was getting canned and I was next, because while West Maxwell owns the entire operation, he only makes appearances when something major's about to go down.

I jot the date at the top of the page and press my pen against the first line, waiting for West to continue the speech I interrupted . . . only his attention veers toward my notebook.

"It's the seventeenth," he says, loud enough that the other end of the twenty-five-foot table can hear him. His jaw flexes as he forces an audible exhalation through his perfectly straight nose. "Not the sixteenth." Scanning the room, he chuffs. "Someone please assure me this young woman isn't one of our fact-checkers."

I ignore his dig as a handful of sorry souls humors him with a chuckle.

Crossing out the date, I correct my *grave* mistake and offer him a subtle nod. "Fixed."

"We good now?" he asks. "You mind if I continue my presentation?"

Prick.

His attention bores into me like a lead laser beam, anchoring me in place while simultaneously burning me from the inside out. But I force the sensations away and divert my gaze to the slide projected on the screen behind him.

"Now, where was I?" He turns away from me, and his black suit coat strains against his muscles as if they, too, would prefer not to be trapped in the inhospitable inferno of his atmosphere. "Ah, yes. I was just getting to the merger."

Merger?

Mergers in the print world almost always mean job cuts.

My core tightens until it burns.

The woman beside me exhales, sinking back into her seat. I scan the sea of faces for my editor, Tom, and pray to be met with a reassuring gaze—only he appears twice as bewildered as everyone else in the room.

"Don't worry." With his signature devilish smirk and wicked glint, West lifts his palms as if he's cheaply entertained by our reactions. "We're not being sold. Would never dream of that. We're buying out a competitor."

A handful of relieved grumbles fills the dense air, and West makes his way to the opposite side of the room as he continues.

"I think you've all heard of a little magazine by the name of *City Gent*?" he asks before shooting a look my way. "For those of us who may not know, *City Gent* is a niche publication with a reader base not unlike our own but with a local demographic. They have a corner on the Manhattan and tristate market and record rack sales at every corner bodega from Harlem to Chinatown. Turns out the diversified corporation that owns them is looking to get out of print media and reallocate those funds to the tech spheres. But their loss is our gain. Happy to share they accepted my offer yesterday afternoon." He points to the woman across from me. "With my direction, Miranda Bonham will be handling every aspect of the merger, so any questions you have can be directed to her. Please know this announcement is hot off the presses, so we may not have answers for you right away. Still working out all the minute details of this merger, but we'll share everything as soon as it becomes available. I have no further information for you at this time."

A man in a cerulean gingham bow tie and matching glasses raises his hand.

"You." West calls on him like he's an attendee at a seminar, because of course he doesn't know any of our names. Then again, I don't know that particular man's name either. Pretty sure he works in accounting and started while I was gone.

"How will this acquisition affect workloads?" the man asks. "Specifically, will we be absorbing more responsibilities, or will we be merging workforces with *City Gent*'s existing staff?"

West steeples his fingers over his nose and stops pacing. "Any *other* questions from those of you who were actually listening to what I just said?"

I cringe inside and avert my attention to my paper, focusing on the scratched-out date at the top.

In the corner of my eye, another hand goes up. I close my eyes and wait for Maxwell to verbally slaughter another well-intentioned staffer.

"No comment, Mr. Maxwell," a woman coos. "Just wanted to offer my congratulations. I think I speak for all of us when I say we're beyond excited for *Made Man*'s new chapter."

Through my peripheral vision, I manage a quick peek at the bold brownnoser, only to find it's a former intern who wanted my job back in the day.

"Thank you . . ." West pauses and squints, as if he's attempting to recall her name, and then, without wasting another precious second, turns on his heel and waves it away. The former intern shrinks into her seat, her humbled face curtained by a wall of glossy honey-blonde hair. "Anyone else feel the need to waste my time?"

Silence blankets the room.

"Ah. Nothing from you?" He saunters back to the head of the table, hands sliding into his pockets ever so casually while a serious expression paints his beautiful face. "After missing the first fifteen minutes of this meeting, surely you have a question or two?"

I attempt to swallow, only to choke on my own spit for half a panicked second. Clearing my throat, I shake my head. After the morning I've had—on top of the bizarre two months I've already endured—getting publicly ridiculed by West Maxwell would only add insult to injury.

"None from me, thanks. I'll find a colleague and get briefed when they have a chance." I flash my editor a look.

Tom lifts his hand. "I'll fill her in after this, sir. No worries."

"Good answer." West folds his cognac leather folio in half and clicks off the projector.

A handful of choice words lingers on the tip of my tongue. I could understand his rudeness if it were warranted. I click my pen and flatten my lips to keep from saying something I might regret.

Besides, a king has no need for the opinion of his peasants, and he'd have no qualms about knocking me off my proverbial high horse in two seconds flat. Not only that, but a man with his kind of influence could take it a step further and have me blacklisted from the entire industry with a single email.

If he wanted to.

I don't know if he's the vengeful type, because at the end of the day, I barely know the man.

And I'm not alone.

For someone under such a spotlight, his personal life is under strict lock and key. Nothing but rumors too outlandish to fact-check contrasted with details too vague to matter. While I have an impressive knack for finding just about anything about just about anyone on the internet, any and all searches on this notorious mystery man lead to a sea of red-carpet Getty images (he's always alone, never with a date) and a handful of carefully curated *Made Man* interviews.

Through picking apart bits and pieces online, I've been able to glean three personal truths about West Maxwell: he grew up in some blink-and-you'll-miss-it Nebraska town; his favorite restaurant is Il Postino on East Sixty-First Street, where he has standing Thursday-night reservations at a private table in the kitchen; and he wears a size 13 shoe.

But what I want to know—all I've ever wanted to know—is what made him so cruel.

"If there are no further questions or comments, you're all free to leave," West drones under his breath as he checks his phone. Peering up at me, he adds, "Except you."

I press a finger into my chest, my heart ricocheting at warp speed. "I'm sorry?"

"Sorry for what?" He delivers his response with a sarcastic sneer as he watches the room clear out.

"You want to talk to . . . *me?*"

I didn't think he knew my name . . .

His full lips curl at one side, flashing a deep dimple that manages to weaken my knees without permission.

There's no denying the man is a work of art.

But he's also a piece of work.

"You write that column for me . . . The Dirty Truth . . . yes?" he asks, referring to the monthly regular I write as a modern woman telling our male readers "what we ladies really think" about their habits, interests, dating moves, bedroom skills, and more.

Only it's all bullshit.

It's only ever things men *want* to hear.

When I first started here, the first thing my editor made clear was that no one is interested in the truth. The truth is painful, and no one's going to drop six bucks on a magazine only to feel like shit for the entire hour it takes to read it.

Made Man's entire business model is centered on inspiring the everyman to be the best version of himself. You don't have to be rich, handsome, good in bed, or successful to have it all—but we can show you how. It is, after all, how our founding father got his start. He was a nobody (rumor has it), and then he became a somebody. Now he has a legion of dedicated followers convinced that if they do everything he did, they'll become everything he is.

If they only knew what he's really like . . .

"Yes." My throat swells, but I manage to swallow. "That's my column."

"The one you turned in last week . . . not your best work." His phone dings, and he steals a glimpse at a long text that fills his entire screen. Pursing his lips, he adds, "I need you to give me something else."

Those articles don't manifest from thin air. They require careful planning. Loads of research. Late-night cocktails and hours-long conversations with colleagues and guy friends to get their opinions before I bite the bullet, topic-wise. I can't just . . . plop down in front of my computer and hammer out a new one.

Not to mention, the one I turned in for next week I wrote while I was out on medical leave. I wasn't even supposed to be working, yet I did it anyway because working here screws with you worse than an abusive ex-boyfriend. You know he's bad for you, and you know you're the one putting in all the effort in the relationship, but you love what he offers you. Financial security, an enviable lifestyle, hope that the life you've always dreamed of is within arm's reach if you keep those blinders up and trudge forward, loyal and true.

"We go to print in three days," I say. The space around us turns blurry and the air thick, hot. "Everything's already been submitted and edited—"

I don't dare ask him why he didn't share his feelings when he first signed off on everything a week ago . . .

He doesn't look up as he taps out a message on his phone. "We'll make it work."

Those articles take me seven days, minimum. And that's if I'm hyperfocused—which I haven't been as of late.

"Can I ask what you didn't like about this one? Maybe I can tweak it to fit what you're wanting?" I slide my pen behind my ear and hug my notebook against my chest. I'm sure I look like a timid schoolgirl, but standing in this man's presence makes me overly aware of every inch of my body, thus making it impossible to stand still.

West shrugs. "I hated every word of it."

No one's ever said they hated my work before—not even my Honest-with-a-capital-H editor. Never in five years have I had to rewrite anything at zero hour. And with my tenure in this role, I understand the expectations of both our loyal readers *and* the man who signs my paycheck.

At least I thought I did.

Glaring at his phone, he taps out another quick text before waving me off. "Just . . . send me something fresh by eight a.m. tomorrow, and we'll be good."

Shoving his phone into the interior pocket of his midnight-black suit jacket, he heads for the double doors, giving them a punishing shove.

"Wait," I call after him before following in step. "Any particular topic you want?"

"I pay you to come up with the ideas, Napier. Not the other way around." West exhales his words in one irritated breath, and I hardly have time to process the fact that he knows my last name. "I'm sure you'll think of something."

The article I wrote last week was for our upcoming June issue, and it was titled "The Dirty Truth about Active-Duty Dating." Tom called it sharp and uplifting—a way to give hope to those overseas. I packed it full of flirty, sexy anecdotes from people I know who've dated someone stationed overseas or on base. I even took it a step further and outlined inventive and romantic care package ideas. Not only that, but I filled a sidebar with a list of highly touted long-distance-dating apps *with* generous coupon codes for active-duty service members.

I didn't just go above; I went beyond.

I wanted to come back with a splash, to prove I still had it despite my two-month absence.

I'm not sure what West could've possibly *hated* about any of that. The man ships tens of thousands of magazines each month to various troops as his way of thanking them for their service, and there was nothing controversial or remotely offensive about my write-up.

Lifting his phone to his ear, West takes a call and leaves me in his leather-and-cedarwood-scented dust before I can muster another hesitation.

Dazed, I pace back to my office.

After locking my door, I plant myself at my desk and stare at a blank Word doc for the better part of an hour.

I don't know what I'm going to write, but I do know one thing: West Maxwell is the worst.

CHAPTER TWO

ELLE

"Whoa. What are *you* still doing up?" My roommate, Indie, shuffles past my room at 3:00 a.m. Rubbing her eyes, she makes her way to my bed and collapses next to me in a yawning heap.

"Searching my soul for the answers to life's big questions." I close my laptop lid and reach for another Dove white chocolate. Unwrapping its tinfoil, I read off the message inside. "'Don't settle for a spark . . . light a fire instead.'"

"That's a good one. You should hang on to it." She reaches over me, helping herself to the half-consumed bag on my nightstand. "What are you really doing, though?"

Indie's always been an insomniac. As a freelance graphic designer, she sets her own hours. And as a creative type, she lets her muse dictate those hours. It's not unusual to both hear *and* smell her making grilled cheese at 4:00 a.m. or to catch her dancing in the living room at midnight, earbuds jammed in her ears. It never used to be an issue, as I typically sleep like a rock the second my head hits the pillow, but tonight I'm pulling an all-nighter to meet Maxwell's 8:00 a.m. deadline. No amount of silence would make a difference.

"I've never seen you up this late." She turns onto her side, head propped on her hand. "Ever."

"Maxwell didn't like the article I turned in last week. He informed me today that he wants a new one." I exhale a slow breath that does nothing to calm the nerves that have been on red alert since that fateful meeting.

"When's it due?" She lifts a brow.

"In five hours."

Her freckled nose wrinkles. "Can you do that?"

I lift a shoulder. "I don't have a choice."

"What's wrong with the one you gave them?"

"Million-dollar question, Indie," I say, settling back against my headboard. "Million-dollar freaking question."

"What if you say no?"

My mouth coils with amusement at the thought. "It doesn't work that way."

"So what are you going to write about, then?"

"Hell if I know."

I run my palm over the smooth silver case of my trusty computer, the one that's churned out dozens upon dozens of Dirty Truths over the last several years. Landing my position at *Made Man* at twenty-five was a dream come true. I didn't know a soul. I didn't intern there. I had zero connections. I simply submitted my work and got lucky, and the rest was history. Naive, bright eyed, and bursting with potential, I subsisted off the adrenaline rush of rubbing elbows with magazine elites and wearing my workaholism like a badge of honor.

During those earliest years, the world was my oyster, and I was certain a stint at *Made Man* was going to catapult me to print-media greatness. Only it turns out print media is dying out faster than anyone ever anticipated. The jobs are fewer and further between, and the competition is stiffer than ever. To have a job in this industry in this day and age is akin to possessing a coveted Willy Wonka golden ticket.

I'd be a fool to walk away from my life's work—but it's the strangest thing . . . because it's all I've been able to think about lately.

The rush is gone.

The fulfillment and satisfaction are nonexistent.

I used to admire my sisters for knowing that a life revolving around family, marriage, and kids was enough to fulfill them, to give them a sense of purpose in this world. And I was so sure that I knew my path was going to be different. There wasn't a doubt in my mind that moving to a big city and chasing some pie-in-the-sky career would flood me with a sense of accomplishment unlike any other. And it did. For a while.

But my cup no longer runneth over.

It's empty. Hollow. Void—not unlike the place I visited during my fleeting encounter with death.

"Maybe it's time to start considering your options," Indie muses.

"What are you talking about?"

She flicks her chocolate wrapper at me. "That's the message I got, but I'm thinking maybe it was intended for you. I want a do-over."

Indie pops the white square into her mouth before helping herself to a second piece from my dwindling stash.

"'Draw yourself a bubble bath.'" Indie spouts off her new quote. "Eh. Did you know white chocolate isn't actually chocolate? It's just sugar and cocoa butter and vanilla masquerading as some extravagant version of the real thing. But no one cares. They see the word *chocolate*, and because they want to believe it's chocolate, it *is* chocolate."

"I did know that," I say. "Isn't it crazy how we're constantly being lied to and we're all just . . . okay with it? We don't bat an eye. It's such a normalized part of our lives that it makes the truth jarring. Like social media filters. Everyone uses them, and everyone knows that's not really what someone looks like, but we all just accept it anyway."

"Yeah. It's annoying. But what can you do?" She pops the second faux chocolate into her mouth and crumples the bubble bath wrapper.

"Once you take your blinders off, it's exhausting having to constantly sift through what's real and what isn't," I continue. "I was reading some of my older articles earlier tonight, and I was just . . . dying inside with every word. Which I know is maybe an insensitive way to put it given the fact that I recently died, but that's how it felt. I wasn't proud of my work—I was disgusted by it."

"Your work is not disgusting, Elle. Promise. You're just stressed right now because of that stupid deadline, so you're overthinking."

If it were two months ago, I'd agree with her.

"They're cringey," I say. "And they're full of lies. And I don't want to write them anymore."

The words are sharp on my tongue, startling us both into a bout of silence.

"Well, *I* don't think they're cringey," Indie volunteers after a brief delay. "I think they're humorous, and it feels like I'm reading a letter from a friend. They're conversational. And poignant."

"I appreciate that. I do. But my column is literally called *The Dirty Truth*, and it's nothing but bullshit." I reach for another chocolate, running my fingers along the creased midnight-blue tinfoil.

"It makes people feel good. Who cares if it's BS?"

I sniff a laugh. "Apparently *I* care."

"That never bothered you before."

I turn to her. "Exactly. That's my point. I never cared before. And now that I do, I can't stop thinking about it."

"Don't be so hard on yourself. You're just doing your job. If they weren't paying you to write this column, it'd be someone else. Do you think every fashion designer loves what they design? Do you think every schoolteacher wants to teach every single grade they're certified to teach? And take me for instance: Do I love every project that lands in my lap? No. At the end of the day, sometimes a job is just a job. And my bills aren't going to pay themselves."

I pick at a loose thread in my comforter. "I've wanted to work in journalism for as long as I can remember. I wanted to write think pieces and inspire change and scoop up the best, most-sought-after interviews based solely on my reputation. What I'm writing now is an insult to all of those things."

"Fortunately, we live in a world where it's possible to have your cake and eat it too. You can still do those things, babe."

"Not if I'm putting in sixty-hour weeks at *Made Man*." I puff a strand of hair from my eyes. "I wish you could have seen the way West Maxwell talked to his staff today. Unbelievable."

"First of all, stop saying his full name, because you're giving that man too much power in your life, and Lord knows he already has more than his fair share." Indie swipes the unopened Dove from my hand. "Plus it's weird. People don't call Oprah *Oprah Winfrey*; they just call her Oprah. And second of all, I doubt he's different than any other power-tripping douche in a three-piece suit—especially in this city. If it's not him, it'll be some other asshole."

Maybe she's right.

Maybe she's wrong.

"He made me feel this small today." I pinch my thumb and index finger together. "You should've seen me, all trembling and nauseous and obedient, letting him grind my confidence into nothing. He's the worst, Indie, and he brings out the worst in me."

"Only because you let him." She spins the impostor chocolate between her fingers before sliding off the wrapper. "Don't let him have that power over you anymore. Don't give him that."

"You're right."

"Always and forever." Indie winks.

"Which is why I should quit." The words send an anxious tingle to my lips, materializing from my mind to my mouth before I have a chance to stop them.

Indie sits up, hand splayed in the air. "Let's not get all crazy, now."

"For the past week, every minute I spend in that office . . ." My voice trails. "It's like the life is being sucked from me all over again. Only slower this time."

The day I died, I was leaving my then boyfriend's Midtown apartment on a Monday morning, attempting to catch a spin class before work. He'd already left for an early-morning meeting, and I'd stayed to catch an extra ten minutes of sleep since we'd been up late the night before. No sooner did I grab my keys off the counter to lock up than the electric thunder shock of pain blasted through my skull like an anvil. I fell to the tile floor, legs useless and vision blurred. I was in too much pain to move, to think straight.

The last thing I remember before blacking out is the door swinging open and a raven-haired woman with the saddest eyes I'd ever seen standing frozen in shock, mouth agape.

Turns out that Matt, my boyfriend of eighteen months, was actually a married father of three from Jersey living a double life.

His wife, acting on a handful of hunches she'd accumulated over the past year, had recently hired a private investigator to have him followed—which had led to the discovery of his secret Midtown apartment, one he'd been paying for with money from her trust fund.

The entire thing makes me physically ill every time I think about it, and I've not spoken to Matt since he attempted to show up in my hospital room the following day. But the most bittersweet part of it all is the fact that had that poor woman not shown up when she did . . . I wouldn't be here right now.

"I'm so tired, Indie," I sigh.

"Then go to bed . . ."

"No, I mean I'm tired of living this weird, filtered version of life where every decision, every move I make, is rooted in fear or every word out of my mouth is some kind of filtered version of the truth." I angle toward her. "We're all guilty of it. Every last one of us. When was the last time you saw a picture online that wasn't filtered and retouched to perfection? When was the last time you gave someone an honest answer when they asked how you were doing? And up until two months ago, I'd never missed a spin class. Not because I love spin. But because I was afraid of what would happen if I stopped going. I'd get soft, I'd have to spend a fortune on a new wardrobe, and what would people say? And that whole thing with Matt." Saying his name out loud makes my teeth grit. "I never thought I'd be one of those people who were afraid to be alone, but even after things got stale with him, I was afraid of being that person who sat alone on a Friday night, missing out on all the fun. I was so scared, in fact, that every time a little sliver of doubt about him would creep into my head or the tiniest of red flags would surface, I'd silence them all with excuses."

Indie presses her lips flat as she listens.

"We're all so consumed with avoiding anything remotely uncomfortable that we lose all touch with reality," I say. "We've been so coddled by articles and ads and relationships that make us feel good. We hunger for pictures that make us think maybe we have a chance at being beautiful with the right lighting, and we hold on to the belief that if we can find someone to occupy our weekends, it means we're worthy . . . but none of it is real."

She glances at the vintage alarm clock on my nightstand. "That was all . . . incredibly deep for three thirty in the morning, babe."

Sinking back against my pillows, I fold my arm over my eyes and gather a long, hard breath.

"But you're not wrong," she adds. "About any of it."

"I wish I were. It'd make all of this easier." I imagine most of us are on autopilot—and two months ago, I was too. I'd climbed a mountain and rested on my laurels, content to sit back and appreciate a job that ticked all my boxes and a man who wasn't perfect but was seemingly perfect for me. Parts of me were settling, of course. But I still had my entire life ahead of me—or so I thought. In my mind, I had plenty of time to continue crafting the life I'd always wanted to live.

Only now that I've seen the proverbial light (without seeing any literal light), there's no going back.

"So what now?" Indie sits up, gathering her wild blonde mane into a high bun and securing it with a purple hair tie from her wrist.

Pitching forward, I crack my laptop open and double-click my empty Word doc. "I finish this article."

"And then?"

"And then I have a decision to make."

Indie slides off my bed, fixes the covers on that side, and makes her way to the door, then stops to read the message on the Dove she stole from me a few minutes ago.

"Huh." Her mouth tugs up at the sides. "'Don't settle for a spark . . . light a fire' again. What are the odds of getting that one twice in one night? Anyway . . . good luck, babe. You've got this."

I wait until Indie shuts the door before scraping my motivation off the floor and running a quick Google image search on West to jumpstart my faithless endeavor. With a hair over four hours to go and not one Dove-chocolate-size ounce of inspiration, I'm left with little choice but to be inventive in chasing my muse. Yawning, I flick through page after page of West Maxwell images, lamenting the fact that the man doesn't take a single bad picture. Or maybe he does and the bad ones have been scrubbed from the internet. Either way, his beauty is distracting, which is why I force myself to replay our exchange again and again—until I'm reminded of his awfulness.

I'm fifty-seven pictures in when it hits me—a tiny spark of madness.

If I didn't know what I was going to write about before, it's crystal clear now.

Two hours later, my article is done.

And my fate? Has officially been set on fire.

CHAPTER THREE

WEST

"Please tell me they make nannies for teenagers." I sink back in my desk chair and soak in the gray cityscape outside.

Miranda glances up from her tablet. "They make anything for anyone if the price is right. Scarlett giving you grief again?"

Dragging my palm along my tensed jaw, I say, "Something like that."

In the past four months, not only have I gained sole custody of my fourteen-year-old niece—I've also amassed an entire set of forehead lines I didn't have before I opened the doors of my Upper West Side bachelor paradise to the spawn of Satan.

Sitting up, I check the tracking app I installed on Scarlett's phone and shoot her yet another text reminding her she's to be at school on time today. When I left this morning, her door was closed and her lights were out. I knocked before attempting to barge in like a human alarm clock, but it was locked—as usual. A minute later, I heard her groan some kind of response before some tinny pop song began to play. I took solace in knowing it at least meant she was home and not gallivanting around the city sans permission for the twentieth time.

In a roundabout way, we both have my dead father to thank for our current situation.

He always used to say, "No good deed goes unpunished." He'd also occasionally drop a classic "Once a Maxwell, always a Maxwell." There was nothing original about that man. Every word that left his beer-slicked lips was a tired cliché. Everything about the way he lived his life was too. Bud "Big Boy" Maxwell was a Natty Ice–drinking, Harley-Davidson-riding, womanizing, wife-beating deadbeat with a narcissistic mud vein a mile wide.

While I owe none of my success to him, I wouldn't be the man I am today if it weren't for that sad sack illustrating how *not* to win at life. I sleep soundly each and every night knowing my current lifestyle is a giant middle finger to the bastard.

Taking my niece in—and getting her out of her appalling circumstances—was also a giant middle finger to the Maxwell name.

Neither of us asked to be born into this family, but it doesn't mean we can't do something about it. Scarlett's too young to realize her fate was already written until I came along and changed it.

Someday she'll thank me.

Until then, she can hate me all she wants.

In fact, she can join the fucking club. There's a spot reserved for her at the end of the line. I'm a firm believer in the idea that you haven't "made it" in life if you don't have a whole slew of people hating your very existence.

"I'm finalizing the agenda for the *City Gent* staff meeting if you want to look it over." Miranda taps her stylus against her screen. "There. Just sent it."

My computer chimes, the screen coming to life, greeting me with an overstuffed inbox of emails I'll never get around to reading. I find hers at the top—above one from Elle Napier, marked with high importance. The subject reads, *New Article As Requested.*

"I'll give it a look in a sec." I motion for her to leave, eyes glued to the screen as I double tap the attachment.

Without a word, Miranda gathers her things and shows herself out. She's one of the good ones: patient, tolerant, and worth her weight in gold. There are instances I don't doubt she knows what I'm thinking before I even think it—an impossible feat.

Sipping my coffee, I wait as Elle's document loads on my screen—and I all but spit it back into my mug when I feast my eyes on the title.

THE DIRTY TRUTH ABOUT WEST MAXWELL

by Elle Napier

What image comes to mind when you think of West Maxwell?

It's okay if you need time. I'll wait . . .

I know there are thousands of them in existence.

Maybe you thought of that Instagram picture from four years ago where he's riding on the back of a camel, pyramids in the distance and an orangesicle sunset coloring the background? What about the one where he's geared up and rappelling down some snowcapped mountain in Switzerland? Or better yet, maybe it's the January 2019 cover of *Made Man*—the one in which West appeared shirtless, leaning against a gleaming Gotham-black McLaren Elva and looking like he'd just won the lottery, his dream woman, and a one-way ticket to paradise, all while pushing his "Ultimate Guide to Your Best Year Ever."

But who's the man behind the filtered image? Who's the man writing the inspirational captions that make you want to set your alarm for 4:30 a.m. so you're not late for tomorrow's grueling CrossFit session? Who's the man that inspires both professional and interpersonal greatness with a single square-shaped, likable, shareable photo?

I bet you think you know who he is.

Or maybe you have a general idea.

Ambitious? Yes.

Attractive? Undeniably.

Intelligent? I'd say so.

Wealthy? Does Saturn have rings?

But what lies beyond that? What drives him? What keeps him going day after day? But more importantly, does it matter?

Spoiler alert—no. It does not matter.

I'm about to drop a dirty little truth bomb—you are not West Maxwell and you never will be.

The West Maxwell you see is a marketing machine's carefully crafted version of the ideal man.

Let me drop another bomb on you while I'm at it: the average woman is not looking for her own personal Made Man. Not even close. She simply wants a partner who listens, who shares her interests, values, and life goals—and bonus points if they're not a jerk and happen to be in close geographic proximity.

I'm oversimplifying, but you get the point.

You want the secret to having it all? You're not going to find it in the pages of this magazine.

Save your money.

Save your time.

And simply be yourself.

There may be a million men trying to knock off West Maxwell, but there is only one you—and that, my friend, is what makes you a genuine catch.

Yours in truth—

Elle Napier

The pen in my hand snaps in two, sending the spring, tip, and ink chamber flying.

I'm two seconds from formulating my response when I notice a second, unnamed attachment.

Dear Mr. Maxwell—

I quit.

Sincerely,

Elle Napier

Jerking my office phone from the corner of my desk, I punch in Tom's extension—until my cell phone rings and *Highland College Preparatory Academy* flashes across my caller ID. Slamming the receiver on its cradle, I take the call on my cell.

"Yes?" I answer.

"Mr. Maxwell, this is Principal Veldhuis at Highland Prep." An all-too-familiar voice fills my ear. He hesitates before beginning again. "It's eight thirty-four, and Scarlett is a no-show again. This is the fifth time this month, number twelve for the semester. Unfortunately there are truancy laws, and—"

"I'm aware. I'll . . . *handle it*. And I'll personally deliver her to you within the hour."

He exhales. "I appreciate that, sir. But I'm afraid if this happens again, we're going to have to take this to the expulsion committee."

"I can assure you it won't come to that." My jaw tightens. I can't assure him of anything because the truth is, four months in I've yet to decode Scarlett's language, unlock her trust, or earn her respect so she'll listen to me once in a damn while. I can command an entire room of adults with a single look, but putting the fear of God into my brother's daughter is an impossible skill to master. It's a daily battle, and so far she's winning—though I'd never tell her that. "I'll make sure of it.

Thank you for the call. Now if you'll excuse me, I'm going to locate my niece."

I end the call and ring Scarlett—getting her voice mail immediately. My vision blurs red until I get my shit together.

When I pull up the tracking app, it appears she's currently in Hell's Kitchen—somewhere along Tenth Avenue. And that's assuming she didn't leave her phone on a bus bench to throw me off; it wouldn't be the first time. I once tracked her to a bodega in Little Italy, only to find it was some thirteen-year-old punk who had grabbed what he claimed was an abandoned phone off a newspaper rack. Pretty sure he pissed himself when he saw me walking toward him.

Heading downstairs, I pull up my email and forward Elle Napier's message to her editor along with direct instructions to deal with it immediately, and then I hail the first Yellow Cab I see.

Scarlett might be in Hell's Kitchen, but she's yet to experience the hellish inferno coming her way.

CHAPTER FOUR

ELLE

"You trying to burn off breakfast or what?" Indie points her cereal spoon in my direction, her mouth half-full of soggy apple-cinnamon Cheerios. "You've been pacing for, like, an hour."

It hasn't been an hour—more like a solid fifteen, twenty minutes.

"I quit my job." I stop patrolling the space by the kitchen island and cover my eyes, peering her way through my fingers. "Twenty minutes ago. I sent the email. It's over. I quit."

My finger shook as I pressed send on that email to West . . . and it hasn't stopped shaking since.

"Excuse me, ma'am, you *what*?" Her spoon lands against the bowl with a loud clink. "You realize this apartment is six grand a month and we just renewed our lease a few months ago . . . right?"

"I have savings. I've done the math. It's all good."

At least, for the next eight or nine months it'll all be good. If I don't manage to find a similar-paying job by then, I'll be packing my entire life into a couple of suitcases and hitching a ride back home to Louisiana to live with my parents. And while I love them dearly, my mother and I are complete opposites, and she's a small-doses kind of person. No good can come from the two of us under the same roof at this point in my life.

But one thing at a time . . .

"I know you were in a weird place this morning with the deadline and everything, but that's a little drastic, don't you think?" she asks. "Just quitting like that?"

I shrug and begin to pace again. Standing still for too long makes my skin hum with anxiety, and moving is the only way to make it stop.

I'm starting to answer her when my phone buzzes in my back pocket. I slide it out to find a call from Tom waiting for me.

"It's my boss," I say before correcting myself. "My *former* boss. My editor. It's . . . Tom."

It rings twice more, then again.

"You going to take it, or are you just going to stare at it a little longer?" Indie asks.

"Hey, Tom." I manage a simple greeting despite my mouth turning to cotton. "What's up?"

"What . . . did . . . you . . . do?" When his words are slow, unrushed, and unminced—never a good sign. "Please tell me this is an extremely belated April Fools' joke and that you are *not* committing career suicide?"

"I'm sorry. I made the decision a few hours ago. I would've called you, but then you would've talked me out of it, and—"

"Of course I would've talked you out of it," he all but shouts into the receiver. "I don't understand, Elle. I really don't. You have no idea what you just did. And"—he lowers his voice—"Maxwell sent me your email and told me to—and I quote—'deal with it immediately.' What the hell does that mean? Does he want me to have HR draft up the termination paperwork, or does he want me to talk you out of it? And what do we do with the article you sent? We go to print in three days, and we can't use that."

"*Tom.*" I strut toward the living room window, take in the gray city-scape below, and swallow a cleansing breath. "Working for that man has been nothing short of a nightmare. We both know it. He needed to read what I wrote, and I needed to write what I wrote. Maybe ending my career with a swan song isn't the most professional thing in the world, but there's no going back now. Just tell him you confirmed my decision and you'll work with HR to find a replacement."

In five years, I've never once had to tell my boss how to do his job.

"Oh Lord." Tom moans into the phone. "Speak of the devil. He's beeping in. I have to go."

He ends the call before I have a chance to say goodbye, though I'm sure it won't be the last time we speak.

"So?" Indie readies a spoonful of cereal. "What's the good word?"

"He's freaking out," I say. "He just needs a full twenty-four hours to process this, and he'll be fine."

"You sure you made the right decision, babe?"

I hesitate, though I'm not sure why. "Like it matters now."

"Am I picking up on a little doubt?" Rising from the table, she pours her milk down the sink and places her dishes in the dishwasher.

"You're picking up on a little bit of everything."

"What's that saying? *Fortune favors the bold?*" She lifts a shoulder and gifts me with a reassuring smile as if it could possibly make any of this less nerve racking.

"Not trying to be bold or brave," I say. "I was thinking about my obituary this morning, after I finished my article."

She chokes. "Your obituary? *Why?*"

"I was thinking about what it would've said had I died two months ago," I say before correcting myself: "I mean if I'd stayed dead."

"Okay . . ."

"It would've mentioned my parents and my sisters and maybe my college and that I worked at a men's magazine . . . but that's *it.*"

Indie shrugs. "You've accomplished more in your thirty years than some people accomplish in a lifetime."

"Maybe, but until you're faced with your own mortality, you don't realize all the time you've wasted on things that don't matter. Meaningless things."

"You think your life has been meaningless so far?" Her voice carries a delicate pitch.

"No," I say. "Not entirely. Just parts of it. So I'm removing the parts that are meaningless and replacing them with things that have meaning. At least that's my plan. I want to write think pieces. Articles that inspire people to take action and move them to change their lives or the lives of those around them. I want my work to have made other people's lives better. Also, I want to make people's lives better. And I can't do that if I'm stuck behind a corporate desk five days a week."

I'm fortunate to be able to work at all. Many people who have suffered my same fate can't say the same. My recovery has been easier than most, which is all the more reason I should dedicate myself to more worthwhile endeavors.

Hunched over the counter, she purses her lips together. "Okay, so you had your three a.m. epiphany and quit your job."

"Exactly."

"And now you're going to find a meaningful job that pays enough so we don't get evicted and we're not living on the streets by Christmas?" She tosses me a wink, though I've known Indie long enough to know she's only half teasing.

"I promise no one's getting evicted." I draw an X across my heart.

"If anyone can make this work, it's you," she says with a resolved sigh, as if she's conjuring nostalgic memories from our college-roommate days.

I first met Indie when she was in my Intro to Journalism class. It took her half a semester before she realized she was terrible at writing and better suited for graphic design. A few years later, when we were making our postgraduation plans, I talked her into moving to Manhattan, despite the fact that she's very much a country girl at heart. It didn't take long for her city wings to spread.

"And for the record," she adds, "I can list a million things you've done in your life that are meaningful. But at the end of the day, all that matters is *your* list. I'm with you either way, okay? You've got my full support. Just don't miss rent, okay?"

Shuffling across the room, I wrap my best friend slash roommate in a tight hug, breathing in her perpetual vanilla-apricot scent.

"Can I just say . . . I'm so glad you didn't die," she says.

Silence settles between us.

And then laughter.

"Same," I say, wiping a happy-sad tear from my eye.

Breaking away, I head to the shower to clear my head and decide what to do with the next several hours of my life. My first taste of freedom may have started on a bitter note, but the second bite will be sweet—I'll make sure of that.

CHAPTER FIVE

ELLE

"The hell are you grinning at?" A white-haired woman walking a fluffy apricot poodle shoots me a glare and clears the sidewalk as I pass. "Psycho!"

I resist a chuckle and continue making my way along West Fifty-Seventh, en route to a little coffee shop I've been wanting to try since last year but never could find the time since I was typically chained to my desk on the opposite side of town.

I've smiled at eight strangers so far this morning. Granted, it's not a very "New York" thing to do, and they probably all think I'm certifiable, but that's the whole point—I'm teaching myself not to care what people think. Smiling at passersby hurts no one. Sprinkling bits of kindness and humanity is the sort of thing we should all be doing.

"Morning." I nod to an elderly gentleman, who spends half a second processing my greeting before his eyes spark. With a slight grin and a tip of his kelly-green fedora, he sends me on my way.

Warmth blooms in my chest as I continue on, squinting to read the street sign half a block down. To my left, a theater sign advertises a one-day-only sale on matinee tickets for some off-Broadway production

I've never heard of. All these years I've lived in the city, I've maybe gone to a total of three shows, which is a shame.

It's wild how a person can be surrounded by so much art and beauty and brilliance . . . only to forget that it's there.

I stop at an automatic ticket machine and purchase a seat for the one-thirty showing of *Unconditional Splendor,* starring Lola Lourdes and featuring Billy Cordova. I don't know who they are or what the show's about, but I've no doubt it'll be magnificent.

Pocketing my ticket, I head to the end of the block and turn left on Tenth. I toss a few more smiles at passing strangers—all ignored, not the end of the world—and continue past a quaint café that smells of cinnamon, cocoa, and fresh-brewed coffee. Seated across from one another at a corner table for two is a young couple holding hands among an assortment of water glasses and tea-light centerpieces. He hasn't taken his eyes off her, and she hasn't stopped blushing. For a moment, I'm reminded of my time with Matt—before I knew everything coming out of his mouth was a bald-faced lie.

I was still newish to the city when a handsome stranger bought me a drink and cozied up beside me at some trendy Lower Manhattan bar. Twelve years my senior, he worked in the financial district as a hedge fund manager, wore pricey tailored suits, towered over me at a perfect six feet two, and smelled like money and top-shelf cologne. He was charming and protective, and having grown up in the city, he loved nothing more than taking me under his wing and teaching me everything he thought I needed to know.

Unfortunately, in doing so, he left his mark all over my adopted stomping grounds.

Every restaurant, every shop, every park, every place we used to frequent now reeks of his memory. But my gripes are infinitesimal in comparison to what his wife must be going through. I can't imagine building an entire life with someone only to have him take a steaming dump all over it.

I think of her often and what I would do if I ever ran into her again—though I don't suppose there's anything I can say that would change the circumstances or make her pain disappear. Sometimes I wonder if she thinks the same about me as well and what she might say if she were to see me again.

Peeling my attention from the lovey-dovey pair, I take a couple of steps only to realize my shoe has come unlaced. Shuffling to a park bench up ahead, I take a seat a couple of feet from a young sandy-haired girl in cutoff jeans and a floral crop top.

"Hi," I say when I feel the unexpected weight of her watchful eyes.

Sniffing, she turns away . . . and I think nothing of it. The city is filled with Manhattanite progeny who ditch school to run amok on their parents' dime. At least she has the street smarts to not talk to strangers.

Kudos, city girl.

"Hi." A small voice offers a faint response.

Tugging the bow on my laces, I glance up—only to be met with mascara-streaked cheeks, a quivering lower lip slicked in cherry blossom lip gloss, and a set of glassy baby blues.

"Are you lost?" I sit up. She can't be much more than fourteen, maybe fifteen.

She shakes her head.

"What's wrong?" I angle toward her, crossing my legs and settling in.

"What *isn't* wrong . . ." She huffs, dabbing a wayward tear with the back of her hand.

I refrain from informing her she reminds me of myself at that age—every setback was the end of the world, no matter how big or how small.

"Can I ask why you're not at school right now?" I keep my tone soft so as not to put her on the defense.

Wiping a tear, she rolls her eyes. "Long story."

"Well, it just so happens I have a little bit of extra time on my hands," I say. "I actually just quit my job, so I don't really have anywhere to be. Except at one thirty—I'm seeing a show. But until then . . ."

I offer a relaxed, gentle smile, studying the tiny quivering thing beside me.

She yanks her crop top down an inch and hunches over, elbows on her knees as she stares at the vintage-style apothecary storefront in front of us.

"I hate it here," she says. "My school's full of snobs and preps. I miss my old friends. And everyone in the city acts like they're constantly having a bad day." Turning to me, she adds, "I've lived here four months, and you're the first person that's said hi to me . . . the first person who didn't look at me like I'm see through."

I'd been here a year when someone told me people move here because they like to feel invisible. Some people want to blend in and not be seen, and you can do that in a city of millions.

"This place isn't for the faint of heart. It'll chew you up and spit you out if you let it," I say. "Where are you from?"

The girl sighs. "Nowhere you've ever heard of."

"Okay . . . so what brought you here?"

"No offense, but it's personal."

I lift my hands. "None taken."

A quiet moment passes between us before she speaks again. "Why'd you quit your job?"

"Because it didn't make me happy anymore," I say. "And my boss was a . . . jerk. He was one of those people—like you said—who act like they're constantly having a bad day."

Her lips twist at the side, as if a little slice of validation was all she needed. "How long did you work there?"

"Five years," I say.

"Where are you going to work now?"

I shrug. "No idea."

"Aren't you scared you won't find another job?" she asks.

"Of course," I say. "But it's all about what you focus on. Fear or hope? Meaning or status quo? That kind of thing."

She wrinkles her nose. "That's weird."

Chuckling, I nod. "It is. I know."

Her phone buzzes on the bench beside her, and without hesitation she silences the call coming through.

"Someone's looking for you," I say. "Bet they're worried."

She blows a puff of air between her lips as a city bus hums past and comes to a stop at the corner light. Up ahead, a shoulder-to-shoulder sea of pedestrians crosses a busy intersection, headed this way.

"Oh *shit*." The girl pops up, slipping her phone in her back pocket. "He found me. I gotta go."

"Wait." I rise. "Are you going to be okay? You're not in any kind of trouble, right?"

Panic colors her baby blues a shade darker as her attention darts toward the crowd. For a split second, I manufacture a mental story about some midwestern teenage runaway being trafficked to New York—because that sort of thing happens more than people realize.

"Scarlett!" a man's voice booms above the city symphony around us.

Glancing up, I see a dark-haired, clench-jawed Adonis in a three-piece suit stalking ahead of the pack, his familiar blue-green gaze piercing in our direction.

West Maxwell.

"You know him?" I speak out of the corner of my mouth, keeping my voice low.

Scarlett exhales. "Unfortunately."

"Wait . . ." I stand frozen. But every second that passes only brings West Maxwell that much closer. "How do you know him?"

"*That,*" she says, her tone salty, "would be my uncle."

Turning to me, she offers an apologetic half smile before dashing off toward him. Within seconds, he hooks his arm around her shoulders and hails a cab, and the two disappear inside.

Surreal.

Ten minutes later, I'm sipping an iced brown sugar latte and thinking about West Maxwell as an *uncle*. Which then makes me think of him as someone's brother, someone's son. It's the strangest thing, imagining this larger-than-life asshole as just a regular guy with the same problems and interpersonal relationships as anyone else.

My thoughts wander, some sillier than others . . . What does he do for Christmas? What's his star sign? Is he a mama's boy? What's his favorite movie? What makes him laugh? What kind of birthday presents does he give? Does he have any family traditions?

The idea of West as an everyman is pure comedy.

Everything I've ever gleaned about the man suggests he's as cold as he is heartless, and everyone knows heartless people can't feel a damn thing.

CHAPTER SIX

WEST

"Don't be mad." Scarlett trots toward me.

"Don't be *mad?*" I repeat her question through clenched teeth. "What the hell are you doing here when you're supposed to be in school? And not answering your phone when I call you—have you lost your damn mind?"

I'd love nothing more than to take that stupid device away from her as punishment, but seeing how it's the only way I can track her down, it isn't an option. I could ground her from her friends, but she claims she doesn't have any of those. Short of making her scrub all ten thousand square feet of my town house on her hands and knees using a toothbrush, there isn't much else I can do to help her realize the gravity of her actions.

Hooking my arm around her narrow shoulders, I direct her to the curb and hail a cab. A taxi screeches to a stop, and I yank open the rear passenger door.

"Get in." I climb in beside her before slamming the door. "Highland Prep on Columbus."

"I'm not going." My niece crosses her arms over her barely there crop top and pouts her glossy bottom lip, a move that makes me realize she left the house looking like a five-dollar hooker today. I shrug out of my jacket and drop it on her lap. "Put this on. As soon as we get there, you're washing your face, and then I'm personally escorting you to the principal's office so you can apologize for ditching school . . . again."

She begins to protest, but I lift a finger.

"You're also going to tell him how much you love Highland Prep and how grateful you are to be a student there." Pulling out my phone, I check my email. Tom was supposed to handle the Elle Napier fiasco this morning, but it's been a solid hour, and he's given me nothing.

"So you want me to lie." Scarlett angles her body to face the window, refusing to look at me, as if it's going to make a difference to her fate.

"No. I want you to *grovel*. They're two seconds from kicking you out of that place, and the next best option has a two-year wait list. There's a six-month wait at Kingman Hall, but that's on the Lower East Side, and quite frankly, I've not heard amazing things."

"I have an idea." Her voice is overly chipper. "You could just ship me back to Nebraska."

"Not in this lifetime," I snap back. Sending her back isn't an option, and even if it were, I wouldn't. I refuse to fail Scarlett. I'm giving her a better life whether she wants it or not. Someday she'll understand. Until then . . .

The taxi slams to an unexpected stop, and we brace ourselves on the seat back in front of us.

"Sorry," the cabbie mutters, his eyes flicking into the rearview.

Ordinarily I'd have my personal driver running me around, but given the fact that Scarlett pulled this cute little stunt and I'd given him the morning off, grabbing a cab was the most efficient option.

"I hate it here," Scarlett says under her breath.

"You haven't even tried to like it."

"I miss my friends."

I chuff. "The ones who hung out at that abandoned railroad depot every night getting stoned? Or are you talking about those little eighth-grade boys who hot-wired that elderly woman's Buick and went joyriding with a case of Busch Light they stole from their dad's garage fridge?"

Silence.

"I refuse to let you grow up to be just another loser from Whitebridge. And you shouldn't settle for that either." A block ahead, her school comes into focus. "If you had any idea how lucky you are to be here. To live in this city, to go to one of the best high schools in the country, to have a wealth of opportunity and privilege at your fingertips . . ." I trail off because I know she isn't listening. Or at least she's pretending not to because she knows it gets to me.

The cab creeps to a stop, and I swipe my card to pay the toll before bolting out of the germ factory on wheels.

Scarlett takes her time getting out—to spite me, I'm sure. And keeps a careful distance from me, teetering on the curb with her arms folded and eyes averted.

"Put the jacket on." I nod to my suit coat, the one currently crumpled in her grip.

"Absolutely not. I'm going to look ridiculous."

"I'll see if there's a spare uniform when we get inside, but for now, you can't go in there with a bare midriff. It's against school policy."

"Since when do *you* care about rules?"

I ignore her attempt at deflection.

Jerking the jacket from her haphazard hold, I drape it over her shoulders and escort her inside, then stop at the restrooms in the front hall so she can wash off her sticky CoverGirl face before we head to the main office.

"I'm not sending you back to Nebraska, Scarlett. Not now, not ever," I tell her when she steps out, fresh faced and looking like a true fourteen-year-old. "The sooner you accept that, the easier this will be for you. There's nothing you can say or do to change that. You may not understand it now, but someday you'll thank me. Until then, you're living under my roof, you're following my rules, and you're not to miss another day of school."

"You realize there are only two weeks left of the school year . . ."

"I'm aware," I lie. I hadn't realized it. I'd been too busy chasing after the *City Gent* merger to pay attention to the school calendar.

A vision of Scarlett wandering the city unsupervised for an entire summer sends a cold sweat down my neck—yet another worry to add to the list of things that keep me up at night.

"Come on." I hook my hand into her elbow and steer her toward the office with long, brisk strides.

Stopping outside the school secretary's door, she jerks away from me. "Why do you care so much?"

"I beg your pardon?"

"Until this year, I'd only met you five times in my life, and I don't even remember half of those. I just have pictures," she says. "I don't get why you care."

If she only knew . . .

Someday I'll tell her. But not here. And certainly not now. She isn't in the right frame of mind to comprehend the depth or seriousness of this situation.

"You're not my dad." Her voice breaks, but her expression is impressively ironclad—delivering the words like a true Maxwell.

"Thank you, Scarlett, for that much-needed reminder. I'd almost forgotten." I get the door and escort my wayward niece inside. "Kill the attitude and get ready to apologize profusely for your actions."

When the shit show's over, I walk the five blocks to my corporate office, where yet another shit show awaits me. Ninety-nine percent of the time, I work from a private office in my home. My reasons have always been comfort, privacy, and convenience. Also, I've found that being absent from the main office as much as possible serves to make my presence that much more impactful.

Besides, my time is priceless, and I reserve none of it for brownnosers, time-wasting chitchatters, watercooler gossip, and office politics.

While I'd normally hand the "little things" off to Miranda, what happened this morning with the staff writer is something I plan to deal with myself.

Sliding out my phone, I dial Tom's number.

"Mr. Maxwell, hi," he answers in the middle of the first ring.

"Expected to hear from you before now." I cut to the chase. "What's the latest with Ms. Napier?"

I called him from the cab on my way to find Scarlett and informed him I'd like a face-to-face meeting with our audacious little staffer immediately.

"Right, so unfortunately she hasn't been answering her phone all morning," he says. "I've called her sixteen times and sent twenty texts, but they're not even showing as read. I think her phone might be off . . ."

Pinching the bridge of my nose, I exhale and stride ahead, passing a slow-walking tourist type and a woman in head-to-toe lime-green Dior.

"I'll keep trying," Tom says. "But I can't make any promises. Let's face it: Elle resigned. I can't force her back here, you know? Unless . . . are you offering her job back? Maybe I could try to talk her into coming back. I will say it's not like her to be this impulsive. Then again, she hasn't really been the same since her little incident a couple months back."

Ah yes.

Her brain aneurysm.

I'm well aware of it—mostly because it was all anyone would talk about at staff meetings for a while, but also because someone forwarded a GoFundMe campaign to the entire company, and it was then I found myself becoming somewhat invested in her story.

But only for a short while—I had a business to run.

"I'm not offering her job back," I say. I would *never* allow an employee to quit with a slap in the face and then offer them the moon and stars to return.

Tom's end goes quiet.

"I'd simply like to have a conversation with her," I say.

"I . . . I can send you her phone number?" he stammers. "I just don't think you're going to get her to come in for a good old-fashioned ass chewing, pardon my French."

"I'm not going to *chew her ass.*" I sniff, approaching the gleaming platinum rotunda of my corporate headquarters. "I'd just like to talk to her. That's all."

"Oh . . . okay," Tom says. "Um, I'll make sure to convey . . . all of that."

"I'd like to speak to her today. This afternoon ideally." I check my watch before entering the elevator. In the seconds before the doors close, I catch a glimpse of a wide-eyed main-floor receptionist making a quick call, warning them off like she always does.

As if I didn't know . . .

"Thank you, Tom," I say. "I trust you'll make this happen."

Ending the call, I press the button for the fortieth floor and darken my phone screen, silently running through all the choice words I'm saving for one Miss Elle Napier.

If she wants the dirty truth . . . I'll give her the dirty truth.

And then some.

CHAPTER SEVEN

ELLE

The afternoon sun blinds me as I step out of the matinee production of *Unconditional Splendor*. Just as I'd hoped, it was magnificent—and it wasn't just the acting. Granted, the performance was superb. But minus three other theatergoers, I had the entire place to myself, prompting one of the ushers to graciously offer me a front-row seat. I was so close to the stage I could smell the pan makeup that caked their faces and the spray paint they'd used on the backdrops. So close I could see the tears rolling down the heroine's face as she professed her undying devotion to her long-lost love.

With my phone off and my never-ending to-do list wiped clean, I found myself present and in the moment for the first time in recent memory. My heart ached for the characters as I watched their love story unfold in the midst of tragedy, and for two straight hours their pain was my pain, their triumph was my triumph, and their joy was my joy.

Had I not quit my job, I'd have missed out on all of that.

Hitting the pavement, I dig my phone from my bag and power it on—only to find dozens of missed calls from Tom with a side of frantic text messages peppered with emojis, expletives, and exclamation marks.

"Hey," I say when I call him back. "What's going on?"

"My God, Elle. I thought something happened to you again." He exhales his words in one long breath. The morning of my aneurysm, he was the first to realize I hadn't shown up to the office, and he spent his entire day calling every hospital and precinct in Manhattan, trying to track me down. "I've been running around my office like a damn lunatic. Was about to start calling hospitals again."

"I went for a walk this morning, and then I caught a show." I suppress a yawn—the all-nighter is finally catching up with me. "Didn't realize you were still keeping tabs."

"West wants to talk to you," he says, monotone.

My smile fades. "What? Why?"

"No clue. He wouldn't say."

Of course he wouldn't say—the man gets his rocks off on being as cryptic as humanly possible.

I stop at a crosswalk and wait next to a couple engaged in a heated argument over whether they should go to the Hamptons for their anniversary in June.

"We go every year." The woman tosses her hands up in drama queen fashion.

"That's the point—it's tradition." Her partner grips fistfuls of air, bending at the knees as if he's going to drop to the pavement in frustration.

In eighteen months together, Matt and I never once fought. Looking back, I realize it's because he was too busy pretending to be Mr. Wonderful and I was too busy playing the part of some cool, modern girlfriend. We were both being the person we thought the other one wanted.

But none of it was real.

Because real couples fight.

Real couples aren't afraid to get their hands dirty.

Real couples don't hide their true feelings—or in Matt's case, their true identities.

"Tell him there's nothing to discuss," I say when I cross the street. "His ego's probably bruised, and he just wants the last word."

Tom sighs. "He says he's not going to berate you, Elle. But he would really like to speak with you."

"I'm sorry, but no," I say. Another call beeps in. "Tom, hold on . . . it's my mom . . . I should take this . . . again, I'm so sorry."

Ever since my aneurysm, my mother has full-blown anxiety fits every time I don't answer her call. If she gets my voice mail, she'll leave a rambling message before firing off a handful of texts asking if I'm okay and demanding I get back to her as soon as possible. And if I don't respond within precisely three minutes, she has my father and sisters blow up my phone, and always in the same order: Dad, then Emma, then Eden, then Evie.

"Hey, Mom," I answer.

"Elle, sweetheart. My goodness, your phone's been off all day, and I called your office, and they said you weren't there. Is everything all right? How are you feeling?"

"Everything's more than all right," I say. "And I'm feeling amazing, actually. Having a pretty incredible day so far. What's up?"

"Well, thank the good Lord for that. Had me worried half to death." Her drawl is sweet and patient. "Anyway, I was just calling to see if you'd received your bridesmaid dress yet? Evie said she mailed it Priority last week. I know you'd had some stolen packages earlier this year, so I thought I'd check . . ."

I picture her strutting along the wraparound porch of our Louisiana colonial, her tea-length dress flouncing in the breeze as she twirls her pearl necklace around one finger.

"I got it Thursday," I say.

"And have you tried it on?"

"I did." I smile and nod at a green-haired teenager in passing, who stares back at me with dead eyes smudged with black eyeliner. "Needs to be let out about an inch in the bust and hemmed a couple of inches, but it's beautiful."

"Are you sure that's all it needs? Did you get a second opinion? Maybe have Indie take a look. The mirror can distort things, you know." Her voice pitches higher with each remark. Bless her micromanaging heart. "You know, if you need, you can send it home, and I can take it to my guy."

"The city has some of the best tailors in the world," I remind her. "I'll find someone amazing, I promise."

"Well, just make sure it'll be done in time for the wedding." My mother lives to plan things, and my baby sister's nuptials are no exception.

Beyond the pictures of cakes and flowers and venues and center-pieces Evie sends in our family group chat, I've yet to get involved in the planning of this lavish affair aside from liking pictures and sharing occasional excitement.

"June twenty-fourth," Mom reminds me, as if she hadn't already given me the date a dozen times before. "You're coming out the week before that, yes?"

"Already booked my tickets."

"Have you sent me your itinerary yet? I'd love to print it off and add it to my file . . ."

"I'll forward it the second we hang up."

"I'll have your father pick you up from the airport that day so you won't have to worry about driving. I know you don't like to drive any-more now that you're a big ol' city girl." She offers a chuckle, though we all know it kills her that I shied away from the Napier-woman tradition of marrying your high school sweetheart, buying a starter home, and popping out your first baby by twenty-four. "So anyway, what's new? How was your first full week back at the office?"

I swallow the lump in my throat. "It was . . . interesting."

"Please tell me you're not putting in those ridiculous twelve-hour days. Remember, the doctor said you needed to ease into everything."

The day of my aneurysm, my mother boarded the first flight out of Baton Rouge and spent every night for two weeks sleeping on the pull-out sofa in my hospital room. When the doctors would come, she'd take notes. When the nurses would make their rounds, she'd tell them every single minute thing they missed between visits. I finally made her go home after a couple of weeks—not because I didn't appreciate her diligence and dedication to my health and safety but because the woman needed a break for her own good.

She was home a mere five days before she boarded a plane back to New York and stayed another two weeks by my side.

Whoever said no one will ever love you as much as your mother was clearly well versed in the Mona Napier school of motherhood.

"There's no easy way to say this," I begin, "but I quit my job this morning."

The other end falls silent for an endless moment, and I check my phone to make sure the call didn't drop.

"Mom?" I ask.

"I'm sorry, you must have cut out. I don't think I heard you correctly," she says. "Can you repeat that?"

"I quit my job."

She gasps into the receiver. I imagine her bent over the porch railing, fanning herself in true Mona Napier theatrics.

"What happened?" she asks. "I don't understand."

Up ahead a man spins a NOW OPEN sign and points to a corner ice cream parlor when he catches my eye.

"Long story. I'll fill you in another time, okay?" I head toward the parlor and scan the menu before immediately settling on two scoops of strawberry Oreo on a sugar cone. For years, I've punished my body with spin classes and fad diets, all so I could squeeze into a coveted New York size 2 wardrobe, when all my body wanted to be was a comfortable 8.

I'm not denying myself life's simplest pleasures just to please everyone around me.

Not anymore.

"Elle, I'm worried you may have made a rash decision," she says. "It's not like you to up and quit. Are you—"

"The world's not going to fall apart if you stop worrying about things," I remind her. "I promise, it's all good."

She clucks her tongue. "Worrying is what I do. It's a mother's job."

Over the generations, worrying has turned into an inheritable trait on my mother's side. Her mother was a worrier, and so was my grandmother and her mother before her. They were all overthinking perfectionists who were absolutely positive everything would fall apart if they relaxed for a minute.

"Do you have another job lined up?" my mother asks. "Or a plan of some sort?"

"No. I don't. But I don't need one," I say.

For the first time in my life, I don't have a plan—nor do I want one.

"Just taking things one day at a time," I add, licking a melty stream of pink ice cream before it reaches the cone.

"Well, you know if you need anything, your father and I are here to help," she offers. "We've helped your sisters out quite a bit over the years, and you've never once asked for anything."

It's true.

They've probably dumped hundreds of thousands of dollars into Emma's and Eden's respective weddings as well as ponied up for the down payments on their first homes. No doubt they're doing the same for Evie. But I've never been the type to ask for anything I haven't worked for, and I never want to feel indebted to anyone.

"I appreciate it," I say. "I really do. But I'll figure it out."

She marinates in that uncertain thought for a moment. "Are you sure everything's okay?"

"*Mom.*" I snort a chuckle. "One hundred percent. I know I made the right decision, and everything's going to work out exactly the way it should. It always does."

We end the call, and I imagine my mother running inside to find my father, hands on her hips as she asks, *Guess what your daughter just did?*

My father will probably laugh, sip his sweet tea as he rocks in his favorite chair, and let her vent until her worries and frustrations absorb into the sunroom's floral wallpaper. He's the opposite of her in every way, and thank goodness for that. Everyone should have someone who balances them out, someone who adores them despite being their polar opposite.

A minute later, I pay for my double scoop in a sugar cone and head for the sidewalk again, ambling home the long way with every intention of taking the most delicious of afternoon naps.

I'm four blocks from my apartment when I pass an empty *City Gent* magazine stand at a corner bodega. It's stark orange and impossible to miss, and it won't be long until those become powerhouse-red *Made Man* racks and West Maxwell leaves his mark all over this city.

Funny how a man can be everywhere and nowhere to be found at the same time.

I think of his niece again. And the mixture of anger and relief on his face when he spotted her. It's strange to imagine someone so cruel caring about someone else in any capacity.

Perhaps he has a heart after all.

Laughing to myself, I shake my head.

Not a chance.

CHAPTER EIGHT

WEST

"I'm sorry, sir, but her mind is made up," Tom says over the phone that afternoon. "And with all due respect, I can't continue to harass her."

I sink into my office chair, cradling the phone on my ear as I tap out a text to Scarlett asking for proof that she's home from school.

A second later she sends me a mean-mugged selfie standing in front of the fridge.

"Did you assure her I wasn't going to berate her?" I ask Tom.

Since this morning, I've read Elle's articles more times than I can count, each time scrutinizing them from all angles. One minute I'm nodding in agreement, and the next I'm stewing at the audacity of her blatant disrespect.

I can't decide if she's brilliant or out of her fucking mind.

Regardless, she doesn't get to kick the hornet's nest and walk away without so much as a sting. She said her piece—now it's my turn to say mine.

"Does she want money?" I ask. "I'll pay her a goddamned consulting fee if she wants. I just want a moment of her time."

"I don't think it's about money, sir," Tom says. "I think she just wants to move on."

"She'll need to come back and collect her things," I say. "Have her assistant box them up for me and send me her address."

He pauses. "A-are you sure? Because I'm sure I can courier them there or send an intern that way. You don't have to—"

"I insist." I cut him off. "And, Tom?"

"Yes?"

"Don't tell her I'm coming. I'd like for this to be a surprise, much like the surprise she imparted to me in my inbox this morning."

"I won't say a word." His voice is marked with seriousness, and I trust he'll keep his promise. He's been with me since the beginning, started as a groundling and worked his way up to a supervising editorial position. Unlike some people here, Tom actually appreciates his career.

Thirty minutes later, I'm finishing up a few emails for the day when a knock at my door brings a trembling assistant with a french braid and a cardboard box.

"Here you are, Mr. Maxwell." The young woman places Elle's things in the middle of my desk and then stands, wide eyed and curious, as if she's waiting to be excused.

"Thank you . . ." I feign an attempt to remember her name, but you can't remember a name you've never learned.

"Leah," she says with a wide, small-town smile.

"Leah," I echo. Waving toward the door, I add, "Thank you. You're free to leave."

She turns to go, nearly tripping over her schoolgirl Mary Janes.

"Wait," I call out.

Leah spins on her heel, hands clasped at her hips. "Yes, Mr. Maxwell?"

"How well did you know Ms. Napier?"

Her face contorts, as if it's a complex mathematical equation I'm asking her to solve and not a simple question.

"Um," she says. "I've been her admin for the last eight months."

"Were you aware of her plans to quit the company?"

Her eyes grow round. "Not at all, sir. I'm just as blindsided by this as you." Taking a step closer, she adds, "And if I may say, I really respected and admired her. She was probably the nicest boss I've ever had. Always available around the clock. Took me out for lunch every week, her treat. Cared about my personal life—was always giving me dating advice. Offered me feedback on this novel I've been working on for the last two years . . . I sent her a text this morning to see if she's okay, but she hasn't responded yet. I'm not really sure what to make of any of this."

I check my watch as she rambles on. I wasn't expecting an essay-length answer to my question.

"Thank you, Leah," I say. "That'll be all."

Rising, I examine the contents of the open-lidded box as the sad girl with the braid departs my office.

A small potted plant. A tin of spearmint Altoids. A tube of lavender hand cream. A framed photo of Elle with three women who look like ice-blonde versions of herself. A book of poetry. A half-empty bag of white chocolates. Cherry blossom lip balm. And an antique gold compact with someone else's monogram carved into the top.

I've never made a habit of getting to know my employees. Besides the fact that there are far too many to get to know, I'm here to run the ship, not rub elbows and make friends.

Pulling out the framed picture, I study the striking face of the woman who rattled my cage with 399 measly words.

I saw her a handful of times over the years, always in passing. She caught my eye every time—though I never made a show of it. A Made Man doesn't grovel, drool, or conduct himself like a shameless horndog in the office.

With her long cocoa-colored hair and striking Pacific-blue gaze and those full, pouty lips the color of ripe raspberries, it was impossible not to notice her, even from across the room. She was quiet, dutiful, and confident, always keeping a safe distance. And she had a smile that always lit the room and drew people in, as if her calming sunlit atmosphere was the antidote to our gray city days.

Little did anyone know, I'd always looked forward to her column every month. Even after I'd approved her work, hers was always the first thing I flipped to when I cracked the spine on a fresh copy of *Made Man.*

And while I'm not the kind to crush on someone (I'm a thirty-seven-year-old grown man, for fuck's sake), I thought about Elle Napier more than I should have. She'd creep into my mind during those quiet, late nights in the office, and I'd let myself conjure up ridiculous fantasy after ridiculous fantasy of all the things I'd do to her if she were mine.

Only I had no intentions of making her mine.

Illusions, in my experience, are always better than realities. I preferred Elle Napier in my dreams, where she could be exactly what I wanted and precisely what I needed and there was no room for bullshit relationship drama or complicated *feelings.*

I text my driver, grab Elle's things, and head downstairs.

Fifteen minutes later, my driver drops me off in front of a brown-brick apartment complex with a small green awning.

I buzz her apartment number—4C—and wait.

CHAPTER NINE

ELLE

"So, uh, there's a man downstairs buzzing up here." Indie leans against my doorjamb, worrying her lip. "Asking for you."

A few minutes ago, I'd just woken from the deepest afternoon nap I've taken in my entire adult life and was appreciating the fact that the most stressful item on my agenda tonight was whether I was going to eat leftovers or make Indie go with me to that new Thai place down the street.

Sitting up, I brush the mess of hair off my face. "What? Who is it?"

"He says he's your boss." Indie picks at a flake of milk-white nail polish on her index finger.

"Hm. As of eight o'clock this morning, I didn't have one of those anymore." I fling the covers off my legs and grab a duster cardigan off the back of my closet door to cover my strappy silk camisole and pajama bottoms. "Maybe he has the wrong place?"

"He asked for you by name. Said he had some of your things from the office."

"Oh." Tom lives on the opposite side of the city and would surely have sent my assistant or an intern to drop my things off, but I could see him making a personal appearance if he's trying to persuade me to come back. "All right. Tell him I'll be down in a sec."

I shuffle to the hall bath, splash water on my face, and run a brush through my hair before stepping into a pair of satin house slippers and heading to the lobby of our complex. Only the instant I step out of the stairwell, I find it isn't Tom waiting for me with a box of my things.

It's West.

My heart stops beating for a fraction of a second, and every last bit of oxygen exits my lungs. While the times I've come face to face with this man have been few and far between, it's nothing compared to finding him here, in my apartment lobby, eyes homed in on me, with zero warning.

Not only that, but he's looking unusually casual in his navy slacks and a white button-down oxford cuffed at his elbows. And his hair— usually nary a strand out of place—is mussed, as if he's been running his hands through it all day.

Only West Maxwell can be having an off day and manage to look ten times sexier.

Squaring my shoulders and lifting my chin, I peel my shock off the floor and manage a simple "What are you doing here?"

"Came to drop off your things," he says, as if it's the most natural thing in the world. "Thought we could have a chat while I'm here."

The main building doors swing open, and the sullen widow from 2B ambles toward the mailbox center, grocery bags in tow and keys jangling. Within seconds, another resident strolls in, yapping on the phone about getting tickets for the next Mets game.

"If this is about my article," I say, "I stand by what I wrote. And if you're trying to get me to come back, my mind's already made up."

"This is absolutely about your article." His aqua irises glint as he studies me. "And don't worry—I wouldn't dream of employing you again."

Humbled yet very much confused, I cross my arms. "Okay, then say what you came here to say."

The woman from 2B loads up her bags and a large stack of mail, and I grab the stairwell door for her just as a family of six bustles in—strollers, diaper bags, and all. But despite the cramped lobby, West doesn't budge or divert his attention off me; he stays anchored in the center of it all, making everyone move around him.

A rock in a stream.

"Is there somewhere we can go that's a bit more"—he flashes a look at the noisy bunch—"private?"

"If you're asking me to invite you up, the answer is no," I say without hesitation. "But we can go outside."

His loaded gaze scans me from head to toe, a reminder I'm not exactly dressed for conversation on a city sidewalk.

A week ago I'd have cared.

Today I couldn't care less.

West places my box by the stairwell before following me outside. We find a little stretch of walkway beyond the entrance and step off to the side.

"All right," I say. "I'm all ears."

West chuffs, speechless for a second. And I can't help but wonder if there's anyone in his life who speaks to him like this.

Doubt it.

"Were you aware, Ms. Napier, that I hand selected you for your position out of more than three hundred and sixty-eight applicants?" he asks.

"I . . . no," I manage. "I was not aware of that."

"You were the twenty-ninth candidate in my stack," he says. "As soon as I read your sample article, I shoved the remaining three hundred and thirty-nine in the trash, picked up the phone, and had Tom make you an offer immediately."

My writer's ego beams quietly on the inside, basking in his bewildering praise.

"I was quite taken with your candidness, and I could tell from the first line you had the sort of perception most writers only dream of," he continues. "It was selfish of me to assign you such a flippant column every month, knowing that you were capable of deeper, more moving pieces, but damn if you didn't make me proud."

"Until this month." I blow a puff of air between my lips, refusing to let his flattery unravel me or soften my stance on him.

"Even the best hitters strike out sooner or later," he says. "Never took you for the delicate-ego type."

"You gave me less than twenty-four hours to write a completely new column, and you refused to tell me what you didn't like about the one you accepted a week ago."

"I didn't accept it—Miranda did," he counters. "Between the merger and a personal matter I'm dealing with, I delegated a few things to her that I shouldn't have. Your article being one of them. And I realize my deadline was extreme, but I had faith in you to pull through. Imagine my dismay when you pulled that little stunt instead."

My jaw slackens. "No."

"No?" His brows knit.

"No," I say again, louder. "I'm not letting you turn this around on me, as if I did you wrong. I did exactly what you told me to do. And it just so happened that in the process, I realized I didn't want to work for *Made Man* anymore—a personal decision based on personal circumstances."

"Funny, because your decision felt very targeted to me," he says. "As if you were writing for one person in particular and not our millions of loyal readers."

"The article was written with *all* readers in mind." I leave it at that, because a beloved journalism professor once said explaining oneself is futile because every reader will infer their own interpretation anyway.

"If what I wrote upset you so much that you had to show up at my apartment to tell me in person how wrong I am about you, then you've done nothing but prove my point. You're not the man people think you are."

His brows slant, yet the rest of his expression is unreadable as he examines me.

"My point in the article—in case you missed it," I continue, "is that no one really knows who you are as a person—they only know you in pictures. And we all know pictures only tell half the story . . . the rest of the story is filled in with assumptions. So when your customers read your magazine because they think they'll be the next you, they're chasing after something that doesn't even exist. Even *you* aren't you."

His silence is deafening and perhaps a sign that Vesuvius is about to erupt, but I can't stop. The words find my tongue faster than I can process them. Years of pent-up frustrations are bubbling to the surface, and there's no going back.

"You're like the Fyre Festival," I say. "Lots of hype but nothing there once you arrive."

His mouth turns slack before his jaw tenses. And maybe that was a little harsh, but it's true.

"You're false advertising of the human variety," I say. "What you see is not what you get."

"Maybe your opinion would hold some weight if you actually knew a damn thing you were talking about." He finally speaks, and his handsome face morphs into a handsome glare. "Tell me, Elle, are you satisfied? Flushing a promising career down the toilet, all for a couple of cheap digs?"

"My career was over the day I returned to the office last week," I say. "My heart isn't in this anymore. You just happened to provide the wake-up call I needed to realize that. And honestly, West? Part of me was hoping I'd inspire a bit of change in you."

He scoffs, hands resting on his narrow hips.

"Between the pages of your magazine, you seem like this upbeat, fun-loving, larger-than-life everyman, but in reality, West . . . you're an awful person," I say, because what's he going to do now? Fire me? "You're cruel and cutting. Unapproachable. Distant. And at times, terrifying."

"Thank you for that insightful and unsolicited opinion."

"Fact," I correct him. "Not an opinion. *Fact*. A fact no one else will tell you to your face because they're so scared of what you'll do or say. You know, when I first started, Tom specifically pulled me aside and told me to tell the readers what they wanted to hear, that they couldn't handle the truth. But it turns out neither can you . . . because here you are, trying desperately to prove that I was wrong because you know I'm right."

A group of twentysomething girls in high-waisted mom jeans and messy topknots passes by, nudging one another and pointing as one slyly pretends to take a selfie to get a shot of West in the background.

But he's so incensed with me, so homed in on me with that unnerving teal gaze, that he doesn't so much as notice what's happening around us.

"I just think," I say, "if you're going to be influencing people, you should be yourself so other people can see that it's okay to be themselves too. West, you have a platform of millions of men who all think the only way to have it all is to look like you and act like you and be like you, and that simply isn't true."

Cocking his head, he says, "What I do goes deeper than you know. And truly, Elle, believe me when I say . . . you know *nothing*."

"Deeper? Really? Because all I see is surface-level bullshit. One minute you're quoting the Stoics, and the next minute you're selling the next hot sneaker and posing in front of the Taj Mahal. Please, tell me what's deep about that."

"Everything I do serves a greater purpose."

"Ah yes. Right. To pad your pockets." I thump the heel of my hand against my forehead. "Of course."

His lips press flat as his incredulous stare bores into me.

"Anyway, I don't want to keep you. I'm sure you have more important things to tend to." I tug my cardigan tight around my pajamas and cross my arms to secure it in place. "Oh, by the way. I met your niece today."

Squinting, he sniffs. "Excuse me?"

"Found her on a bus bench on Tenth when I was on my way to grab a coffee. She was upset, and we had a nice little talk."

Disbelief colors his chiseled face.

"Sandy hair, big blue eyes, lots of makeup, tiny clothes," I elaborate. "Said she just moved here and things weren't going well . . . then you showed up looking all angry and—"

"She was ditching school."

"She hates it here." I toss my hands in the air. "This city's not for everyone."

"Not that it's any of your concern, but she doesn't have a choice," he says. "I'm her legal guardian, and she's stuck with me for the next four years."

Just when I thought the most self-centered man in the world couldn't be more self-centered, he pitches a curveball that begs to differ.

"It's weird thinking of you as an uncle," I muse aloud, taking him in under the fading early-evening light.

"What's weird about that?"

"Because it implies you have a soft spot . . . and there's nothing soft about you. You're all edges, West. You're ice cold. A person could get frostbite just looking at you."

"Poetic."

The journalist in me is dying to know the story behind this iron-hearted media mogul taking custody of his teenage niece, but I don't dare ask unless I want him to rip off my head and spit the answer down my neck.

"You know, I've probably googled you a hundred times," I say. "And there's nothing. It's like your past has been completely scrubbed clean."

"I pay good money to keep it that way."

"What are you so afraid of? Is your past so colorful that it could shatter this perfect illusion you've built up?"

"Not afraid of anything," he says. "I value my privacy."

"I'm sorry, but don't you lose some of that when you plaster your own face on the cover of the most widely circulated men's magazine in modern history? You're basically a millennial Hugh Hefner—minus the girlfriends and orgies. At least I assume. No one really knows for sure . . ."

"I've had to put a pause on those." His mouth turns up in one corner. "It's a little difficult to host orgies when I'm sharing the roof with my fourteen-year-old niece."

Choking on a laugh, I say, "So you do have a sense of humor . . ."

"Excuse me . . ." A man in ripped jeans and a designer T-shirt stops by. "I don't mean to interrupt, but are you West Maxwell?"

West gives a subtle nod, hardly attempting to disguise the annoyance emanating from him in waves.

"Would you mind if I got a selfie with you? My roommates are never going to believe this . . ." The guy readies his phone, but West waves him off.

"Not right now, man," West says in a bro-to-bro kind of tone he must reserve for his fans and stans.

The smile evaporates from the poor guy's face, and he slides his phone away as quickly as he got it out.

"Of course. Sorry," he mutters, lifting a hand and offering an apologetic wave.

"He only takes pictures he can photoshop," I tell the guy before he scurries off.

West shoots me a pointed look.

The guy stops in his tracks, carefully reaching for his cell. "I can use one of those Snapchat filters . . ."

"Yes, great idea. Give me your phone." I wait for him to ready the filter before grabbing his phone, and then I motion for the two of them to stand closer. "Okay, one . . . two . . . three."

The guy wears an ear-wide smile and flashes a peace sign while West gives his signature devil-may-care smirk.

"Here you are." I hand the phone back. "And don't worry, West—your skin looked flawless in that one. No Photoshop necessary."

Not that he needs it anyway . . . he's the epitome of human perfection in its physical form.

The guy heads off, and I shoot West a wink.

"You just made his day," I tell him. "Do you always say no to selfies?"

"Plenty of people say no to selfies . . ."

A tepid draft of early-evening wind ruffles my hair and sends a chill through my thin pajamas—a wordless push to wrap things up and get inside.

"So?" I ask. "Did you say all the things you came here to say? Wait . . . what did you come here to say?"

His perfect nostrils flare from his perfectly straight nose, and he gifts me with weighted scrutiny.

"You didn't hear a word I said, did you?" he asks. "Too busy giving me what for."

"To be fair, your presence is unnerving," I say, purposely neglecting to add that his looks are distracting. "But I think you came here to tell me you're not superficial and I was wrong."

"Close enough."

We linger in some surreal sort of limbo, unmoving, eyes locked.

"Also, I'd like to remind you of the NDA you signed when you first started as well as the five-year noncompete clause in your contract." He checks his phone and slides it away.

I'd almost forgotten about the noncompete clause, the one that prevents me from working at another magazine for a period of five years after leaving *Made Man*. When I first signed it, I was told it was an industry standard. Now I know it was just a manipulative tactic on West's part to keep people from leaving. I suppose you don't build a media empire by being Mr. Nice Guy.

Either way, I'm done with magazines.

I'll write phone books if I have to.

Anything to keep from working for West Maxwell ever again.

CHAPTER TEN

WEST

"Who were you talking to on that bench earlier today?" I ask Scarlett when I get home. Of course I didn't see her talking to anyone at the time, but now that I know about her little exchange with Elle, I want her to think I have eyes all over the city.

"Hey to you too, Uncle West." She rolls her eyes, flipping through an old issue of *Made Man* as she reclines on the vintage leather Chesterfield in my study.

"I don't want you talking to strangers anymore, you understand?" I loosen my tie.

"Yeah, yeah, yeah. Stranger danger." She fights a teasing grin.

"It's not a laughing matter, Scarlett. The city's full of insidious types who'd love nothing more than to make your life a living nightmare. Gangbangers. Traffickers. People ready to exploit you without a second thought. Or worse."

As much hell as this kid gives me, I'd never forgive myself if something happened to her.

Taking care of her is the only thing anyone has ever asked me to do in this life—and that's exactly what I intend to do. Keep her safe.

Educate her. Prepare her for the real world while also ensuring she's molded into a respectable (and self-respecting) member of society.

"Anyway, no more talking to people you don't know." I jerk my tie from my neck.

"That lady was really nice." Scarlett licks a finger and flicks to the next page. There's nothing in that magazine that could possibly be of interest to a high school freshman. "She said she just quit her job . . . that her boss was a jerk."

Sounds about right.

An image of Elle flashes in my mind's eye—the way she stood there on the sidewalk in her pink satin pajamas, her cardigan barely covering her nearly transparent camisole and her hair a bedheaded mess at five o'clock in the evening. While she stood there giving me what for (and then some), the woman didn't have a care in the world. She stood up for herself and her beliefs, and whether or not I agree with her, I have to admit it was sexy as hell listening to that pretty little mess with great big opinions put me in my place in a way that hasn't been done since a lifetime ago.

"Inspiring," I say before moving on. "You have homework, I presume?"

She lifts a shoulder. "Eh."

Smart-ass.

"Uncle West, can I go back to Nebraska this summer?" Her round eyes plead as she softens her tone. "Please? I miss my friends. I literally have zero friends here . . ."

"Maybe if you weren't so busy skipping class, you'd actually have some by now. Kind of hard to get to know people when you're never there."

"They suck." She pouts. "And the feeling is mutual because they all think I suck too."

"And you know that how?"

"No one talks to me. Sometimes people stare," she says. "And most of the time I eat lunch in the bathroom, but on the days when someone blows it out, I can't, so on those days I just don't eat at all, and then by the middle of the afternoon my stomach is growling super loud, and it's *so* embarrassing."

She shrinks back against the leather with a dramatic groan.

"Some people have real problems, Scarlett." I fold my tie and shove it in my pocket. "Pretty sure my day was worse than yours."

I'm not one to one-up a teenager, but I'm making an exception today in hopes that sharing some common ground might help her relate to me a bit more. It doesn't matter who someone is or how much money they have; no one is immune to bad days.

"Try me." She flicks to another page.

"I'm in the middle of an enormous merger, and my best staff writer quit without warning," I say. "And not only that, but she made it clear on her way out that she thinks I'm the worst kind of human being."

"Since when have you cared what anyone thinks of you?"

Her point is fair, though I can't begin to answer the question. While the internet is littered with all varieties of opinions about me, Elle's words cut deeper than all of them combined.

With a single article, she undermined my entire life's work and reduced it to garbage.

If she only knew . . .

"You're, like, emotionally bulletproof," Scarlett says. "That's what Grandma always used to say."

Yes, my mother did use to say that about me. Though it was never intended to be a compliment, I learned to use it to my advantage, and it's served me well.

"Oh my God." My niece bolts up, the issue of *Made Man* carelessly wrinkled between her petite hands. "It's her! It's the lady from this morning."

Flipping the magazine around, she all but shoves it in my face, and sure enough, it's Elle's column from February of this year . . . "The Dirty Truth about Valentine's Day." I feast my gaze on the professional headshot of Elle tucked in the corner of her write-up, a flawless portrait of a gorgeous brunette with glossy waves and juicy red lips tugged into a sultry, sexy grin.

Years ago, I selected her based on her writing prowess alone, and when readers began writing in about how much they loved the column and how they wanted to see the face of the woman behind it, I had Tom book her a photo shoot with full hair, makeup, and wardrobe. From then on, I instructed my team to include her photo alongside her column.

The readers went nuts—understandably so.

Not only were Elle's articles witty, personable, and on point, but her beauty was second to none. She wasn't so stunning that she felt plastic and out of reach for the average reader, but she was, without question, a bona fide head turner. The quintessential girl next door with an edge. Almost immediately readers wrote in asking if she was single, and I even fielded a few calls from associates all over the world wanting to know if I'd arrange a meetup for them next time they were in town.

I refused, of course, in the name of boundaries and professionalism. But deep down, I couldn't stand the thought of someone I knew having the one thing I couldn't.

I drag in a hard breath and clench my fist around my tie.

Elle Napier has royally screwed me over, not just professionally but personally.

With her sharp, pointed chin and piercing ocean eyes, she owns you without even trying—though I get the sense she's not exactly aware of the kind of power she wields with a single glance.

"Wait . . ." Scarlett's nose wrinkles. "That lady said she quit her job today . . . you said your best writer just quit. She writes for your magazine. Are *you* the jerk boss?"

"Smart girl." I head for the doorway.

Scarlett cackles. "Idiot uncle."

"I'm going to change. Why don't you get cleaned up for dinner? We still need to finish our conversation from this morning."

"And after that we can discuss me moving back to Whitebridge for the summer."

Halting in my spot, I lift a hand. "Not a fucking chance."

"Two weeks?" She clasps her hands together. "Just two weeks to see my friends?"

"I can't even trust you alone for two hours."

"Then come with me." She cocks a hip and folds her arms. "You can supervise me, and you'll know everyone I'm with at all times."

"You can't pay me enough to set foot in that town ever again." It was bad enough I had to fly to Nebraska for the court hearings and proceedings in my three-year battle to gain full custody of Scarlett. Compound that with a shitty childhood and two decades of bad memories, and I've had a lifetime's fill of Whitebridge.

In an instant, her eyes begin to well, her lower lip quivers, and she tips her chin down.

My chest tightens.

I can't do tears.

And I especially can't do them from my niece, who's been through unimaginable circumstances in her short fourteen years.

"Scarlett . . ." I drag my palm along my five-o'clock shadow. "We'll talk over dinner, okay?"

She dries her tears on the back of her hand, and I realize I just gave her hope. False hope. The Fyre Festival equivalent of hope, as Elle Napier would say.

"So you'll think about it?" she asks.

"I said we'd talk."

"So that's a no . . ." The lilt in her voice is gone, replaced with a quaver.

I need to figure out what to do with her this summer—anything to avoid sending her back to that shithole town.

"You're better off here than there, Scarlett. I promise," I say. While this stage of our relationship is still shiny and new, until she learns to trust me, my words are empty. Sound and wasted air. I'm hopeful that with time she'll learn that I did what I did *for* her. For now, I'm just some long-lost uncle who ripped her out of the only home she'd ever known and dropped her into a strange and unwelcoming universe. I don't blame her for resenting me. "Now, I'm going to get changed. Meet me in the dining room in ten. I asked Bettina to make that dish you liked from the other week—those filets with the balsamic reduction."

Scarlett lifts her hands as if she's "raising the roof"—a sarcastic move if I've ever seen one.

I let it go, disappearing into my room to peel out of my work clothes and change into jeans and a T-shirt.

When I get back, Scarlett's dining chair is vacant.

Once again, she's nowhere to be found.

CHAPTER ELEVEN

ELLE

"I didn't realize where we were . . ." Indie bites her lip and offers an apologetic wince as we approach Matt's apartment building on Sutton Place.

An hour ago, I was standing outside having one of the strangest conversations of my life with West Maxwell. I was so worked up when I got back to my place that Indie insisted on a walk-and-talk. Only now we've been walking and talking for an hour, only to wind up mere yards from the place where my life almost came to a permanent end.

"It's fine." I nudge her along and motion for her to keep going. "I doubt he lives here anymore anyway."

"Unless his wife kicked him out and he has no choice but to live here . . ."

"This is true." I think about her again. Claudia is her name—a detail I only learned recently after a late-night deep dive into Matt's real identity. Even the last name he gave me when we were together was fake—which makes sense in retrospect given that I could never find anything about him online. Early in our relationship, he told me he hated social media and that he preferred to live his life away from all that "nonsense."

Like a fool, I adored that about him. "It's okay. I'm bound to run into him sooner or later. This city's like a giant small town."

"What would you even say?" Indie asks. "Have you thought about that?"

As soon as I stopped taking Matt's calls and had my mother change my phone number, he sent me letters for weeks, detailing his marital problems and professing his love for me. He claimed he only stayed with Claudia because of the kids but that his heart would forever be mine.

I shredded each and every letter he sent after the first one without so much as opening them.

"Oh, I have fictional confrontations with him in my head all the time," I say. "Or I used to. I'm starting not to care as much lately. I think about his wife more than I think of him now . . . can you imagine? Marrying him and having his babies, and *that's* how he repays you? By spending your trust fund money on a city apartment so he can screw some younger woman?"

"So cliché." Indie shakes her head.

"And revolting." I grip my throat as it burns with bile. "It makes me sick that I was even a part of that equation."

"Babe, you had no idea."

"Yeah, but I should've known. Instead I was following him blindly all around town and believing every word that came out of his mouth without a second thought."

"Love makes people do stupid things. It's science. There's a chemical involved or something."

"Is it even love if you can flip it off like a switch?" I glance up at a fourth-floor window I know to be his, and my stomach drops when I find the light is on.

We'd been together a whirlwind three months when he dropped the L-word, and I was so inspired by his bravery and conviction (because in my experience, most men would rather take a dull butter knife to their genitalia than utter that word so soon) that I even wrote an article called "The Dirty Truth about Saying I Love You."

Without naming his name, I sang his praises like a lovesick puppy.

"Feels like a lifetime since I've been up there." I sigh, stopping by the doors I used to traipse through with a million-dollar smile on my face and my finest perfume wafting behind me. Ernie, the doorman, would greet me with his usual "How you doin' tonight, Miss Napier?" And I'd stop to catch up with him for a minute or two, letting him fill me in on his baby grandson's latest milestone. "Can't believe it's only been a couple of months."

"A lot has changed since then."

"Everything has changed."

"Why are we stopping?" Indie eyes the front door, pointing. "You're not going up there, are you?"

"Hell no." I laugh at the notion. "I was just thinking about that day."

Funny how a single moment in time will live forever in my memory as simply *that day.*

My mother once referred to my aneurysm as an earthquake, reminding me that sometimes you survive the damage and sometimes you don't, but once you've been hit, things are never the same. You have to rebuild. And she went on to say that no earthquake is without aftershocks—little waves that affect everyone in your vicinity in some capacity.

Clips of that fateful morning play in a loop in my memory, some more vivid than others.

The blinding, searing pain in my skull.

The jangle of my keys as they hit the tile floor before I did.

His wife in the doorway with her sad, dark eyes.

The wailing of the ambulance sirens.

The darkness blanketing me.

The smell of antiseptic that filled my nostrils as I woke to an array of wires and machines spouting off my vital signs in some Manhattan hospital room.

The silver-haired doctor who told me how lucky I was to be alive—after he told me I'd died.

I asked for Matt for days before my mother finally told me the truth—at least the truth as it had been relayed to her second- or third-hand. Apparently after I'd blacked out, his wife had called 911, and as they'd loaded me inside the back of the ambulance, she'd told a young paramedic, "The only thing I know about this woman is that she's been fucking my husband." And then she disappeared into the crowd of onlookers that had gathered to watch the spectacle.

I don't blame her for leaving.

She didn't owe me a damn thing.

A Matt-size shadow fills Matt's apartment window, jerking me back into the present moment. Hooking my hand into Indie's elbow, I jerk her along and get the hell out of there before he notices.

I'd hate for him to think I'm standing here missing the way we were.

Maybe I can't rewrite the past, but today I turned the page on a new chapter.

Fingers crossed this one doesn't end with another earthquake.

CHAPTER TWELVE

WEST

"I swear to God, Scarlett," I say the second the cops leave. "I had the whole damn city looking for you; do you realize that?"

Her gaze drops to the marble-inlay floor of my entryway as the antique grandfather clock to the left chimes thrice—as if I needed to be reminded it's the middle of the longest damn night of my life.

"And what the hell were you doing at Penn Station?" I circle her, my fingertips digging into my temples. "Did you think you could just . . . hop a train back to Whitebridge? That's not how it works. You could've gotten yourself killed. Is that your goal here? Because if it is, you're well on your way."

I didn't spend all my time, effort, money, and energy rescuing her from a grim and perilous existence only to stand back and let her take a one-way ticket back to that hellhole. She's safer with me than she'll ever be with anyone else, and that's a verifiable fact.

She responds with flinching shoulders and silence, as usual.

"What's it going to take, Scarlett? Tell me. Because short of injecting you with a microchip tracking device, you're leaving me no choice"—I pause—"but to send you to a boarding school with twenty-four-hour security."

Working for years and spending a small fortune to ensure my niece was in good hands only to ship her off to be someone else's problem is far from ideal, but my options are waning.

As if I've flipped a switch, her jaw falls and her pale eyes grow wild. "You're seriously going to ditch me?"

Ignoring the piercing tightness in my chest and the urge to look away, I speak through gritted teeth. "The choice is yours, Scarlett. If you choose to run away again, you're choosing boarding school. If you choose to go to school and live by the rules I've set in place for your own safety, then you'll stay here and finish high school in the city."

"You're just trying to scare me." Her nose crinkles with infuriating teenage defiance.

"Test me." I step closer, narrowing the gap between us.

She smells like the night air with a mix of train-station filth and drugstore raspberry body spray.

"Get cleaned up and go to bed," I say. "You have school in the morning. And I'm arming the apartment tonight in away mode, so if you so much as step out of your room for a glass of water from the kitchen, I'll know."

"I hate you!"

"Someday you won't. Until then, good night, Scarlett."

My temperamental niece storms down the hall, and within seconds her door slams shut and angsty emo shit blasts at full volume.

Heading to my study, I pour two fingers of scotch from a limited-edition bottle of Macallan and settle into a chair to collect my thoughts and calm myself in hopes I'll be able to nab a couple of hours' sleep before my day begins.

Parenthood was never something I wanted to check off my list, and being a father—or father figure—is something I've gone out of my way to avoid in my thirty-seven years, because a man knows his strengths just as well as he knows his weaknesses.

Marriage, kids, domesticity, patience—those things have never been on my radar. But a few years ago, I flew home to attend my mother's funeral, and that was when I saw Scarlett. I hadn't seen her since she was a curly-haired baby, barely walking and never without a pink pacifier in her mouth. But after seeing her at the memorial, emaciated and unwashed, shadowing her mother—who was clearly in the throes of addiction again—I had to intervene.

I couldn't, in good conscience, depart Whitebridge and leave my only niece to grow up in drug-addicted squalor. Once upon a time, I thought it was enough to send a check every month—believing that it was more than enough to provide them a comfortable life. Denial allowed me to turn a blind eye to reality, and my fixation on chasing my own dreams only fueled that. But I wouldn't be the man I am today if I didn't have the capacity to learn from my mistakes and admit when I need to change course. The instant I understood the circumstances surrounding Scarlett's living conditions, I didn't hesitate to call my attorney and piece together a plan to get her away from Lexi and under my custodial care.

Unfortunately, the court doesn't simply terminate parental rights because someone's an unfit parent. Turns out there's an entire elaborate system and a million hoops to jump through in addition to a myriad of opportunities for the parent to prove to the courts that they're fit.

Scarlett's mom put up a good fight, but in the end, she loved the pipe and the bottle more than her daughter, and she couldn't keep the facade going any longer.

My only regret is that I waited as long as I did, but given the fact that I avoided my hometown like the plague, I'd never known how bad it was for Scarlett.

They say ignorance is bliss, but sometimes that very same bliss will screw you over.

I take an unhurried sip of liquor, letting the thick amber liquid burn on the way down, and then I remind myself Scarlett never learned boundaries from her mother. She never knew the love of a father—seeing how hers died when she was a baby—and her mother never could keep a decent man around longer than a few months at a time.

I also remind myself that I'm new at this, that Scarlett didn't come with an instruction manual.

My brother, Will, was nineteen when he knocked up his seventeen-year-old girlfriend. The situation was less than ideal, of course, but in small-town, backwoods Whitebridge, that sort of thing happened all the time.

As his older brother, I wanted better for him. I told him to man up and do the right thing to take care of his family. Given that school was never his forte and the best jobs in Whitebridge hardly paid livable wages, we both decided the army was the next logical step.

Or rather, he hemmed and hawed, so I decided for him.

His heartsick girlfriend, Lexi, wrote him letters every day when he was at boot camp, sending update pictures of her growing belly with each passing week. Fortunately, Will's first return home coincided with the birth of their baby. But within the first six months of Scarlett's life, her father was stationed overseas.

For as long as I live, I'll never forget sitting in Mom's garage, sipping beers as he tried to act brave and I tried to act brave for him. By the end of the night, we'd each polished off a six-pack, and I'd promised—on my life—to watch over his girls should he not make it home alive.

With a punch to the arm and a healthy dose of denial, I'd told him to shut the hell up with that kind of talk.

And then I'd promised.

Five months later, he and eight other soldiers were taken out by a roadside IED after handing out water and blankets to civilians in some war-torn Middle Eastern city.

Not a day goes by that I don't hate myself for pushing him into the military.

If I hadn't been so damn adamant and had let Will think for himself for once, he'd still be here, and I have no doubt he'd be one hell of a father to Scarlett.

The kind she deserves.

He was always so good with kids—maybe because he was just a big kid himself. But they always seemed to gravitate toward him, toward his gigantic smile and willingness to make a fool of himself for a couple of laughs.

We were night and day, Will and I.

But he was my best friend.

And I'd give everything I have right now for one more day with him.

I may have stepped into Scarlett's life a little later than I should have, but I can't let my brother down again. I can't ship his daughter off for someone else to deal with after I gave him my word.

I have to make this work.

If I don't, I've failed Will *and* Scarlett—the only family I've ever given a damn about.

Tossing back the remainder of my scotch, I rest the empty tumbler on a coaster—next to the copy of *Made Man* Scarlett was paging through earlier in the evening. In her haste to leave, she left it open on Elle's February article.

Grabbing the magazine, I examine her photo, but this time in a different light.

Intelligent, accomplished, and unapologetically honest, she's precisely the type of influence Scarlett needs in her life, and given that Elle is currently without a job . . .

I fold the issue and place it back on the coffee table.

Elle would *never*.

Unless I make her an offer she can't refuse.

CHAPTER THIRTEEN

ELLE

"Hello?" Because it's a lazy Friday morning and I have nothing better to do, I answer a random number that I fully expect to be either spam or my doctor's office calling with an automated appointment reminder.

"Elle." A man's velvet voice fills my ear. "Didn't think you'd answer. And on the first ring, no less. Lucky me."

"Who is this?"

"Really?" The caller sniffs. "You worked for me for five years, I darkened your doorstep less than twenty-four hours ago, and already you're forgetting the sound of my voice? That's a shame."

"West?"

Indie glances up from her laptop on the sofa, shooting me a quizzical look.

I shoot one back.

"Why are you calling?" I rise from my chair and pace our small living room in hopes that a little movement will keep my heart rate under control. This man has an uncanny ability to send my blood pressure to the damn moon.

"I have a proposition for you," he says. "An offer."

"I'm not coming back," I say before he can elaborate.

"Nor am I asking you to."

Returning to my chair, I swallow a deep breath as my knee bounces. I'm not sure what kind of offer West could possibly have in mind for me, but every second that passes tortures my curiosity.

"Normally I'd present the offer in person, but seeing how you're averse to being in the same room as me lately, I'll cut to the chase and lay it out for you now," he says. "My niece, Scarlett—the one you met yesterday in Hell's Kitchen?"

"Yeah, what about her?"

"She's in need of a decent influence in her life. A grown woman she can look up to," he says.

My jaw falls. "And *I* was the first person you thought to call?"

"You're not perfect, Elle, but you're what she needs," he says.

I choke out a laugh. "Seriously? All that money and all those connections? You could make a phone call and have someone at your door within the hour, ready to shape her into whatever you want her to be—but you want *me*?"

"She likes you," he says. "Which means she borderline respects you. Which means she'll listen to you. She neither likes nor respects me, and she sure as hell doesn't listen to me. Short of sending her to some boarding school, you're my next best option."

"I don't understand what you're asking. Do you want me to babysit her? She's kind of old for that, yeah?"

"I want you to spend time with her. Get to know her. Let her get to know you. Fill her head with all that shit about being fearless or whatever it is you're doing now," he says. "And while you're doing all of that, keep tabs on her. Make sure she's safe and keeping out of trouble. Teach her how to navigate the city like a local. Treat her like your kid sister, and I'll pay you double what you were making at the magazine."

"You're insane."

"Triple."

"Officially off your rocker." I rise from my chair again, this time patrolling our tiny New York kitchen.

"Name your price."

"I don't even . . . I'm not trained to work with teenagers . . . I wouldn't even know where to begin . . . and this entire thing is absurd, honestly . . ." I trip over my thoughts, each one hurtling faster to my lips than the one before.

"You have sisters," he says.

"How do you know?"

"There was a picture in your box, you with three women who looked just like blonde versions of you."

I hunch over the island. "You went through my things?"

"At least I'm being honest . . . that's your whole thing now, isn't it? Transparency?"

"Yeah, but I didn't need to know that. Now I'm just picturing you rifling through my belongings, and it's creeping me out."

"I can assure you my intentions couldn't have been further from . . . creepy," he says. "So tell me, Elle. What's your price? And would you be willing to start at three o'clock today?"

"Today?"

"Highland Prep dismisses at three ten. You can wait there with her driver. I'll send her a text and let her know I've hired her a companion," he says.

"She's going to see through this," I say. "Any teenage girl with half a brain cell would. And not only will she see through it, she'll hate it twice as much."

I don't know much about teenage girls, but once upon a time I was one. And the last thing I wanted back then was to be under someone's lens. Constant supervision doesn't exactly allow for a girl to find her voice and figure out her place in this world.

"She ran away last night. Again. She's run away so many times in the past four months I've lost count. The police found her at Penn

Station. I think she was trying to get back home, but she's fourteen, for God's sake. She doesn't know the first thing about the real world, and she wouldn't. She . . . had a bit of a rough start. Her father—my brother—died when she was a baby, and her mother . . . let's just say Scarlett drew the short straw in that department."

I sink onto the nearest barstool, hunched on my elbows as West opens up. He's giving me an abbreviated version of her story, sparing any and all details, but it's like a sliver of light peeking out from a closed door, a microscopic glimpse into West's humanity.

For the first time in five years, my heart aches for this boardroom tyrant and his poor, sweet niece. She's clearly grieving the loss of her old life. And he only wants to keep her safe.

"I don't know," I say. "As much as I'd love to be that touchstone in Scarlett's life, you're not exactly the easiest person to work for."

"I'm aware." He clears his throat. "But I'll make it more than worth your while."

"Not everything's about money," I say. "Maybe to you, but not to everyone. There's not a salary you can give me that'll make it worth suffering through your moods and your underhanded remarks."

West responds with a rare bout of silence.

Or maybe he's got nothing to say because he knows a tiger can't change its stripes.

You can't be an epic asshole your entire life, snap your fingers, and suddenly become a kindhearted gentleman with a heart of gold.

"I'm not a man who has to beg for anything," he finally says. "But I'm not above making a fool of myself if it means securing Scarlett's safety. So please. I'm begging you to do this—not for me but for her."

Burying my face against my palm, I gather a hard breath into my lungs. "Your offer is extremely generous, and I'd love to be a positive role model for Scarlett, but I'm sorry, West—I can't work for you."

"Elle—"

"Which is why I'll do it for free." I sit up and find Indie's mouth agape as she slams the lid on her laptop. "I'm not working; I've got nothing but time right now. I'll spend time with her because it's the right thing to do and because Lord knows this world is starving for authentic influences. But I can't work for you. There'll be no boss-employee dynamic between us. Not now, not ever. Understood?"

Indie waves her hands from across the room, frantic as she attempts to flag me down, eyes wild with unspoken protests.

I'm sure she thinks I'm making a grave mistake by associating with that man in any way, shape, or form, but I want to do this. If I'm not doing anything else, I might as well make a difference in someone's life.

"Those are your terms?" he asks after a moment of contemplation.

"Those are my terms."

Exhaling into the phone, he says, "Thank you, Elle. This means more to me than you could possibly understand."

We end the call, and I get lost in my own thoughts while Indie fires off question after question about whether I'm making the right decision. I agreed to this for Scarlett—and only for Scarlett. But I'd be lying if I said I wasn't looking forward to unearthing the real West Maxwell in the process.

A dozen questions pollute my thoughts, followed by a hundred doubts and a million reasons to change my mind before it's too late and I'm in over my head.

But something won't let me.

An hour later, I'm lying in bed, replaying West's phone call in my head until I have it memorized backward and forward, and I've deduced only one thing: West loves Scarlett.

Perhaps the tin man has a heart after all.

CHAPTER FOURTEEN

ELLE

"This is so weird." Scarlett grips her backpack straps as we walk after school, her gaze trained straight ahead. She won't look at me.

"Totally." I sip my iced coffee, strutting alongside her as if this is the most natural thing in the world.

"So . . . like . . . what do we do?"

From what I understand, West told Scarlett I'm her "summer mentor," and she immediately saw through it, proclaiming she was too old for a babysitter. It took a bit of convincing, but he managed to get through to her. That and he told her it was either this or boarding school.

I shrug. "We can do anything you want."

I figured we should start slow, and I should let her call the shots instead of planning out activities like a nanny would do for her charge.

"What do you usually do after school?" I ask.

She rolls her eyes. "Nothing."

I nudge her. "Come on. I doubt you do *nothing*."

"Uncle West expects me to go straight home, but sometimes I hang out at Central Park or stop at the Duane Reade and look for a new lip gloss or get one of those celebrity weekly magazines with the fake arti-cles. Mostly boring stuff."

In a city chock full of life and culture and adventure and fascinating people, being bored is a punishable offense in my book.

"Ah, so you like magazines?" I muse. "A girl after your uncle's heart . . ."

"I mostly like the pictures. All the stories are made up. Like, most of those relationships are for publicity or whatever. But it feels like you're catching up on your favorite show, you know? One week Sabrina Carpenter is with Joshua Bassett, and the next week she's moved on to someone new. And there's always drama."

Of course. Drama is what sells. Nobody's interested in the mun-dane everyday lives of the people they idolize. They want the glamour, the tears, the joy, and the heartbreak, and they want it with a side of glossy, photoshopped images.

"You remind me so much of myself at your age it's scary."

Scarlett gives me side-eye, fighting a temperamental smile. "I hope that's a good thing."

"Me too," I laugh.

"You must be doing something right if Uncle West trusts you with me," she says. "He's such a control freak."

"Yeah, well, he didn't become the man he is today by leaving every-thing to chance." Defending West Maxwell is the last thing I thought I'd find myself doing, and yet here I am. The words are foreign on my tongue, though delivered with the ease and confidence of someone who actually knows the inscrutable titan.

"I guess." She blows a tuft of sandy hair from her eyes, her voice monotone. As much as I'd like to squeeze every ounce of West Maxwell intel from her young little mind, I won't do that. It'd be wrong. And she's insanely savvy—she'd see through it in a heartbeat.

"You ever check out any museums?" I change the subject. "Or join an after-school club? What are you interested in?"

Scarlett chuffs, her white Converse scuffing along the pavement. "Nothing, really."

"What kinds of things did you do back home? Nebraska, was it?"

"Just mostly hung out with friends, I guess."

"But what did you do when you were hanging out?"

A half smile tugs at her lips. "Stuff Uncle West doesn't approve of."

"I get the sense there isn't much he *does* approve of."

"Right?" She perks up as if she's pleased to finally have someone with whom to commiserate. "Nothing I do is ever good enough for him. He's constantly telling me everything I'm doing wrong, and he just gets all annoyed no matter what I say, and it turns into a fight every time."

I'm sure there are two sides to Scarlett's story, but as her mentor, I choose hers.

"He was the same way in the office." I point my coffee south, toward *Made Man*'s headquarters. "So don't take it personally."

"You're lucky you got away from him. Wish I could just quit being his niece . . ."

"You're family. At least he's morally obligated to be nice to you."

Her eyes widen, and she shoots me a cocked glance. "You obviously don't know my uncle."

"You're right. I don't know him at all." I sip the last of my iced latte before chucking it in a nearby garbage can in passing. "It's kind of his whole thing. Closed off or whatever."

We stop at a crosswalk and wait for the light. I have no idea where we're going, just that we seem to be headed toward the Upper West Side. Either way, I'm following her lead and taking this one step at a time—literally.

"Then why'd you agree to mentor me? Or whatever you guys are calling it so it doesn't sound like babysitting . . ." She mutters the last part under her breath.

"Long story." A story that begins with me dying and ends with me quitting my job after pulling an all-nighter. Mind-numbing stuff to a fourteen-year-old, I'm sure. "Where are we going, by the way?"

"Home." She tugs on her uniform polo. "Not walking around the city looking like a preppy clown."

We round the corner to Seventy-Third Street and make our way up a picturesque tree-lined street with narrow but statuesque townhomes shouldered up to one another.

"It's this one." Scarlett waves me to the last unit in the set and tramples up the pristine limestone steps before holding a shiny silver fob against the glossy jet-black door. The dead bolt clicks, and Scarlett pushes her way inside, motioning for me to follow.

Within seconds, I'm standing on the black-and-white-checkered marble floor of West Maxwell's foyer. A familiar trace of his cologne fills my lungs—a small reminder that he was recently here. And that, perhaps, he still is. After all, the man works from his home office 99 percent of the time. But before I have a chance to process the surrealness of this moment, Scarlett punches a button on the wall and steps into an elevator I hadn't realized was there.

"My room's on the fifth floor," she says when I step in beside her. "Kitchen's on the first, along with the living room and dining room. Second floor is laundry and staff quarters. Uncle West's room is on the third. Fourth floor is his office—I'm not allowed to go there. Fifth is my room plus his study. Sixth is the media room and home gym. Seventh is the terrace. There's a basement, but I don't go down there because it's creepy as hell and I swear the furnace looks like a monster . . ."

My mind spins so fast that I don't have time to whip up a mental floor plan or process the fact that one man requires so many floors, so many rooms.

The elevator glides to a stop and deposits us on one of West's superfluous levels, one that doesn't look much different than the first.

Polished marble floors. Wainscoted walls the color of midnight along with burnished black light fixtures accented with dimmed Edison bulbs.

"Gonna change. I'll be right back. You can hang out in the study if you want." She points to a room on the opposite end of the narrow hall before disappearing into her room.

I linger in the hallway for a few moments before eyeing the doorway to West's personal study. Scarlett basically told me to make myself at home . . . and waiting out here while she gets dressed feels like something a nanny (or creepy stalker) would do, so I opt to give her some space and take her words to heart.

A second later, I step inside a tall-ceilinged room trimmed with black-painted wood, built-in bookcases, and leather gentlemen's club chairs. A soapstone fireplace anchors the center of the far wall, and a library's worth of *Made Man* issues fill a bookcase to my left.

Taking a seat in one of the buttery-soft vintage-looking chairs that flank the fireplace, I fix my gaze on an open issue of *Made Man* spilling over the side of the glass coffee table. Sucking in a breath when I realize it's open to my February article—"The Dirty Truth about Valentine's Day"—I attempt not to read too much into it. Surely West Maxwell has better things to do with his time than flip through old articles.

Especially *my* old articles.

I cross my legs, check my watch, and sink into the chair, which cradles me with a kind of crème de la crème luxury only reserved for the luckiest. No wonder West prefers to work from home—if I had rooms like this at my disposal, I'd never leave either. Closing my eyes, I'm the portrait of relaxation, entirely too comfortable to move a muscle, when a cleared throat pulls me out of my trance.

When I glance up, a masculine figure in a three-piece suit looms over me, his shadow covering me like a blanket of ice.

"You're in my chair," West says.

Reminding myself I no longer report to him nor do I work for him, I offer a polite yet curt, "You have an abundance of chairs in this room. Surely you can find another?"

He studies me for an uncomfortable moment before turning away and making a beeline for a brass bar cart in the corner. Pouring himself two fingers of whiskey-brown liquid from a crystal decanter, he returns a second later . . . and takes the seat beside me.

"Scarlett told me to hang out in here while she changed," I say.

He pulls a sip between his perfect lips, staying silent.

"You off for the day?" I ask, eyeing his drink.

Something tells me the man despises small talk.

"What gave it away?" West takes another sip before placing his drink on a marble coaster next to the splayed February issue of *Made Man*—which he promptly flicks shut.

I don't bother asking if or why he was reading it—I'd have better odds of him serenading me with a love song than getting a truthful response.

"Any plans for the weekend?" I sit up, clasping my hands over my knee and pretending none of this is painfully awkward. "I mean, what does the world's most elusive yet fascinating man do in his spare time? Inquiring minds want to know."

"Inquiring minds should worry about their own itineraries," he shoots back. "How was the walk home with Scarlett?"

"Fine." I wave my hand, leaving out the early stroppy bits. "I'm trying to get an idea of what her interests are . . . thought maybe I'd take her around the city tomorrow? Maybe grab a show or hit up the Museum of Natural History? Unless you wanted to do those things with her . . ."

He sniffs. "Be my guest."

As he's a private yet insanely well-known man, I could understand his not wanting to risk exposing his niece to the public eye. But he can't expect her to spend her days hiding away like some princess in a tower.

"Maybe one of these days you could join us?" I offer. "Once Scarlett and I get to know each other better, I mean."

His lips draw up at the corners, as if the mere thought of the three of us cavalcading around the city is comical. And maybe it is. But I think it'd be good for Scarlett. While it's wonderful that West can provide for her materially, she's going to need more than that.

"All right, fine," I say. "Think about it and let me know."

He swirls his drink, staring blankly ahead as if he's lost in thought. Or maybe he's picturing how much fun he could have if only he'd allow it.

"Good Lord, that was painful. I know seventh graders with more game than you two." Scarlett's slight figure takes up the narrow doorway to the study, and I waste no time rising and gathering my things. "Anyway, can we leave, Elle? I'd like to get out of here sometime before my eightieth birthday."

West shoots her a disapproving look, and I ignore her comment.

I'm not sure how Scarlett inferred flirting out of any of that, but I'm sure she was just being a typical teenager trying to get a reaction.

"Yeah, we should bounce," I say, knowing how lame I sound but playing it cool and casual for Scarlett's sake. "Your uncle needs his peace and quiet so he can catch up on some more of my articles." Turning around, I point to his collection of archived magazines. "Highly recommend the one from October 2018."

"Burn!" Scarlett hovers a palm over her glossy lips, fighting a chuckle as we head to the elevator.

In all honesty, I don't recall what I wrote for that month's issue. I'm just messing with him—mostly because I can but also because he looks like he could use a healthy dose of *silly*. For a man with all the money in the world, it would seem he bears the weight of said money on his shoulders.

Behind the curtains of West Maxwell's beautiful and privileged life is a dark and heavy portrait I wasn't expecting. There are no panties hanging from lampshades. No hired hands prepping for a Friday-night party with the who's who of the city. There's no town car waiting to courier him to JFK for a weekend getaway to Saint Thomas or a scantily clad Brazilian runway model waiting to flank his side and usher him into weekend mode.

It's funny—the whole world celebrates this man.

If they only knew . . . he doesn't even celebrate himself.

I follow Scarlett to the elevator and wait for level five to disappear from view as we make our way to the main level.

"Is he always like that?" I ask.

She lifts her overplucked brows. "Like what?"

"Sullen."

The doors glide open, depositing us onto the checkered marble foyer floor.

Scarlett bounces toward the front doors as if she can't get out of here fast enough.

"Yeah," she says when the late-afternoon sun wraps us in its warmth.

I shake off the chill that followed us from West's apartment.

"Now do you see what I'm dealing with?" Scarlett asks. "He acts like he has it so bad. Dude's allergic to happiness or something. Reminds me of this Ken doll I used to play with."

I snicker at the analogy. West could totally be a Ken doll with his dashing good looks and perfect physique.

"He always looked pissed off at the world," Scarlett says. "I don't know if they painted him wrong at the factory or something, but no one ever wanted to play with him. Or if they did play with him, he was always the bad guy. The cheating husband or whatever. Then one day my mom's boyfriend's dog chewed his head off, and we threw the rest of him away."

"Oh." I lift my brows. "Well, that's a plot twist I didn't see coming."

"Anyway, where are we going?" She tightens the strap of her little denim purse over her left shoulder and shoots me a quizzical look. "I should text Uncle West and let him know our exact coordinates, or he might send out the search hounds again."

"Maybe he won't be so bad now that he knows you're not alone."

"Doubtful." Scarlett adjusts her bag. "He loves to make my life miserable. Did you know he had me watched the other day?"

"What do you mean?"

"He knew I'd met you before I even told him. Talk about psycho."

Biting my tongue, I opt not to tell her I was the one who spilled those beans. It wouldn't be the worst thing in the world for a rambunctious fourteen-year-old to think her uncle has eyes on every city block.

"So . . . where to?" Scarlett yawns as she checks her phone. Not only is she bored with the city, but she's already growing bored with me as well. Then again, I doubt she slept much last night, seeing as how she was hanging out at Penn Station at 3:00 a.m.

"Let me think . . ."

A million options flood my mind, but one stands out more than the rest. I'd been dating Matt for two months and dealing with a bout of homesickness when he took me to 97 Orchard Street.

Leading her down a flight of stairs and into the belly of our famed subway system, I swipe my MetroCard and grab us two seats headed for the Lower East Side.

"Where are you taking me?" she asks once we're settled, eyes glinting with curiosity.

"To get a little perspective."

CHAPTER FIFTEEN

WEST

Trailing my finger along the spine of my personal *Made Man* library, I stop at the October 2018 issue, slide it out from its protective sleeve, and settle into my favorite chair for some much-needed quiet time—and to find out exactly why Elle recommended this particular article to me as she dashed out the door with my niece.

THE DIRTY TRUTH ABOUT FIRST TIMES

By Elle Napier

In light of our Halloween-themed issue this month, I wanted to share a terrifying tale. But it's not the kind of terror that makes you sleep with your head under the covers and a baseball bat under your bed. It's the kind of dread that makes your chest ache and your heart drop to the floor when you spend a little too much time reminiscing down memory lane.

That's right—we're not talking about ghosts or masked intruders. This month we're talking about first times and the emotional goblins of regret that haunt us long after the moment has passed.

I was a knobby-kneed eight-year-old when I had my first crush. He was the boy next door, he was an impressive two years older than me, and his name was Elijah. With his giant cocoa-brown curls, a grin that took up his whole face, a swaggering confidence in his long stride, and eyes the color of Pacific Northwest evergreens, he made all the girls on Longmont Street swoon and plan their future nuptials. I should also mention Elijah was a grade A certifiable jerk—but he was my grade A certifiable jerk, therefore I was more than willing to overlook his less favorable traits and let the things I adored about him shine through instead.

Perspective is everything.

Let me say it again louder for those in the back: PERSPECTIVE IS EVERYTHING.

Eight-year-old me didn't know it at the time, but the boy with the contagious laugh, questionable table manners, and unfiltered vocabulary would go on to be my first kiss, my first boyfriend, my first prom date, my first taste of ethereal teenage love, and also my first experience with crippling heartbreak that sent me into a bittersweet blue period until my sisters and best friends slapped a little perspective into me.

There's that word again . . .

Perspective.

Our firsts have a tendency to live loud in our memories, unfairly drowning out the seconds and thirds and fourths. I can tell you exactly what I wore the first time Elijah took me on a real date to see *House of Wax* at the local two-screen movie theater: a pale-pink spaghetti strap tank top, cutoff jean shorts, a mood ring on my right ring finger that stayed yellow (a.k.a. nervous) all night, and an abundance of my mother's Kai perfume.

I vaguely remember the guy who came after him—despite us dating for six months and him being my first college boyfriend. His name was Mark, and he was from Toledo, but most of my memories after that grow hazy.

What I do remember, though, is being so terrified Mark was going to discard me the way Elijah did that I never fully embraced what we had or made it a point to make our relationship meaningful in any way. I showed up for the relationship, but I was never fully there. Never fully committed. Only half-present. My memories of Elijah were much too vivid at the time, and I was convinced nothing could ever hold a candle to all of those "magical" firsts. For six months, I simply bode my time until our inevitable breakup, and I applauded myself for having the foresight to not get too attached.

In retrospect, I only cheated myself.

Mark was a great guy—at least from what I remember.

I was the one who sucked because I let all of those firsts with Elijah steer the ship.

Anyway, all of this is to say, I can confidently tell you that the firsts never stop, and they never get easier—or less terrifying. Think about it . . . every first date is followed by an eventual first kiss. Then a first time between the sheets (which begs its own dedicated article). Possibly the first time mustering the courage to say, "I love you." The first time meeting your significant other's friends and family. It goes on and on and it never stops.

Life is literally just a series of first times.

If we continue to let our firsts get in the way of all the other firsts that come after them, we're doing ourselves a huge disservice—and to me, that's downright terrifying.

Here's to embracing all of the firsts—past, present, and future.

And remember: perspective is everything.

Yours in truth—

Elle Napier

I fold the magazine, swirl my bourbon, and sink back into my seat. I distinctly recall reading that article years ago, as it came on the cusp of a nasty breakup with my then girlfriend. She called me *emotionally unavailable* and *damaged* and a slew of other much-deserved words that I let ricochet off me with zero reaction.

After she was finished pitching her fit, I checked a few work emails as she packed up her things into a set of designer luggage and hailed a cab to somewhere else. I deleted and blocked her number after that, noting the relief that washed over me like a cool drink of water I hadn't known I needed.

And I took Elle's words to heart: *perspective is everything*.

I've never been relationship material, though like a fool I've tried my hand a time or two.

People aren't meant to be alone; of that much I'm certain. But when you've been alone most of your adult life, it becomes as natural as breathing air. You don't think about it until someone tells you to think about it.

Elle's October 2018 article made me think about my aloneness.

But only for a moment.

Then I put that shit into perspective and moved the hell on.

My phone chimes from across the room. Placing my bourbon aside, I return the issue of *Made Man* to its rightful place between September and November before retrieving my device.

MIRANDA: Merger update for you. Apparently twelve people at City Gent turned in immediate resignations upon learning they were going to be working for you. Once again, your reputation precedes you.

I smirk, thumbing back a quick response.

ME: Good riddance.

MIRANDA: We lost some decent ones in that batch . . .

ME: We'll replace them with better ones.

MIRANDA: On it. I'll get with HR immediately.

ME: Monday.

MIRANDA: ???

ME: Take the weekend off.

MIRANDA: You feeling okay?!

ME: Never better.

I debate inserting a smiling emoji to emphasize my point but think better of it. I don't do that shit.

In the context of everything that's been going on with Scarlett lately, I feel like a proverbial million bucks. Knowing she's trotting around the city with a responsible adult means one less worry polluting my mind. For the first time in months, something akin to warm relaxation spreads through my veins. Or maybe it's the bourbon. Either way, I'm here for it.

MIRANDA: Send me a pic to prove it's really you and not Scarlett . . .

Scarlett wouldn't dare touch my phone—and honestly, she's too preoccupied with her own to care. My boring business dealings don't hold a candle to the superfluous amount of candy-colored apps and games littering her screen.

ME: Take the weekend. We'll talk Monday.

Closing out of my messages, I pull up a moody Chopin playlist on my phone and stream it through the built-in speakers above and around me. Within seconds I'm enveloped in another place, another time, escaping to a world away from the picture-perfect one I've spent my entire life building.

Liquescent in my chair, I empty my thoughts. Or rather, I attempt to. It's the strangest thing . . . every time I close my eyes, all I see is *her*.

CHAPTER SIXTEEN

ELLE

"You doing okay?" I ask Scarlett. Our two-hour tour of the Tenement Museum concluded a half hour ago. Now we're a block from West's home, and she's yet to say a single word. "A lot to take in, I know . . ."

"That was, like, probably the most depressing thing I've ever seen," she finally says.

"I was going for something more along the lines of eye opening."

Scarlett rolls her eyes. "I thought we were going to be doing fun things. Not . . . that."

"We will." I eye West's glossy front door in the distance, and my stomach clenches with dread while the rest of me tingles in curious anticipation. Never has a man given me such a mixed bag of emotions with the mere idea of his presence. "I just wanted to show you that generations ago, people left everything they knew and everyone they loved to come to this very city to start a better life. They endured poverty and sickness and disease and death and heartbreak and government corruption . . . so that their families could someday have a better life. They weren't even shooting for the stars—they just wanted *better*. So when you think about how hard things are right now, I want you to think about those thousands of families who started there, at those tenements. Think of their strength and their determination and know that you're capable of conquering hard things too."

While it's lopsided to place the plight of refugees and immigrants next to a fourteen-year-old moving to a cushy Manhattan apartment and attending a posh private school, I can't think of a better way to give her some immediate perspective.

I'll never forget the day I bemoaned to Matt how I'd been missing home and was thinking about packing up and heading back. It'd been a stressful couple of months at work, and the city was feeling particularly grumpy lately. Not to mention one of my sisters had just delivered her first baby and I was missing out on priceless family gatherings. But Matt wasted no time hauling me to 97 Orchard and promptly telling me that if I gave up on my dreams over a couple of minor inconveniences, I'd be throwing mud in the face of all those people who sacrificed so much more for so much less.

"Someday you'll look back at this, and you'll—" I begin to say before she lifts a hand.

"No offense, Elle, but I'm really freaking tired right now, and I just want to go to bed." Despite the fact that it's barely 7:00 p.m., Scarlett trots up the steps to West's apartment, swipes her key card, and disappears inside. A moment later, she pops her head out. "You coming in or what?"

"Am . . . am I supposed to?"

She motions over her shoulder. "Uncle West says he'd like a word with you, so probably."

With my heart in my teeth, I glide up the narrow limestone stairs and step into his world once again.

CHAPTER SEVENTEEN

WEST

"I read your article," I say as we settle into my study. Upon the girls' return, Scarlett promptly announced she was skipping dinner and going straight to bed, and I took the opportunity to invite Elle in for a drink and a debriefing on their evening together. "The one from October 2018."

"Oh." Her dark brows arch. "I was joking when I told you to read that . . . what was it about? They all kind of blur together over the years . . ."

Figures.

"'The Dirty Truth about First Times,'" I recite, my back to her as I top off my bourbon. "What's your poison?"

"Gin and tonic," she says without hesitation. "Please."

"Scarlett was decent for you tonight, I presume?" I mix her drink, give it a stir, and deliver it with a monogrammed cocktail napkin.

"She was . . . quiet."

Our fingertips graze in the exchange, and our gazes hold.

Her lips slip into a coy smile as she sinks into the chair next to mine. "I took her to the Tenement Museum, but now I'm worried I traumatized her."

I take a seat. "The Tenement Museum. Interesting choice."

While I'm well aware of its purpose and history, I've yet to visit it myself, and it's one of the last places I'd whisk a teenager off to on a Friday night.

"I was hoping to give her some perspective." Elle takes a careful sip. "This is amazing, by the way."

"What kind of *perspective* were you hoping to give her, exactly?"

"I just wanted to show her how lucky she is to be here," Elle says. "And how so many people sacrificed everything they had for a chance at something better in this very city."

"And do you think it resonated with her?" I fight a chuckle.

Elle rests her elbow on the arm of the chair and her pretty face on her hand as she exhales. "No. I don't. She didn't say a single word to me on the walk home, and when I asked if she was okay, she told me it was really depressing and she wanted to go to bed."

"Sounds about right."

"I was thinking tomorrow we'd do something lighter," she continues. "There's this really fun vintage flea market in SoHo the last Saturday of every month—so tomorrow. I don't know if she's into that kind of thing, but at least it won't be depressing. Vintage Pucci and Halston never are."

"Excuse me, sir." Bettina stands in the doorway, hands clasped at her hips. "Dinner is ready."

Pointing at Elle's cocktail, I say, "Why don't you join me? It'd be a shame for Scarlett's plate—or that perfectly good gin and tonic—to go to waste."

"Are you sure?" Elle rises, her movements jagged and uncertain.

"I am," I say. "But apparently you aren't. Don't feel obligated to stay out of politeness."

I've eaten thousands of dinners alone; one more won't kill me.

Elle's lips move, but no sound emerges. And her eyes scan the room as if she's looking for an exit, though her feet remain firmly planted. She's a beautiful portrait of confusion with those deep ocean eyes and windswept chocolate strands framing her face.

But indecision has always been my biggest pet peeve.

"Guess I'll decide for you." I head for the door. "You're staying for dinner."

A quiet elevator ride later, we're situated at the dining table as Bettina serves her signature coq au vin with haricots verts. Simple, timeless, and impeccably presented.

"Thank you," Elle says to Bettina once we're settled.

Silence envelops us, punctuated by the occasional tinkle of silverware against china.

"You know, it's ironic that my October 2018 article was about firsts." She breaks that silence. "Because this week has been full of firsts for me."

"And are you embracing those firsts?" I recite one of her lines.

"What do you mean?"

"You ended your article with a sentence about embracing past, present, and future firsts," I remind her.

"Oh. I don't remember that line." She prongs a green bean. "But it sounds like something I'd write." Elle pauses in contemplation. "It's inspiring, though, right? I mean, that's what your readers want to hear. They want to be uplifted. Easily digestible advice from the city girl next door—that's how Tom always framed my column."

My jaw tenses. "Yes, Elle. You did your job, and you did it well."

I offer a figurative pat on the back in the form of an approving nod.

"So aside from your semifictitious advice, was the boy in the story real?" I ask. "Elijah?"

Reaching for her gin and tonic, she sniffs. "Very much so."

"You still keep in touch?"

Elle takes a sip. "No. But his kid brother is marrying my kid sister next month, so there'll be ample opportunity for us to catch up."

Her tone is dry and flat and laced with sarcasm.

"I take it you're not looking forward to that reunion?" I slice into my chicken and wait for her response.

"Elijah . . . he's a very charming person. Very persuasive. He has this way about him that makes you forget what a toxic narcissist he is," she says. "I've spent the last twelve years going out of my way to avoid him for that very reason, so no. I'm not looking forward to spending a week in his presence."

"A *week*?"

"In my family, weddings are a weeklong endeavor. Lots of dinners and cookouts and brunches and parties and after-parties." She exhales. "It'll be every bit as exhausting as it sounds, but it's the Napier way. When it comes to special events, we only have one mode. We don't do anything halfway."

I conjure up a mental image of Elle twirling on some parquet floor in a pastel-blue bridesmaid dress, surrounded by giggling children as she teaches them the proper way to dance the macarena.

Weddings have never been my cup of tea. In fact, I've been known to go out of my way to schedule a conflicting travel arrangement if it gets me out of RSVP'ing yes to an invite. But I respect a woman who truly knows how to celebrate.

At least, in my head she does.

Pulling in a generous sip of bourbon, I tell myself that the Elle in my head is likely much different than the woman sitting across from me. Fantasizing about what she does or doesn't do at a wedding that hasn't even happened yet serves zero purpose.

"Have you ever been married, West?" she asks between bites of chicken, her voice as casual as if she were asking about tomorrow's weather forecast.

I resist the urge to remind her my personal life is not small-talk fodder, until I remind myself she isn't a tabloid journalist, nor does she work for me. She's simply a woman doing me a generous favor out of the kindness of her heart.

"No." I take another drink, focusing on the still life painting on the opposite side of the room and pretending I don't feel the blanketing weight of her stare or the silence of all the additional questions she'd probably kill to ask.

"Ever been engaged?" She follows up with a doozy.

Brazen, this one.

"Once," I say.

Briefly.

A lifetime ago.

But I keep those details to myself.

"Who ended it?" Elle asks.

"Forgive me for changing the subject, but I imagine your food is getting cold."

Her full mouth pulls at one corner, and a second later she's resting her elbow next to her plate and her cheek against her fist as she stares at me in amused wonderment.

"I'm sorry," she half laughs. "I thought it was crazy before, the idea of you being some doting uncle, but the idea of you being in love? Of wanting to settle down? That's absolutely wild to me. I cannot wrap my head around it."

"Fortunately, you don't need to." I toss back the remains of my bourbon. "It's ancient history."

"You're like an advent calendar. All these little rooms with little doors and little surprises inside each one."

"I thought I was a human Fyre Festival. Which is it?"

"Both." She flashes a slow, teasing grin, and her eyes glint in a way that suggests her gin and tonic is kicking in. "You're also a padlocked diary, and I have every intention of picking that lock."

"Good luck with that."

Many have tried; none have succeeded.

"Challenge accepted," she counters, flashing a dazzling smile that hitches my breath and dismantles me like a bomb—but only for an instant. "You're like a three-thousand-piece puzzle. Once I get the frame situated, I'll start working on the inside. And sooner or later, I'll have the whole picture."

"How optimistic of you."

"For the record—and not that it matters—but you can ask me anything you want, and I'll give you an honest answer," she says. "I'm so over filtering everything to make other people happy. Seriously, ask me anything."

"I'll take your word for it." The last thing I'm in the mood for is a volleyball game of personal questions.

"So your engagement—who ended it? You or her? You never answered."

"It was mutual."

She rolls her pretty blue eyes. "Well, that's boring."

"I'm sorry my personal life couldn't be of more entertainment to you." I take the last bite of my chicken and dab the corners of my mouth with my napkin before placing it over my plate.

"Were you in love?" she asks next.

"In love enough to propose, I guess." I can't believe I'm answering her questions; then again, it's not like I'm giving her any real information. I'm careful to leave out the fact that her father hated me with the passion of a thousand Floridian suns and her mother once got drunk off too many vodka sodas and grabbed my package behind their pool house.

I'm also careful to bite my tongue about all my ex's narcissistic tendencies and my moronic belief that our insane sex life and picture-perfect exterior would make up for the tumultuous roller coaster that was our relationship behind closed doors. When we weren't fighting, we were fucking. And when she wasn't getting my attention, she'd make damn sure to get someone else's. She was creative like that. A total mind fuck. In the end, instead of sucking my cock every night, she was sucking my soul from my marrow.

I hated the man I was becoming.

And I'd become a passenger on my own ship—with her drama and nonsense behind the wheel. It was no way for a man to live. And given my ex's batshit-crazy MO, I had to set the stage for a mutual breakup, or she'd have never let me go. It needed to feel like it was her idea and not just mine, or the woman would have dragged it out for an eternity before throwing lies in the air like confetti and writing a tell-all book when it was all over.

But none of those things are any of Elle's business, nor am I in a mood for a jaunt down memory lane.

"What was her name?" she asks.

"Heather," I say. It's a common enough name that I'm comfortable sharing it.

"How long were you together?" she asks.

"Too long." And that's the God's honest truth.

She clucks her tongue at my ambiguity. "What'd the ring look like?"

"I'm not sure what that has to do with anything . . ."

"Did you pick it out yourself, or did she tell you what she wanted?"

"Again, I'm not sure what that has to do with anything."

She squirms in her seat, inching closer to me like an excited child who can no longer contain herself. "I'm just trying to get a visual here. I can't picture you walking into a jeweler and choosing a ring. I feel like you probably had people who did that for you."

"I chose it myself. Six carats because six was her favorite number. Flawless. Brilliant cut because I wanted to ensure the glimmering facets could be seen from the International Space Station." Younger and insecure, I wanted the entire world to know she was taken the instant she walked into the room. It's comedic in retrospect—how terrified I was to lose one of the worst things to ever happen to me.

Elle's jaw falls, and she reminds me of that ridiculous GIF of Andy from *Parks and Rec*—the one Miranda sends me anytime she wants to rouse some semblance of a smile from me.

"This is big." She slaps a hand on my polished dining table. "Like, that's normal-people stuff. *You* picking an engagement ring."

I can't help but chuckle at her reaction, though I wipe the ridiculous amused expression from my face as soon as it appears. I've spent a lifetime building a fortress around myself—I won't let some cute brunette tear it down with a playful line of questioning.

Flattening my mouth, I clear my throat and straighten my shoulders.

"I feel like I'm making you uncomfortable," she says. "So I'm going to stop. But you should know I'm going to spend the rest of my night trying to picture what she looked like and what kind of fiancé you were, and by tomorrow I'm going to have this whole narrative in my head, and if it's wrong, I'm going to be incredibly disappointed."

"Or you could use that time to not think about me."

Her eyes flash, and her cheeks turn a deeper shade of pink. "I'm sorry. I . . . I got carried away. I shouldn't have asked all those questions."

Folding her napkin, she lays it aside before pushing her chair out and rising to leave.

"I really like Scarlett," she says. "For the record, I think she's a great girl in a tough spot, and I'm going to do everything I can to help her grow confident with her place in this world."

"Appreciate that."

"If you wouldn't mind sometime, maybe you could fill me in a little more on what she's been through?" She lifts a shoulder to her ear. "I think maybe it'd help me to understand her better?"

"Sometime, yes."

"And I'm so sorry about your brother," she adds. "I know you said he passed when she was a baby, but that had to have been so devastating. And then to look at her every day and see a part of him . . . that's got to be tough for you."

I know where this is going.

"It was. And it is." I rise from the table and head to the doorway, tension burning into my shoulders. She can question me about my failed engagement until she's blue in the face, but I'm not in the mood to play twenty questions about my dead brother. "Thank you for joining me for dinner, Elle. If you don't mind, I'm heading upstairs for the evening. Please show yourself out."

I leave before she has a chance to protest.

CHAPTER EIGHTEEN

ELLE

"Sweetheart, you never did send me your flight itinerary," my mother drawls into the phone Saturday morning as I'm en route to West's to pick up Scarlett.

"Shoot. I'm so sorry. It's been a crazy couple of days . . ."

Quit my job . . .

Gave one of the most influential men in the world what for . . .

Volunteered to mentor his teenage niece despite not having a clue what I'm doing . . .

Had cocktails and dinner in his private residence on a Friday night and then proceeded to grill him on his personal life . . .

"That's fine, Elle. I know you have a lot going on, but I'd appreciate it if you could prioritize that one little action item for me." She speaks like a true planner. "Would really mean the world to me." And in true Mona Napier fashion, she sprinkles a little sugar on top too. "Will only take a second."

"I'll do it as soon as we hang up," I promise, fighting a yawn. As soon as I got home last night, I spent way too much time browsing Nebraska obituaries in search of West's brother's, only to find a three-sentence tribute and a name—William Michael Maxwell. Given how private West is, I'm not surprised he had it scrubbed from the internet just like everything else.

"You know," Mom says, her voice inching up a mischievous octave, "I was at the Winn-Dixie yesterday, and you'll never believe who I ran into."

"Oh yeah?" I weave between a dog walker and a slow walker. "Who'd you see?"

"Elijah. You remember Elijah, right? Your high school boyfriend."

Wish I didn't . . .

"Yeah," I say. "What's he up to?"

"Oh, he was in town visiting his family. You know he's a dentist now. Has a practice up in Saint Louis."

"I think someone was telling me that not too long ago." That "someone" being Facebook. I totally internet stalked him after a bottle of wine on a snowed-in Wednesday night last year. "Good for him."

"Yeah," she continues. "And Elle, I'm telling you, the man looks cuter than ever. He's got all these muscles. And this pearly-white smile. Well, he always had that perfect smile. But he just . . . well, you know some people don't age well. Not Elijah."

"Good for him," I repeat because there's nothing else to say.

"Oh, and guess what?"

"What?"

"He's single. Never been married. Can you believe that?" she asks.

Yes. Yes, I can believe that, because his lying, cheating ways would be an impediment to that sort of lifestyle . . .

"He asked about you." My mother chuckles, speaking with breathless words as if the excitement of this admission is getting the best of her. "Says he can't wait to catch up with you at the wedding. Oh, and he asked if you're bringing a date. I told him no . . . and you should've seen the look on his face, Elle. It's like his eyes just *lit* from within. Like fireworks. Then he said he's coming solo too."

"I hate to disappoint either of you, but there's not going to be any kind of running-toward-each-other-in-slow-motion reunion happening. I'll say hi and I'll be cordial, but the Elijah-and-Elle ship has sailed."

"Oh, Elle. Don't be so negative. Everything happens for a reason. Maybe you'll feel differently when you see him again. It's been, what, twelve years?"

"Not long enough."

My mother chuckles, and I picture her waving me off as she paces her giant yellow kitchen while a china cup of hibiscus tea cools on the windowsill above the sink.

I round the corner to West's apartment, instantly spotting Scarlett perched on the bottom steps, head in her hand. As soon as she notices me, I give her an overenthusiastic wave and ear-to-ear grin—an attempt to start the day off on a positive note to offset the depressing ending to our Friday night together.

"Hey, Mom. Sorry to cut this short, but I'm meeting up with someone," I say when she begins to ramble on about Elijah's muscles for the second time. If she likes him so much, maybe she should marry him? Not that my father would be cool with that, but the way she's fawning over Elijah, it seems Dad might have a little competition. "I'll call you later, okay? And I'll text you that itinerary right now."

"Okay, but don't forget, sweetheart."

"Doing it right now." I end the call and flick through my email in warp speed until I find the flight confirmation and forward it off. "Hey, Scarlett." Tucking my phone away, I slide my hands into my back jeans pockets. "You all rested up?"

Her pale-blue eyes are a little brighter in the morning sun, and her hair is shower damp and pulled back. Without giving myself too much credit, I think it's safe to say she's somewhat excited to hang out with me today, which means I didn't completely bomb it with the Tenement Museum fiasco.

Scarlett gives me a thumbs-up before tucking her phone into her bra.

Gazing past my shoulder, she says, "Hey, Uncle West."

From the corner of my eye, I see a glistening, shirtless Greek god of a man trot in our direction before settling to my right.

Only slightly winded, he pulls a white earbud from his left ear before stretching a muscled arm overhead—a move that only serves to accentuate his chiseled torso and picture-perfect Adonis belt (no Photoshop necessary).

"Hey," I say, keeping as cool as I can despite the air around us suddenly growing ten degrees hotter. "I didn't take you for a Central Park–jogger type. Figured you were one of those private-home-gym guys."

"He is," Scarlett says under her breath. "He's totally a private-home-gym guy. What's with this?"

"A man can't get some fresh air without coming home to the Spanish Inquisition?" He adjusts the black sweatband currently pushing his thick, dark hair off his forehead. "Where are you two headed?"

I nudge Scarlett. "Thought we'd hit up this designer flea market in SoHo. I promised my roommate I'd find her a vintage Hermès scarf."

"Whatever that is," Scarlett says.

"Oh, honey. If you're going to be a New Yorker, you have to know your designers." I snake my arm around her and manage to wrangle a smile out of her. "You want to join, West?"

"As enthralling as an Hermès hunt sounds, I'll pass," he says. "But thank you."

"He has people who shop for him," Scarlett says, head tilted. "Unlike us peasants."

West gives her a playful punch on the shoulder before retrieving a key fob from a zippered pocket in his shorts and heading inside. It takes all the strength I have not to picture him in the shower.

"Did you have breakfast yet?" I ask Scarlett as we head off.

"I don't really eat breakfast."

"What? Why?"

She lifts a shoulder. "My mom never really made it, and we never had a lot of food in the house, so I got used to skipping it. I don't get hungry until about noon."

West's words from last week play in my ear—without giving away too much, he implied that her mom was less than amazing. I imagine things had to have been pretty horrid for him to end up with sole custody.

"So what was life like back in Nebraska?" I ask. "Tell me about the good stuff, the stuff you miss."

"It was amazing."

"Really? How so?"

"My mom was never home, so I kind of got to do whatever I wanted." She speaks of it with a braggadocio lilt in her voice, as if it's the kind of thing that might impress someone. "My mom's not strict at all—unlike Uncle West. She trusts me."

That or she doesn't care . . .

"I could hang out with my friends all the time," she continues. "Seven days a week. Anytime I wanted."

"Where was your mom?"

Her lips twist at one side. "Sometimes working. Sometimes hanging out with her friends."

"What did you do if you needed to get ahold of her?"

Scarlett doesn't answer me right away, taking a moment before exhaling a short breath.

"You literally sound like the people who took me away from her. You're asking the exact same questions," she says.

Shoot.

"Yeah, you're right. Sorry." I bite my lip and search for the right words. "I'm just trying to understand where you came from so I can help you figure out where you're going."

118

"And now you sound like the therapist Uncle West sent me to when I first got here." Her dirty Converse sneakers scuff along the sidewalk.

If I can't catch a break with this child, I can only assume West has it a hundred times worse.

"Scarlett." I stop and place my hand on her shoulder. "I'm not a therapist or a DHS worker. I'm just a thirty-year-old staff writer that your uncle—for some insane reason—thinks will be a good influence for you this summer. Please know that I'm on your side. I'm here *for* you and *because of* you. I can't make you trust me, but I can show you that I'm worth your trust. Just give me a little grace, and I'll do the same with you, okay?"

Arms crossed, she still refuses to look at me, but as promised, I give her a little grace and let it go.

"It's not the worst thing in the world to have someone who cares about you," I say, soft and gentle. "Everyone needs at least one of those."

Her attention fixes on a crack in the pavement.

"You have your uncle West," I add, "and I have Mona Napier. Two sides of the exact same coin. Believe me, I'm no stranger to having every second of your day micromanaged."

Scarlett sniffs.

"We're going to have fun this summer." I lighten my tone. "I promise."

"Fine." She relents a little, her posture less rigid as we trudge ahead. "So who are the good designers?"

With pep in my step, I tell her all about the classics—Halston, Pucci, Chanel, and Dior—as well as how to spot fakes from a mile away. By the time we're looking around at the flea market, our morning rough patch has been honed to a polished-marble finish, and my sullen teenage charge is wearing a proud smile as she showcases a colorful Pucci pocket square.

"I'm ninety-nine percent sure Uncle West will never wear this," she says before cracking a devilish grin. "I'm totally going to make him wear this to work next week."

"Just make sure you take a picture since I won't be there to see him."

"For sure."

We head to the checkout, where an iPad-wielding woman in a seventies-era sundress swipes my card for the thirty-dollar pocket square, and we're on our way.

"What next?" she asks, waving the vibrant fabric like a makeshift flag.

"Oh," I say. "I didn't have a whole day planned . . . thought we'd head back to your place, but we can stop for lunch at this new café I keep hearing about. I've been dying to try it. Supposedly they have this—"

"It's okay," she says. "I get it. I wouldn't want to spend an entire weekend with me either."

"*Scarlett.*" I nudge her arm. "Stop. You can't guilt-trip the inventor of guilt trips. I was practically the queen of guilt trips when I was your age. As a result, they no longer work on me because I see through each and every one. Anyway, we've got an entire summer to fill. No need to rush it."

"Fine." We cross an intersection, and she strides ahead a few steps, forcing distance between us. And I think I get it now—she pushes people away because she's testing them.

She runs away because she wants West to find her to prove he cares.

And now she's doing the same thing to me, albeit on a lesser scale.

"Scarlett, wait up." I jog ahead to catch up, and once there, I give her a little bit of grace yet again and let it go. "So I was thinking, maybe this week we could check out that new Sabrina Carpenter movie? Maybe a matinee after school on Monday?"

"Yeah, sure."

"When you get home, why don't you make a list of all the things you want to do this summer? Like an NYC bucket list. And I'll do everything I can to help you clear it."

"I want to go home," she says without hesitation. "To Whitebridge. For a week. That's all I really want to do. And every time I ask Uncle West, he says, 'Never.' He doesn't even say no—it's always *never*. But maybe if you go with me?"

Scarlett turns to me with hope-laced baby blues.

"School's out in two weeks," she says. "We could go right after that."

"My sister's getting married end of June, and I'm going out there the week before," I say. "I could squeeze in a trip to Nebraska before that . . . but one thing at a time. We're still in the trust-building phase. Your uncle has to trust me with you, and he has to trust that you're not going to do anything crazy again—like run off to Penn Station at three a.m."

I give her a wink, but I mean business.

"You do your part; I'll do mine. Deal?" I extend my hand, and she looks at me like I'm crazy. *"Deal?"*

After a quick bout of hesitation, she finally slides her hand into mine. "Deal."

Nebraska, here we come.

Maybe . . .

CHAPTER NINETEEN

WEST

"Back already?" I ask Scarlett as she appears in the doorway of my study shortly after noon on Saturday long enough to give a quick wave and dash away. Rising, I follow. "Where's Elle?"

Turning back, she offers a shrug. "She had other stuff to do; I don't know. I'm not her keeper."

"Did you get anything at the farmers' market?"

"Flea market," she corrects me before digging into her left pocket and displaying a crumpled square embossed with some psychedelic pattern. "This is for you. It's Gucci or Pucci or something. I don't know. Elle says it's cool, and we both think you should wear it to work next week."

"The two of you discussed this, did you?" I swipe it from her hand and give it a careful exam as the scents of mothballs and *time* fill my lungs.

The day I saunter into corporate with a smelly and comically vibrant pocket square is the day I officially lose all credibility with my team.

"And what else did the two of you discuss today?" I ask.

"Maybe you should've joined us; then you'd know."

"There's a thin red line between spirited conversation, Scarlett . . . and blatant disrespect."

Throwing her hands in the air, she groans in true Scarlett fashion. "Ugh. I can't win with you!"

A second later, she disappears behind a slammed door. Steeling my nerves, I retreat to my study, close the door like a civilized gentleman, and text Elle.

ME: How was she?

ELLE: We had a good time!

ME: That's not what I asked . . .

ELLE: I know. I was answering your question based on what you should have asked.

Smart-ass.

ELLE: Friendly reminder—I'm not her babysitter and I don't work for you. ☺

ME: Friendly reminder—I'm her uncle and sole caretaker and prefer to know if she's being respectful to the adults in her life.

Three dots fill the screen before disappearing completely. A full minute passes before she replies.

ELLE: She was great . . . all things considered.

Shifting in my chair, I cross my legs and huff.

ME: All things considered? Care to elaborate.

ELLE: Is that really necessary? You know more about her situation than I do. I'm sure you understand this isn't easy for her.

ME: Of course.

I set my phone aside, lean back, and wait for her response. Only when my phone vibrates again, it isn't Elle filling my screen.

It's Nadia.

My fuck buddy—for lack of a better term.

NADIA: Hey, stranger. Haven't heard from you in a while. Hope all is well. I'm in town for the week . . . lmk when you want me to come over. ;-)

Dragging my hand along my jaw, I force a hard breath through my nostrils as a river of blockaded tension floods through me. It's been over four months since I've had a true *release*. A record for me. But hosting hookups with Scarlett under my roof feels wrong on a myriad of levels, and leaving Scarlett alone for more than a handful of hours at night is completely out of the question given her track record.

NADIA: Btw, I had the craziest dream about you the other night . . . I'll tell you all about it when I see you. Maybe we can recreate it.

NADIA: Spoiler alert—it involved handcuffs and that thing you do with your tongue . . .

If it were this time last year, I'd be sending a car to pick her up *immediately*. We'd be holed up in my bedroom for an entire weekend, subsisting off takeout and multiple orgasms. Nadia is the only woman I've fucked who has been 100 percent okay with my no-strings requirement—unlike her predecessors, who have played the part before inevitably springing "the talk" on me when they start to grow attached.

As she's an international jet-setter and bona fide Russian oil heiress, there's nothing I can offer Nadia that she doesn't already have. And settling down is akin to nonsexual handcuffs in her book. At twenty-five, she has no interest in relationships, nor does she attempt to get to know me on a personal level. We can talk caviars, fine wines, and foreign films until four in the morning, and not once does she ask the kind of stirring, soul-rousing questions that suck the life out of a good time.

I reread Nadia's messages, my thumb hovering over the keyboard, frozen.

What could potentially be a few hours of mental and physical freedom doesn't hold the same lure it once did. My heartbeat doesn't falter from its steady tempo. My cock doesn't strain against the inside of my boxer briefs. There's no sense of urgency. No hedonistic desire saturating my core.

Darkening my screen, I push the thought of Nadia away. Until everything with Scarlett is sorted out, gone are the days of meaningless liaisons.

Exiting my study, I head up to my private office and lose myself in work for the hours that follow. This week we'll begin a search for Elle's replacement and discuss our new staff structure and chain of command once the merger is finalized, and I'll stop by the photo shoot for August's cover. We booked a temperamental, egotistical A-list actor for that month's feature, and those types are typically offended if I don't make a personal appearance.

Years ago, when I was first launching this rag, I used to live for those moments. They validated all my late nights and obsessive dedication. They confirmed that everything I'd sacrificed wasn't for naught. Only somewhere along the line, the shiny parts of this endeavor lost their luster. I thought, perhaps, I was going through a funk.

Everyone has a blue period.

It happens to the best of us and often without warning.

I've consulted the best of the best in both Eastern and Western medicine and swallowed overpriced supplements I couldn't begin to pronounce, but my blue period has only intensified, growing from a dusky cerulean to a dark midnight Atlantic.

But everything in this world is temporary.

Nothing ever lasts.

Of that much, I'm certain.

CHAPTER TWENTY

ELLE

"Ugh. That movie was horrid," Scarlett's friend Piper groans Monday afternoon as we leave the Sabrina Carpenter matinee. "Like, I cringed the entire time."

It wasn't *that* bad.

Maybe if she'd looked up from her phone screen once in a while, she could've gotten into it . . .

Scarlett was entranced every minute of it, mindlessly snapping off bits of Twizzlers as her eyes fixated on the teen-targeted storyline unfolding on the big screen.

"Yeah, it sucked," Scarlett says, though I don't believe her for a second.

Biting my tongue, I keep my commentary to myself and stay a couple of strides behind them. Two hours ago, I met Scarlett at Highland Prep after school, only I didn't expect her to have a chatty, red-haired pal in tow. At first, I was tickled that Scarlett had made a friend, and I was maybe a little too enthusiastic about inviting her along to the show, but a block into our walk to the theater, I'd heard her new buddy name-drop three celebrities (her father is a talent manager), make fun of their chemistry teacher's "jiggly Buddha belly," and wax on about how much she hates her ex–best friend for posting an unflattering picture of her on Instagram without permission.

I'd wager this girl was ousted by her friend group for being woefully unlikable and has now latched on to Scarlett because the new kid is always the lowest-hanging fruit.

Still, I keep quiet, noting the extra bounce in Scarlett's step as she chats with her new friend—and the fact that she hasn't stopped smiling in hours.

Piper may not be the ideal insta-friend, but Scarlett needs this.

"Hey, you should come over to my place for a little bit." Piper taps out a text on her gigantic purple iPhone. "My mom said it's cool."

Whipping around, Scarlett lifts her brows. "I'm going to Piper's."

My jaw slackens as I search for the appropriate words to say. I'm not her keeper, so I can't exactly tell her no. But if I tell her yes, I'll have West's wrath to deal with.

"You should ask your uncle first," I say, advising her the way a good mentor should. "He's the boss . . ."

Pulling out her phone, Scarlett dials West and puts the call on speaker before thinking better of it. Thirty seconds later, she hangs up.

"He didn't answer," she sighs. "I'll just text him and let him know where I am."

"Wait," I say. "Let me try him."

Scarlett squints, wordlessly questioning my involvement in this. And I don't blame her. It's weird. And it's confusing. And these dynamics are new to all of us. There's no manual, no precedent to follow.

"You know how he is," I say with a casual wave of my hand. Pulling up his contact, I press the green call button—only to get his voice mail after a few rings. It's a Monday, so he's likely swamped.

"Come on. Let's just go," Piper says before turning to me. "Thanks for the movie, Ellie."

"Elle," I correct her.

"Same thing," Piper giggles before linking her arm into Scarlett's. They're halfway down Lexington Avenue before I realize I don't even know Piper's last name.

Still, I remind myself I'm not her nanny.

With quivering fingertips I fire off a text to West, letting him know we left the movie and Scarlett's going to her friend Piper's house for a little bit. Exhaling, I wait until the message shows as delivered before heading home. And I'm halfway there when my phone buzzes in my pocket, sending a shock-like startle through my center.

But the number flashing on the screen doesn't belong to West.

"Hello?" I answer.

"Hi, is this Elle Napier?" a woman's voice responds. "This is Connie Marsden with Winlock Media Group. We received your application over the weekend for the social media content coordinator position, and I'd love to set up a time for an interview at your convenience."

That was fast . . .

I was browsing jobs online yesterday when that position popped up under *gigs for writers*. The description said it'd be supervising a team of content creators contracted to manage the social media pages of high-profile clientele, which would include not only coordinating posts and schedules but developing creative content—the social media equivalent of editors and writers in the print world.

It certainly didn't sound like a life-altering gig that would flood my existence with purpose and meaning, but it mentioned a flexible schedule, and Winlock is notoriously philanthropic with generous opportunities to give back to the community, so I thought it might be a good lily pad to occupy while I figure things out.

"Hi, Connie. Thanks so much for calling; that would be amazing," I say, tempering my excitement so as not to scare her away. "My schedule is pretty free at the moment—what works for you?"

"How about nine a.m. this Friday?"

"Perfect."

"I'll send the calendar invite as soon as we hang up. Looking forward to meeting you!" Connie hangs up, and within seconds, an iCal invite pings my inbox. My mother would adore this woman.

I float home on a hopeful breeze—my stomach prickled with butterflies as I climb the stairs to my apartment, ready to proudly inform Indie that I've already landed a job interview—until my phone rings with a call from West, and all the giddy energy is sucked from the stuffy stairwell.

"Hey," I answer, holding my breath.

"When you sent my niece off to some random person's house, did you happen to get a last name or an address?" His words are curt and his tone is punishing.

"First of all, I didn't *send* her anywhere. She was invited. I told her to ask you, but you didn't answer when she called." I straighten my shoulders. "Second of all, I'm not her nanny. I can't tell her what she can and can't do; I can only help her make the right choices."

I imagine if I'd told her no, it would've tarnished all the trust we've built up so far, and she would've wasted no time placing me in the same category as her "control freak" uncle.

"Either way," he says, "she's not answering my calls or texts, and her phone is off, so I can't track her."

I take a seat on the steps, massaging the tightness from my temples. I thought I was getting through to her, that she understood she had to walk a fine line if we had any chance at all of making this Nebraska thing happen.

"West," I exhale. "I'm so sorry. When I left, they were on Lexington. That's all I know."

The silence between us is deafening as the heaviness of his anger radiates through the phone.

"I'll help you find her," I add. "Give me twenty, and I'll meet you at your place."

"Don't bother," he says. "I'm picking you up in five."

West ends the call, and I make a vain attempt to call Scarlett before heading downstairs to wait. Four minutes later, a black town car pulls up in front of my building, and a uniformed driver steps out to get the passenger door.

"Well?" West asks, his aqua gaze slicing into me. Everything around him is dark, from the onyx leather accoutrements of the interior to the jet-black suit that hardly contains his muscled physique. "Are you just going to stand there, or are you getting in?"

He checks his watch—a black stainless steel band accented with a black diamond-encrusted bezel.

For a moment, I'm taken back to that day in the boardroom last week, when he made me feel like a speck of dust in his universe—and I allowed it.

"I think we'd get more traction if we split up." I remain planted on the sidewalk.

"Excuse me?"

"I'll walk the Lexington area," I say. "And I'll let you know if I see her."

"It'll take you twenty minutes just to get there." West scoffs at my suggestion. "Just get in. It'll be quicker."

"No." As a habitual people pleaser and lifelong yes-woman, the word is foreign on my tongue but satisfying nonetheless. "I'll let you know if I find her."

I leave him with a polite yet firm wave before heading north, but I barely make it to the corner before the soft scuff of leather dress shoes on pavement follows. Turning, I find my former boss barreling after me, a man on a mission.

The crosswalk flashes white, and the small crowd around me dashes off, but my legs turn to lead.

"I don't understand the obstinance," he says, jaw pulsing as he towers over me. "Get in the damn car, Elle, so you can help me find my niece."

"I'm not getting in your car." I fold my arms to hide the fact that I'm trembling. "I'll look for your niece, but not with you. Not when you're acting like a certifiable psychopath."

His perfect nostrils flare and his lips arch into the sneer of a man not used to disobedience or insubordination. I imagine if a person is used to always getting their way, it'd be infuriating to deal with pushback. But I stopped catering to his whims a week ago, and I'll be damned if it was all for nothing.

The crosswalk flashes to white again.

"I'll let you know if I find her," I say before leaving him to seethe on the corner of Sixty-Eighth and York.

It's dark by the time I get home three hours later, and my legs are aching for respite.

Still no Scarlett.

And no word from West other than periodic texts informing me she's yet to be found.

Peeling out of my clothes, I run a blazing-hot bath and pour in two capfuls of Indie's Tahitian Vanilla bubble bath. With each passing minute tonight, guilt has stacked on top of guilt. By the time I got home, I convinced myself this was all my fault, that if I'd have put my foot down, none of this would've happened. And when I wasn't coming up with a million worst-case scenarios involving Scarlett, I was busy replaying my sidewalk exchange with West.

While there's no denying the man was a grade A asshole, I can't help but wonder if it was nothing more than a mask to cover up the sheer helplessness he was feeling inside. For a confident, intelligent, and wildly successful man to be brought to his knees by a fourteen-year-old rebel can't be an easy pill to swallow. And it doesn't excuse his behavior.

But maybe at the end of the day, he's just like anyone else, doing the best he can.

Sinking into the water, I slide lower and lower still. Until the hot liquid seeps up my collarbone, trails up my neck, and fills my ears—almost drowning out the shrill, faint ring emanating from my phone by the sink ledge.

Exploding out of the depths of my aquatic despair, I all but slip out of the tub on my way to answer, and I swear my soul exits my body the instant I find Scarlett's name flashing across my screen.

"Oh my God," I answer, bathwater dripping from me in rivulets and forming a pool at my feet. "Where are you?"

CHAPTER TWENTY-ONE

WEST

I'm pacing the foyer when Elle and Scarlett arrive. An hour ago, Elle phoned me to let me know she'd finally heard from my niece and that she'd be delivering her personally. Apparently she was with her "friend" Piper, who had decided to meet up with some boys. Scarlett knew I'd say no, so she turned off her phone.

But evidently, after dragging her to some park on the Lower East Side, Piper ditched her when her old group of friends showed up.

Scarlett, not knowing where she was, went to turn her phone back on—but the battery had died. After that, she found a Duane Reade, where a kindly cashier let her charge her phone on his personal charger in the break room.

Afraid of facing my wrath, the second she was powered up again, she called Elle.

The entire thing sounds terribly . . . *convenient.*

I haven't had a chance to sort fact from fiction.

"Uncle West, I—" Scarlett begins to protest a verbal lashing I haven't even begun to deliver.

"Go to your room." My jaw clenches so tight it sends a shock of pain down my neck.

"But I—" she attempts again.

I lift a hand. "Honestly, Scarlett. I'm too upset to speak to you right now. And I'm afraid of what I'd say if I even tried. Go to your room. We'll talk in the morning, when I've calmed down."

Scarlett shoots Elle a look, who simply nods with a pained wince—as if she's in agreement that it's the best course of action for all involved.

Skulking to the elevator, Scarlett slams a palm on the call button before disappearing between the double doors.

Dragging in a long breath, I wait for my vision to change from red to clear again before turning to Elle.

"Thank you," I say. "I'm not good at this . . . feeling-like-my-heart-is-walking-around-outside-my-body thing. I shouldn't have been so demanding before; I shouldn't have taken it out on you."

Her blue eyes slide to the tile floor, and she wrings her hands. "West, I'm sorry, but I think I may have bitten off more than I can chew. Scarlett has some complexities that I wasn't really prepared for. Every time I think I'm making progress with her, she does something like this. I think it's time to consult a professional."

"Don't you think I've already done that?"

Her gaze flicks to mine. "Maybe try someone more specialized?"

"When she first came here, she met three times a week with a three-thousand-dollar-an-hour so-called *specialist* who couldn't break through and ended treatment after two months of making zero progress," I say. "It's the Maxwell in her. We're obstinate. The stubbornness is simply bred into us." I step toward her, closing the space between us. "But if you turn your back on her now, Elle, you'll just be another name on a list."

Clasping her hands over her heart, she frowns. "That would've been nice to know before . . ."

"You'd have walked away. Any sane person would," I say, then pause. "Through your columns over the years, I've come to appreciate your unique perspectives and insights—particularly when it comes to interpersonal relationships, motivations, causes, and effects. You don't see things the way everyone else does. I'd hoped you'd be the one to get through to her."

She's quiet for a beat, soaking in my words perhaps.

"If this is going to work . . . you're going to have to let me in. You're going to have to shed some light on what she's been through—and what you've been through. Otherwise I'm just feeling around in the dark and getting nowhere."

My jaw sets.

It's been a lifetime since I've let anyone in, but I'm at the end of my rope with Scarlett.

"Tell me about her parents," Elle says. "Her father was your brother, right? What was he like? And what was her life like back in Nebraska? What did she go through that was so awful you had to take her in? I need context, West. She's not just some troubled teenager—she's so much more than that. I just want to know why."

"Come with me."

I take her to my study, where I pluck a small leather-bound photo album off a corner shelf. The thin binder holds fifty photos, maybe less. But it's the only window I keep to my past.

"Here." I place it in her hands, our fingertips brushing.

She cracks the spine, flipping to the first page—an image of a grinning toddler version of myself holding my newborn brother.

"Will, Scarlet's father, was my younger brother," I begin. "He was nineteen when he got Scarlett's mother pregnant. She was a junior in high school at the time. Keep in mind, this wasn't out of the ordinary for people in Whitebridge. Anyway, Will was . . . different than me. He was funny and witty and the friendliest kid you'd ever meet, but he was also very unsure of himself. Deep down he was lost, just like everyone else. So he always lived in my shadow. Anywhere I went, Will would follow. But after I went away to college, Will found someone else's shadow to live in. Took him down a darker path for a year or so, and he'd gotten into some hard drugs for a while, dropped out of welding school, lost his motivation to make anything of himself. By the time I got him clean again, he was head over heels with the high school girl who worked part time at the gas station making pizza. I didn't see what the fuss was, but Will was spellbound. Obsessed. You could tell him the sky was blue, and he'd insist it was orange if Lexi said it was orange. Anyway, they hadn't been together more than a couple of months when she got pregnant."

Elle traces her finger along a picture of the two of us standing side by side at Will's graduation. I soak in the familiar image of Will grinning proudly in his red cap and gown, standing just a couple of inches shorter than me.

"He looks just like you," she muses.

"Yeah, we were spitting images of each other—on the outside."

"That must be your mom? She looks just like you two." Elle points to the woman standing off to the side, her position an ironic and inadvertent metaphor because my entire life, my mother was always standing off to the proverbial side. Close enough but distant at the same time. "What's she like?"

"Dead."

She sucks in a breath, the album frozen in her hands. "I'm sorry. I didn't know."

"Of course you didn't." I flip to another page. "She died three years ago . . . lung cancer. She smoked two packs a day for as long as I can remember—a slow, drawn-out suicide."

"That's heartbreaking."

"Can't force someone to be here if they don't want to be."

"Everything you do, everything you've done . . . is it for them?"

I gather a long breath. "That's a loaded question."

Leaving her vanilla-bubble-bath-scented side, I make myself a drink and toss it back in one go.

"What about your father? Is he still around?" she asks.

I give her a terse shake of the head. "My past is like one of those depressingly cliché country songs. There's a reason I keep a tight lid on it. No one wants to hear about that shit. And I sure as hell don't want to be some sob story, nor do I want it reduced to some sad little paragraph on my Wikipedia page."

"There's nothing wrong with being vulnerable. You're not made of steel, West. Even if you pretend you are. Maybe you can fool the world, but you can't fool me."

Charmed and a bit bemused, I mix her a gin and tonic—a wordless invitation to stay a little longer. Anyone who can hold her own around me is worthy of the privilege. Besides, every second in this room with her is one less second I'm alone with my current reality.

"So tell me, Superman," she says, settling into my favorite chair. Intentional? Perhaps. Her cherry blossom lips curl into a mischievous grin, and I'm taken back to the first time I saw her wandering the halls of my corporate headquarters. The confident bounce in her step, the sway in her hips, the contagious laugh. The curve-hugging blue sweaterdress. "What's your kryptonite?"

I pause to contemplate my answer. "I have none."

Elle squints. "Liar."

"Believe it or not, I have more important things to do than sit around categorizing my weaknesses." I sip my bourbon and sink into a chair that isn't my favorite.

"It's your heart," she says. "That's your kryptonite."

I attempt to swallow, only to choke instead. "And what makes you so sure?"

Examining me, she twists her mouth to one side before shrugging. "Gut feeling."

Rolling my eyes, I huff. "Right. Of course."

"My father always told me the harder you are on the outside, the softer you are on the inside," she says. "And you, West, are the hardest person I've ever met."

Elle takes a drink before rising from her chair and striding to mine. "Get up," she says.

"What?"

"Get. *Up.*" Elle motions, uncharacteristically impatient, until she finally slides her hand into mine and all but yanks me to a standing position. Without warning, her fingers glide through my hair, ruffling it into a tousled mess, before working the top button of my shirt. "There."

"What . . . are you doing?"

"Making you a little less perfect." She stands back to admire her work, a pleased smile painting her pretty face. "See? It's that easy. Just take something you always do and then do it in a different way. It's life changing. I promise."

Lifting a hand to my hair, I attempt to finger comb it back into place, only to have my efforts thwarted.

"Stop," she says, coming closer. Her lithe fingers circle my wrist as her soft scent invades my lungs. "Leave it."

"I don't like this."

"I know." Her eyes search mine, though for what I'm not sure, and she's yet to let me go. My heart pounds in my ears when I calculate the narrow distance between our bodies and how satisfying it would be to punish those pillowed lips with a *hard* kiss. "But you need this. You need to be softened up a bit. For your own good . . . and for Scarlett."

My thoughts turn a shade cleaner with the mention of my niece.

"Is this what you want, West?" she asks, voice breathless. "To control every aspect of your existence until you've suffocated the life out of it?"

I don't respond.

"And what are you teaching Scarlett? That if something's not perfect, it's not worth it?" she adds.

"I'm teaching her to want more for herself."

"More what, exactly?" she asks. "More money? More accolades?"

"More than the wasted potential she'd have if she stayed in Whitebridge."

"Okay, so you're doing that by micromanaging every second of her day and flying off the handle when she makes a mistake?"

"Running away is a little more than a *mistake*, wouldn't you say?"

Elle releases my hand. "Don't you see what she's doing? She's running away because the only time she feels loved is when you chase after her . . . when you worry about her."

My heart stops beating in my chest as the gravity of her words grab hold of it.

"Maybe if you showed her your softer side more often or you let her know how much you care about her in more meaningful ways, she wouldn't be so quick to test you," Elle says. "She's always saying she wants to go home to Nebraska, right? To see her friends? Maybe that's because in some heartbreaking sort of way, those friends were the only family she had, the only place she felt loved and wanted. And she just wants to feel those things again."

Sinking into my chair, I let her words seep into the deepest, hardest parts of me.

It's been a lifetime since showing someone I cared about them didn't involve opening my wallet.

"You know, it's probably getting late." Elle places her drink on a coaster before flinging her bag over her shoulder and heading for the door. "And I don't know about you, but I think I've had enough excitement for one day."

I follow her to the elevator without objection, but never before have I longed so desperately for an excuse to make someone stay. Up until now, it's exclusively been the opposite.

She presses the call button and turns to face me, peering up through a fringe of dark lashes.

"Thank you for the drink. And thank you for letting me in . . . I know it wasn't easy for you." With an exhausted yet playful glint, she reaches to flick another button on my shirt. "Just making sure there's no *S* on your chest, Superman."

The doors part, and Elle steps inside, leaving a hollow vacancy in the space she occupied mere seconds before. Gone are her warmth and candor, leaving a noticeable nothingness in their place.

"Go easy on Scarlett tomorrow," she says. "And think about what I said, okay?"

Sliding my hands in my pockets, I offer a nod in the seconds before she disappears.

And when she's finally gone, I retire to my room to think about what she said.

I think about it all night.

But mostly, I think about her.

CHAPTER TWENTY-TWO

ELLE

I'm paging through an out-of-season Christmas issue of *Better Homes and Gardens* in my neurologist's waiting room when a text from Tom pings my phone.

TOM: Okay, something weird is going on.

ME: What's up?

TOM: Head honcho is here . . . for NO reason . . . and he brought catered breakfast . . . from Beauvais.

ME: Maybe he just wanted to do something nice for a change?

Sounds like someone took my words to heart last night . . .

TOM: We're clearly not talking about the same person.

ME: Stranger things have happened.

TOM: Someone overheard him making SMALL TALK with Anita's assistant. Just random small talk. Like it was completely normal.

TOM: I feel like I've stepped into a parallel universe. Is this real life??

ME: Enjoy it!

Closing out of my chat with Tom, I shoot West a text.

ME: So freaking proud of you.

Within seconds, he responds.

WEST: No idea what you're talking about.

ME: Liar.

"Elle Napier?" A young nurse in bright-pink scrubs calls my name from the door beside the reception desk. Tucking my phone away, I head back for my checkup. "Let's grab a quick weight on you."

She stops at a scale, and I slip off my shoes and close my eyes before climbing on. A year ago, I'd have cared about the number and based my entire day around whether it was within a certain range. I've since learned I have more important things to worry about, and I'll be damned if I let a number put a damper on a perfectly good day.

"Okay, we're going to head back to room number three," the nurse says.

We settle into a small room with salmon-pink walls and a portrait of a buck in a forest.

"Just going to get a blood pressure on you," she says as I perch myself on the edge of the exam table, paper crumpling beneath me. A minute later, she jots down a number. "Perfect, perfect. Any questions or concerns you want to bring up to Dr. Breckenridge today?"

"None at all." I lift my hands before clapping them on my lap. "Everything's been going really well. I had some fatigue those first few weeks at home, but it seems to have resolved in the past month."

"No headaches, eye pain, dizziness, blurred vision . . ."

I shake my head. "No, none of that."

She taps a few notes into her laptop before shutting the lid and packing up. "All right, the doctor will be with you shortly."

I rest on the edge of the exam table, my shoes barely scuffing the footrest, as some elevator music version of a Taylor Swift song pipes in from above. A few minutes later, a knock at the door is followed by the man of the hour.

"Dr. Breckenridge," I say. "So good to see you."

"And you as well, Ms. Napier." He offers a honey-warm smile as he washes his hands and settles into a rolling stool. "So what's the latest? How's everything going?"

While Matt's wife was the one who called 911 after I collapsed, it was Dr. Breckenridge and his team who saved my life when I got to the hospital. They were the ones who quickly figured out what was happening and prepped me for emergency surgery after I ruptured and coded in the exam room.

"Any changes since the last time?" he asks, retrieving a penlight from behind his ear. "Blurred or double vision?" He shines the light into my left eye, then my right.

"None."

"Any new numbness or tingling or weaknesses?"

"Nope."

"And your fatigue?" he asks.

"Better."

"And how's work? You went back the other week, right?"

"Yeah. Two weeks ago. But I quit last week."

His gray eyes search mine. "Wait, why? They wouldn't accommodate you?"

During my recovery, he told me it was crucial for me to avoid stress or anything that could raise my blood pressure, and he wrote me an order not to work long hours anymore. Though I suspect the order was more for me than for HR.

"No, it's not that," I say. "It just wasn't what I wanted to do anymore."

He exhales. "Yeah, that's one of the side effects they don't write about in textbooks. Sometimes after traumatic or life-altering experiences, people make huge life changes. A lot of times their loved ones will chalk it up to a personality change from brain damage or something like that. Everyone always wants a medical explanation. But most of the time that brush with death was their tipping point to do the things they'd always wanted to do or live a better life than the one they'd had before. Looks different for everyone, of course. But it's completely normal."

"Yes," I say, pointing. "That's exactly it."

"You're a very fortunate young woman," he says, pushing up from his stool. He told me the same thing in the week that followed my surgery, and he informed me that 60 percent of aneurysm-rupture patients have some sort of permanent disability afterward. "One of the lucky ones, that's for sure."

With no long-term issues (so far), all I have to do is come in for regular follow-ups and head to the ER at the first sign of pain behind my eyes or double vision.

"We'll check you again in a couple of months." He washes his hands on his way out, shaking them dry over the sink before dabbing them with recycled paper towels. "Can't wait to hear what you're up to next time. Sure it'll be something big."

Yeah, maybe.

Hopefully.

I head for the checkout desk and make my next appointment before heading home. On my way, I stop for an iced latte and a quick visit to Central Park for a little people watching. Grabbing a seat on a bench next to an elderly couple, I nonchalantly watch as they hold hands, rub noses, and share a turkey sandwich on rye that she pulls out of her purse. I bet they've been together their whole lives. No easy feat. When they're finished, he helps her up before pushing himself to his feet, grabbing his four-legged wooden cane and hobbling off beside her along the path.

A dreadlocked man on neon Rollerblades whirs by with a pack of at least eight dogs, beachy music blasting from his headphones. And behind him is a leggings-clad mom pushing a double jogging stroller. Three women in pantsuits and serious haircuts power walk past, and I catch wind of their conversation—something about reports and changing drop-shipping protocols. On the other side of the green space is a preschool class cozying up under a shade tree for an afternoon picnic.

Statistically one of every fifty people in this country has an unruptured brain aneurysm.

I look at all these people, just out here living their day-to-day lives, blissfully unaware that all of it could be gone tomorrow. How many of them would waste no time becoming the best versions of themselves if they knew?

Drawing in a late-spring breath, I think of West. I meant what I said when I told him I was proud. He took my advice, stepped out of his control freak comfort zone, and softened up a bit. It may only be breakfast and small talk, but for a man like him . . . that's huge.

Grabbing my phone, I shoot him a message.

ME: Where'd you go to college?

Seven whole minutes lapse before I get a response.

WEST: It's a matter of public record (if you dig hard enough). But the University of Nebraska. Why?

ME: What'd you major in?

WEST: Again, matter of public record.

ME: Easier to go to the source.

WEST: Business Management. Why?

I send him a puzzle-piece emoji. I meant what I said about piecing him together—edges first, then the inside.

WEST: Cute.

There are no sarcasm emojis, but if there were, and if West were an emoji-using man, he'd have tacked a hundred of them onto his comment, I'm sure.

ME: I'm jealous that the staff got Beauvais for breakfast this morning. I've tried to get a table there for years and the second I quit . . .

WEST: I'll make a call and get you a table.

ME: Oh. I wasn't hinting at that. But if you're offering . . . 😅

A full fifteen minutes pass before he replies.

WEST: Ten AM tomorrow.

CHAPTER TWENTY-THREE

WEST

The scent of buttermilk waffles and croque monsieur fills the halls of *Made Man*'s corporate office Tuesday morning as I make my rounds. All morning I've made it a point to acknowledge anyone who isn't hiding away from me. I've managed to corner an intern, two personal assistants, and the entire accounting department. While they were wild eyed and gape mouthed, as if seeing a unicorn in real life for the first time, they all engaged in conversation and emerged unscathed.

Little do any of them know, they have Elle to thank for this.

She wants me to show my softer side, to do things I wouldn't normally do, and she promised it'd be "life changing." I don't know about life changing, but clearly whatever I've been doing isn't working.

Scarlett avoided me all morning, but I managed to catch her on the way to school. She said she wanted to walk, and while I'd have preferred to give her a ride, I decided to take it easy on her and simply told her to be safe and that I looked forward to hearing about her day later. The hardened look on her face faded in real time when she realized I wasn't going to berate her, and she even managed some semblance of a smile on her way out.

There's a chance Elle isn't wrong about Scarlett.

But only time will tell.

"Hey." I stop at Tom's office, leaning in at the doorway like a man with all the time in the world. While shooting the breeze grates against every fiber of my soul, I promised myself I'd try it out for a full twenty-four hours.

"Mr. Maxwell." Tom spins in his chair, angling his computer monitor away before folding his hands on his desk. "What's going on?"

"Just felt like coming in today." I hook my fingers through my belt loops and try to find a casual, comfortable stance, but nothing feels natural. "Do you still keep in touch with Elle?"

"Sparingly . . ."

"How's she doing since her untimely departure?"

Tom flicks a hand in the air. "You know, she hasn't said. I think she just wants to move on and kind of forget about this place."

I worry the inside of my lip and play dumb. "Ah, so she isn't working for anyone else?"

Tom chuckles. "It's only been a week."

"Didn't know if she had something else lined up," I say, silently relieved that she isn't blabbing all over town about helping out with Scarlett. Not that I thought she would. But it speaks volumes about her character that she isn't turning my personal situation into cheap fodder for her social circles.

"After everything she went through, I don't blame her for wanting to start fresh," Tom says, legs crossed as he shakes his head.

"The aneurysm," I say. "I heard."

"Not just that but the boyfriend thing too." He leans forward, lowering his voice.

"What *boyfriend* thing?" I distinctly recall reading her GoFundMe story a handful of times, and not once did it mention any kind of significant other.

My skin heats at the thought of Elle gifting some faceless man her contagious smile, pressing her body up against him, eyes twinkling as his hands are in her hair and his mouth is seconds from crushing hers.

"Well, she was with this guy for, I don't know . . . almost a couple of years?" Tom says. "She was actually at his apartment the morning of the aneurysm. He'd already left, but she was getting ready to go when it happened . . . and then apparently the boyfriend's wife showed up."

"Wait, what?" I never took Elle to be a home-wrecker. "So her boyfriend was married?"

Tom splays his hands on his desk as he inhales. "Yes. But Elle had no idea. This guy—Matt was his name—was living a double life. Had an apartment in Manhattan and a wife and kids back in Jersey."

Fucking punk.

"And get this: he was even paying for his love nest with his wife's trust fund. How screwed up is that? Needless to say, Elle was devastated. She really loved the guy. To die and lose the person you thought you were going to spend your life with all in the same day?"

Lifting a hand, I say, "Pause. She *died* too?"

Whoever wrote her GoFundMe story was clearly not a fellow journalist, as the article left out several crucial details.

"For three minutes, yes," Tom says. "She coded, but they brought her back."

It makes sense now—Elle's quest for a truthful, meaningful existence.

Rapping on the doorjamb before I go, I sniff. "Let me know if you hear from her again, Tom. Tell her I hope she's found that *purpose* she was looking for."

His thin brows knit as he presses his fingertips lightly over his heart. "Will do, sir. Will do."

CHAPTER TWENTY-FOUR

ELLE

"Your menu, madame." My authentically French server hands me a breakfast menu printed on linen paper before topping off my goblet of artisanal still water. "Will be back to take your order shortly."

Beauvais is every bit as glamorous as I'd hoped. Crystal chandeliers. White tablecloths. Natural light. Herringbone floors. Delicate french-blue wainscoting contrasted with saddle-leather seating.

Indie was supposed to join me this morning, but at the last minute she backed out—sidelined by a migraine. There was a time in my not-so-distant past that dining alone was a social prison sentence for me. I wouldn't dream of it. It always seemed like such a lonely endeavor. But today I'm excited to embrace it—like a date with myself. I even took the liberty of wearing a midlength black dress with buttons down the back, twisting my hair into a sleek chignon, and finishing off the look with a swipe of matte-red lipstick.

Trés chic.

I'm debating between the brioche french toast and the berries-and-crème oatmeal when something catches the corner of my eye. Glancing up from my menu, I'm forced to do a double take when I realize the man at the adjacent table is none other than my ex.

Steeling my nerves and focusing on the words on the linen paper in my hands, I ignore the bastard, though from my periphery I can't help but notice his every squirm and the way his gaze flicks in my direction every two seconds.

The woman sitting across from him—with her back to me—wears designer jeans and a Chanel bouclé jacket, and when she gets up to use the restroom, her hair is blowout fresh, bouncing with each step. I can't see her face, but I'm sure she's beautiful—and I'm also sure she's not Claudia.

I scan the room in hopes that my server is making his way over, but no dice. Tapping my fingers, I wait. And I continue to pretend Matt's penetrating gaze isn't getting under my skin and dampening this once-in-a-lifetime breakfast experience I'm about to enjoy.

Reaching for my water, I take a sip and purposely angle my body away from him, giving him a literal cold shoulder. But evidently the message isn't received loud and clear, because within seconds, the audacious asshole is seated at my table.

"Elle," he says under his breath. He leans in as if he's trying to make this an intimate moment. His familiar cologne, the kind I selected for him last Christmas, assaults my air space.

I lean back. "Excuse me, what is this?"

"You have no idea how good it is to see you." He ignores my obvious disgust, reaching for my hand, but I retreat before his fingertips have a chance to brush mine. "Tried to contact you, but you changed your number."

"Right. The number I'd had since I was eighteen." It was a huge pain in the ass to switch it, especially in the midst of recovering from a freaking brain aneurysm. Granted, my mom did most of the work. But still. It took me weeks to memorize the new one, and my bank shut down all my accounts for a couple of days because they thought it was a fraudulent change. I wouldn't have changed it if he hadn't blown up my phone twice an hour, every hour for the first forty-eight hours like a complete psychopath.

"You could've just blocked me," he says.

I sip my water and remain calm. "So you could call me from a different number?"

"I just wanted to make sure you were okay." A frustration bleeds through his words, as if *I'm* the one who has wronged *him* in this situation.

"I am. Thanks to your wife. She saved my life."

"Yeah." He hesitates, dragging a palm along his square jaw as he sucks in a breath—a move I used to find sexy as hell. "I heard."

I hope Claudia gave it to him and then some.

"I'd love to thank her myself," I add, "but that might be awkward given the circumstances."

"I'm really sorry about everything." His voice softens, and his gaze is relaxed, as if he's trying to disarm me by showing he gives a damn. "I think about you all the time, Elle. Every day."

I nod toward the table where the beautiful brunette sat a minute ago. "Yeah, seems like you're really struggling to move on. All that guilt must really be getting to you."

He rolls his eyes. "Come on. She's a client."

"If you say so . . ." Not that I care or that it matters, but once a liar, always a liar.

His expression intensifies, the corners of his mouth pulling into a disappointed frown.

"I really am sorry, Elle," he repeats, as if I didn't hear him the first time. "I'm sorry I hurt you. I mean that. I want you to know that."

"I'm not the one you should be groveling to. I'm not the one who took vows with you or birthed your children."

His gaze lands on the salt and pepper shakers that divide us, and he raps his fingers on the tabletop.

"Claudia left me," he says under his breath.

"Smart woman."

"Ah, you must be the pencil dick I've been hearing about. Nice to finally put a face with a name," a man's voice interjects from behind me, and within seconds West Maxwell appears at the side of our table, his muscled hand digging into Matt's shoulder before giving it a friendly yet not-so-friendly squeeze. "Thanks for keeping my seat warm. But I'll take it from here."

My surroundings grow blurry for a second, and I pinch the underside of my wrist to make sure this isn't a dream.

"Sometime this century would be great." West sniffs before stooping down to kiss my cheek.

West Maxwell kissed my cheek.

His rich scent invades my lungs and clings to the air around us as if he's staking his territory.

Matt's gaze flicks from West to me and back, and he offers a smirking huff, as if he thinks this is a joke—but his amusement vanishes the second West motions for him to hurry it along.

Matt slides out of the chair, eyeing the two of us with the trepidation of someone being pranked. But the joke is on all of us, because I have no idea what West is doing here or why he's suddenly playing the part of my knight in shining armor.

"You ready to go, babe?" Matt's breakfast date slash client sidles up to him, slipping her arm under his. "We should get going—we're touring that loft in a half hour, remember?"

West doesn't hesitate to take his spot, sliding into his seat and unbuttoning his suit coat in one fell swoop.

"Will you be paying for your new place in cash, or will you be financing it with your wife's trust fund?" West blinks as he delivers his casual question.

Matt's "client" wrinkles her elegant nose. "What's he talking about, babe?"

Babe.

"His wife left him," I chime in. "Two months ago. Because she caught him with another woman." I press my fingertip against my collarbone. "In my defense, I had no idea he was married because he failed to mention that the entire eighteen months we were together."

The Chanel-clad beauty takes a step back. "Matty, is that true?"

Matty.

"It's a bit more complicated than that—" he begins to say before she tosses her hands up and heads for the door. He chases after her in damage control mode, like a dog with his tail tucked.

"Good teamwork," West says once they're gone.

"Okay, two things." I lift an index finger. "First of all, why are you here? And secondly, I had everything under control. You didn't have to swoop in and rescue me."

"I was doing that thing you told me to do," he says, "where you do the things you wouldn't normally do."

"Ah. So that was all for *your* benefit."

"One hundred percent." There's an unusual air of playfulness in his tone.

"Seriously, though, what are you doing here?" I scan the room for my server once again, who is apparently missing in action.

"A man's got to eat." He catches the eye of someone in the distance, lifting his fingers as if to casually wave them over. A second later, a man in a burgundy suit and shiny black loafers approaches us. "Étienne, good to see you again."

"Mr. Maxwell," the man says, extending his hand.

"Thanks again for squeezing in that catering order yesterday. I know it was last minute, but it meant the world to my team and me," West says. "They've been working extra hard this year, and I wanted to reward them with the best breakfast in Manhattan."

Étienne glows with West's praise, nodding and thanking him profusely, as though West's emergent order yesterday were doing *him* a favor.

"Will you be having your usual, sir?" Étienne asks.

"Of course," West says. "And the same for my guest, please."

Étienne leaves us with an accommodating nod before strutting off to the kitchen.

I cock my head. "You didn't have to order for me."

"I know."

"How do you even know I'll like what you're having?"

His mouth lifts at the side. "You will."

Before I have a chance to respond, our server appears out of nowhere with a fresh carafe of coffee, two porcelain mugs, and a tiny pitcher of cream.

"By the way, how did you know about Matt?" I squint.

He pours steaming coffee into a mug with expert precision. "I have my ways."

"And how did you know *that* was Matt?"

His exotic gaze slips onto mine. "Again, I have my ways."

"So it's okay for you to pry into people's pasts, but they're not allowed to pry into yours?"

"Generally." He tips a splash of cream into his cup before giving it a stir. "But I think we've moved past that, don't you?"

Leaning back, I take him in.

"I don't know whether to be flattered or creeped out that you checked into my relationship history," I say.

"Tom mentioned it yesterday morning when I asked if he'd heard from you lately." He takes a sip. "He told me you were moving on, and then he went into great detail as to everything you'd been through lately."

I wince. Sounds like Tom.

Once he gets nervous, he word vomits all over the place.

"Oh." I play it cool. "So you weren't googling me . . ."

"I don't google anyone." He takes another sip. "I have people who do that for me."

"Just like you have people who shop for you," I say. "Do you have people who date for you too? Like a proxy type thing?"

He flashes a half-second smile. "Now that's an idea."

"*Do* you date?" I lift a brow.

"What exactly are you asking, Elle? If I've gone on dates in the past or if I'm actively dating at the moment?"

My cheeks flush warm under the intensity of his gaze, though I get the sense he isn't annoyed with my question this time.

"Both," I say.

"Yes." His eyes flash. "And no. Not seeing anyone at the moment."

"Mademoiselle. Monsieur." Our server arrives with an array of artfully arranged croissants, jams, poached eggs, fresh berries, and butters, spread across a myriad of plates—enough to feed a family of five. "Can I get you anything else at the moment?"

"No, thank you, Alain," he answers the man, though his gaze is trained on me. "I believe we have everything we need."

CHAPTER TWENTY-FIVE

WEST

"How'd it go tonight?" I ask Scarlett Wednesday evening when she returns from spending time with Elle. "What kinds of trouble did you two get into this time?"

I toss her a playful wink in an attempt to keep things light.

"Elle's roommate locked herself out, so we had to run to her place, and we just ended up hanging out there," Scarlett says, leaning against the doorway of my study. "We ordered pizza and did peel-off face masks and watched this really cheesy movie on Netflix. But it was fun."

"Ah." I imagine the three of them gathered around Elle's living room—not that I know what it looks like, but I picture it like something out of a chick flick. Quirky throw pillows. A velvet sofa in some whimsical color. Potted plants. A flickering candle that smells like boutique perfume. "Well, that sounds like a lovely time."

"They've been best friends since college," Scarlett volunteers. "They've lived together for almost a decade or something like that. And they've only gotten into two fights ever—both times over stupid stuff."

I page through the magazine in my lap and offer a simple "Riveting."

While Elle is nothing short of intriguing to me, I'd be doing myself no favors becoming invested in her personal life.

"Elle showed me a picture of her sisters," Scarlett continues. "Did you know she has three? And she's the oldest. Her youngest one's getting married at the end of next month. And all of their names start with *E* . . . Emma, Evie, and . . . I forget the other one's name."

Her lips twist at the side as she snaps her fingers.

This is the most I've heard her talk about anything in months.

"Eden," she says. "That's the other one. But Evie's the one getting married. And she's marrying Elle's ex-boyfriend's little brother. Isn't that crazy?"

"Absolutely wild." I flick another page before glancing up. "Oh, Scarlett. Your English Comp instructor emailed me today about the paper you recently submitted. Said it was your best work yet—and not only that but the best one in the class."

Her eyes light, and a faint smile paints her lips.

"Very proud of you," I say. "You know, if writing is something that interests you, I'm sure Elle could give you a few pointers."

Dragging in an exhausted breath, she tucks a strand of hair behind her ears. "Yeah. Guess I've never really thought about it before."

"You have plenty of time to figure out what you're good at in this world, but the sooner you find out, the easier life gets," I say. "I speak from experience. Learn your strengths and never look back."

I learned long ago that acting like you had it all was a one-way ticket to having it all. I'd been out of college a few years, working dead-end jobs and barely making rent, when I'd stumbled upon an article about YouTubers making millions of dollars creating videos about mundane, everyday things. They were mostly ten- or fifteen-minute day-in-the-life sorts of things, but I quickly realized the ones with the fancy houses in the background and the killer wheels and the slick haircuts were racking up all the views. Not only that, but the most successful vloggers were spilling content over to other social media platforms, growing their fandoms and doubling down on affiliate commissions, promotional contracts, and overall notoriety.

While I didn't have a dime to my name, I had connections.

A best friend with a vintage Porsche.

A cousin in beauty school needing to practice men's cuts.

A local photographer trying to build his high-fashion portfolio.

A buddy with a rich uncle who let me rent out his luxuriously appointed guesthouse for dirt cheap as long as I kept an eye on his place when he was gone on business.

For two solid years, I *Great Gatsby*'d my way to a multimillion-user following, and in the proverbial blink of an eye, I found myself making cameos and appearances, being interviewed on morning talk shows and for various men's magazines.

Just like that, a certified nobody named West Maxwell became an international household name. But all the money, sex appeal, media coverage, and influence in the world could never fill the void Will left when he died.

The satisfaction of my milestones was always short lived. Little bursts of wonderful would always sizzle out. I've found that's been a running theme in my life so far—nothing ever lasts.

Honestly, I'm not sure how long *Made Man* will be around. If it were up to me, it'd be forever. I'm doing everything in my power to push it to the top, working around the clock to secure the hottest talent for our covers, pushing my writers to churn out the most relevant content, and listening to my readers' invaluable feedback. Our third year in business, we blew our competitors out of the water fivefold in sales, and ten years in, we're number one in our niche. But print media is dying a slow, painful death. Sooner or later, I imagine we'll be strictly online, and I'm prepping a team who will take us wholly into the digital stratosphere over the coming years.

But I've never been good at letting go of the past—or accepting defeat.

"You should get to bed," I tell Scarlett when she yawns.

"Yeah." Her eyes grow heavy lidded.

"When are you seeing Elle again?" I ask before I forget.

She begins to respond—until her cell phone rings and her eyes widen.

"What? Who is it?" I ask.

Lifting her phone, she swallows. "It's Mom."

I grip the arms of my chair and bite my tongue. In the four months I've had custody of Scarlett, Lexi has reached out maybe twice. And the only reason she contacted me the second time was to ask if I'd cover her past-due electric bill, as her power was about to be shut off and it was the middle of winter.

"Hey, Mama," Scarlett says, picking up on the fourth ring as our eyes lock from across the room. "Been trying to call you, but your phone was shut off . . ."

I don't have to hear the other half of the conversation to know Lexi's feeding her daughter a buffet of bullshit excuses, but I withhold a reaction for Scarlett's sake.

Scarlett's silence tells me her mother's asking questions, and she looks to me, eyes growing glassy.

"Oh, you know, it's . . ." Scarlett's voice breaks when she tries to speak. "Hang on, Mama. Uncle West, I'm going to my room."

"Good night, Scarlett." I watch her disappear into the hallway, swallowed up by the darkness, and then I listen for her door to close.

The thought of Lexi filling her daughter's head with false hope and empty promises washes my thoughts in tension before drowning them completely. And I know from experience, given that my mother was the same way. She wasn't addicted to the hard stuff by any means, but she was all talk and no action. I lost track of how many times she'd sworn to me she was coming to my baseball game—her eyes all light and her smile stretching wide—only to pull a no-show. She did the same to my brother too. He was more forgiving, always giving her a million chances.

He and Scarlett are cut from the same cloth in that way.

No matter what Lexi says or does, Scarlett's going to love her . . . hell, even idolize her. It's just the way it is. As a child, Scarlett doesn't have the capacity to know the difference between her mother's love and her mother's blatant carelessness. It doesn't help that it's easy to like Lexi, despite her flaws. She's a good-time girl. Always smiling. Forever the life of the party. When she talks to you, she makes you feel like she's known you a million years.

Despite her numerous fuckups and gross parental negligence, I often have to remind myself Lexi was nothing more than a kid raising a kid. She didn't have the resources or emotional capacity to give Scarlett everything she needed. I hoped, with time, she would grow into it. But some people are just sort of . . . stuck.

I suspect Lexi will forever be stuck at seventeen in mind and spirit.

In the early years, when Scarlett was a toddler and I was beginning to rake in money from my social media channels, I'd send Lexi cash now and then. And as my income stream billowed with every passing month, I'd send more. Eventually I purchased a small house for the two of them and a reliable and economical car for Lexi, and set up an automatic monthly stipend so she didn't have to work.

Erroneously, I believed that if I gave Will's girls everything they needed, they'd be set. Lexi wouldn't have to work or worry about money, and Scarlett would have a full-time mom dedicated to her every need.

But everything backfired as soon as Scarlett hit kindergarten. Once she was in school full time, Lexi saw an opportunity to reclaim her youth and wash her hands of responsibility, if only for a few hours a day.

A hometown acquaintance of mine kept tabs on them at my request, filling me in on Lexi's latest activities and comings and goings. At the time, I was still building my empire, putting in eighty-hour weeks and in no condition to so much as think about raising a child. So I continued to write checks and wire money and keep an eye on things from afar. But nothing was improving. If anything, Lexi's day drinking and partying were growing worse by the minute. By the time Scarlett hit second grade, I'd hired a full-time nanny to help Lexi—a stand-in for myself. A responsible adult to take her to school on time, make her three meals a day, and ensure she had clean laundry and some semblance of a "normal" childhood at all times.

But no one ever stayed more than a few months at a time. I suspect Lexi found Scarlett bonding more with the nanny of the month than with her, and her jealousy was triggered. One by one, she ran them off.

In trying to make things better for my niece, I'm certain I made them worse.

While there's no rewriting the past, I can only hope I'm making up for it now.

In my younger days, I was convinced money could do anything you told it to do. But as the years ticked by, I learned the hard way that it only magnifies us. If we're good people at heart, it makes us better. But if we are selfish, lazy, and unmotivated, it only enriches those qualities tenfold.

Rising from my chair, I switch off the lamp and close the door to my study before making my way to the elevator.

"I want to see you again, Mama. I miss you so much," I hear Scarlett say from the end of the hall.

My chest tightens as I press the call button and step inside the elevator car.

I may have sole physical and legal custody of Scarlett and intend to see her into adulthood and beyond, but depriving her of her relationship with her mother would be cruel. She'd never understand and she'd never forgive me, and I don't know that there's anything to be gained from withholding that from her as long as their exchanges don't put Scarlett in any kind of danger.

I step off on my floor and head to my suite, stopping at the door to gather my thoughts. Scarlett's been begging to go back to Nebraska since the second she stepped off the plane at JFK months back.

While I have no desire to make my presence known in Whitebridge ever again in this lifetime, now that Elle's in the picture, I might be willing to arrange for a quick weekend getaway. Scarlett would need to be fully supervised, of course. And she'd need to continue to walk a straight line through the end of the school year.

But I'll consider it.

I wash up for bed before shooting Elle a text, proposing this idea.

ELLE: I'm more than willing to take her. Poor thing is so homesick, West. It'd be a game-changer for sure. Would really lift her spirits.

ME: How was she tonight?

ELLE: Again, not her babysitter . . .

ME: Well aware. I'm asking if you think she's doing better. She seemed to be in a good mood tonight when she came home.

ELLE: We had fun. ☺ And for the record, she didn't complain about you once tonight which is a first. I think you're making progress . . .

I begin to type a response, something along the lines of how this wouldn't be possible without her help—but I delete it all. I've never been a sentimental sap. No need to start now.

ME: I'll book the flights tomorrow. Good night, Elle.

ELLE: Good night, Superman.

I darken my screen and hit the pillow with a ridiculous grin commandeering my lips. And then I roll to my side, facing the empty half of my bed. Squinting, I imagine her beside me. The warmth of her body, the cashmere feel of her skin beneath my palms, the heat of her mouth against mine, her sugar-sweet scent dragging into my lungs.

Reaching for my phone, I spend the next several hours googling the ever-loving fuck out of Elle Napier.

While I've been content to maintain the "perfect" version of her I conjured up in my head the first day I laid eyes on her, I'm finding it difficult to stop thinking about her lately. Perhaps if I found something less than savory about her, a flaw or black mark of some kind, a reason to keep her from running laps in my mind . . . I could snap some sense into myself.

Ninety minutes later, I emerge from a wholesome rabbit hole of Napier family social media photos. Like a damn stalker, I flicked through every public photo Elle, her mother, and her sisters posted with eagle-eyed scrutiny, zooming in and out in search of anything and everything that could possibly signify that Elle isn't all she seems.

But she's all carefree smiles and good times.

And the Napiers are just a regular, tight-knit family from some small town in Louisiana.

They love boating. Fourth of July celebrations. Family trips to the mountains. Reunions and anniversaries. Christmastime, weddings, and babies.

From what I can gather, Elle Napier is the kind you keep. The prettiest girl in the room, though she never acts like it. Witty and brave. An uncomplicated breath of fresh air. A yes-woman in the best of ways.

Will would've loved her.

And maybe I could, too, if I were capable of that sort of thing.

In the moments before I finally succumb to the day's exhaustion, I paint a mental picture of the life Elle deserves. A blue-blooded, pedigreed man to sweep her off her feet and place a permanent light in her ocean eyes. The kind of man she can take home to her parents and who would fit into those mile-wide family portraits they hang above their mantel each year. A guy who can roll around in the grass with her nieces and nephews and play a mean game of boccie ball with her brothers-in-law before drinking an ice-cold IPA with her father on the porch.

I'm not that guy.

I never will be.

But if I were, I'd make her mine in a heartbeat.

And I'd never let her go.

CHAPTER
TWENTY-SIX

ELLE

It's a forty-minute drive from the Omaha airport to Whitebridge. Scarlett sits beside me in the back seat of our Uber, all but leaning out the window like an excited Labrador, pointing at every landmark and narrating every mile of the journey.

As soon as my cell gets a good connection, I fire off a quick thank-you email to Connie with Winlock Media. Our interview went well this morning—at least, I think it did. It all happened so fast, and this day has been a blur ever since.

"There's a garden at that park with a maze," she says when we pass the **WELCOME TO WHITEBRIDGE** sign. "And a place on the corner that has the best ice cream. Crazy flavors like cinnamon chocolate raspberry and Twinkie sprinkle. My mom used to take me there when I was little."

Speaking of Scarlett's mom, Scarlett's been firing off texts to her since the second we stepped off the plane. As far as I know, however, she's received no responses. West told me to leave my expectations at the door when it comes to Lexi. That she has a tendency to make promises she can't keep. But I'm keeping an open mind and giving her the benefit of the doubt. She hasn't seen her daughter in almost half a year—I can't imagine she'd flake out on her like this.

"I told my mom we're almost there, but she hasn't sent anything." Scarlett checks her phone again, her lips pressed into a flat line. "Maybe she's stuck at work?"

West made arrangements for us to stay at the Whitebridge Best Western tonight and tomorrow, but our first stop is supposed to be Lexi's house.

"There it is." Scarlett opens the passenger door before we come to a complete stop, dashing up the jagged concrete walkway toward the sinking front stoop.

"Thank you," I say to the driver before grabbing our weekend bags and climbing out. I follow Scarlett, keeping back as she tries to barge her way through the locked door.

"That's weird." She turns to me after a few futile attempts. "Mom never locks the house."

Stepping back, she flips the front doormat over—perhaps searching for a key—before skipping down the steps and peering into a front window. Her palms leave imprints against the murky glass.

"It's dark in there," she says, dusting cobwebs off her hands. "I'll check the back door."

The Uber driver backs out of the driveway and disappears down the street as Scarlett dashes around the side of the house. A minute later she returns, eyes sullen and shoulders deflated.

"Back door was locked too," she says.

"Scarlett, is that you?" a woman in a mauve terry cloth robe calls from the front porch next door. Pinching a cigarette between her lips, she offers a quick wave.

"Hey, Dede. Have you seen Mama?" Scarlett asks.

"Not for a few weeks now," she says, nodding toward the front yard. "Grass is getting long. Thought about asking my stepson to mow, but I wasn't sure what was going on."

Scarlett swipes her phone from her back pocket, dialing Lexi for the millionth time.

"It's ringing . . ." Her eyes widen as she pinches her bottom lip between her thumb and forefinger. "And ringing . . . and ringing . . ."

"Maybe she's working?" I give the benefit of the doubt to someone who likely doesn't deserve it. "Just leave a message and let her know we'll be at the Best Western. She can meet up with us there."

Sucking in a breath, Scarlett leaves a message for her mother. And while her words paint a picture of excitement, her tone is laced with disappointment.

"I guess I should call us a ride?" I glance around the sparsely populated strip of street. The sign on the way into town said Whitebridge had a population of 1,400. I'm willing to bet Ubers aren't a thing here.

Snatching her bag off the gravel driveway, Scarlett heads for the sidewalk. "We can walk. It's only a few blocks from here."

For the next ten minutes, we walk in silence, the wheels of our bags droning against the sidewalk.

"Maybe we can order in and watch a pay-per-view?" I offer when we get closer. "That could be fun, yeah? And you can invite a few of your friends over. I think there's a pool at the hotel. It's warm enough to swim if that's something you guys are into."

Scarlett stops, releasing the handle of her bag before retrieving her phone.

"Yeah," she says, monotone. "It's just . . . I don't have anyone's numbers anymore. Uncle West made me get rid of my old phone when I moved, and I never had them memorized because I didn't need to . . ."

Honk . . . honk-honk-honk . . . honkkkkk . . .

A screeching horn, crunching tires, and a coughing muffler barge into our moment without warning. By the time I turn to see what all the commotion is, I'm met with a tiny bottle-blonde flying out the passenger side of a rusted El Camino.

"Mama!" Scarlett drops her things on the pavement and dashes toward someone I can only assume is her mother. Though from a distance, it would be easy to mistake Lexi for one of Scarlett's friends. She's not much bigger than her daughter, and with her cutoff shorts and skintight tube top, she's dressed more like a high schooler on summer break than a grown adult woman meeting up with her daughter.

But I'm not here to judge.

"Mama, this is my friend, Elle," Scarlett introduces us a moment later.

"Hi." I wave. "So nice to meet you."

Lexi waves back, grinning wide as she slides her hands into her back pockets. "Likewise. Scarlett told me all about you over the phone. You guys want a ride?"

She points to the open back of the El Camino, and I steal a peek at the man sitting in the driver's seat in his wraparound sunglasses and no expression on his face.

"We can just walk." I point in the direction of her house. "Just a couple of blocks."

"No, no," Lexi says. "I insist. Just hop on back. We're going to Jared's anyway."

"Why was the house locked up, Mama?" Scarlett asks. "Dede said she hadn't seen you in weeks."

Lexi pushes a casual breath between her lips before laughing. "Dede needs to mind her own business, doesn't she? I've been living with Jared. The house just feels so lonely without you there."

Lexi reaches for Scarlett's hair, dragging her fingers through a strand before tucking it behind her ear.

"You look so much older since I last saw you," Lexi says in a bittersweet yet proud tone. "Getting so pretty too."

Lexi's driver shifts his car into park before crossing his arms and making no effort to hide his impatient annoyance at having to wait.

"Should we go somewhere and catch up?" I ask. "We're staying at the Best Western. We were just talking about ordering in tonight, maybe watching a movie. You should join us."

The light in Lexi's eyes fades a shade, and her attention weaves from Scarlett to me and back. I don't mean to make her feel like a third wheel, but I can't let the two of them go anywhere alone together. I promised West.

"Lex, hurry up. I'm fucking starving," her driver says. "Wrap it up."

Scarlett takes a step closer to her mom, threading her fingers with hers. "You're going with us, right, Mama?"

Lexi turns toward the douche in the car. "It's my kid. She's only here for the weekend."

The man grits his teeth before pounding his steering wheel. "Not my problem, Lex."

My heart hammers hard in my chest as my surroundings grow murky. Everything inside of me wants to call Lexi out for not making Scarlett a priority, and everything else inside of me wants to go animal on this douche for making her choose between him and her own flesh and blood.

But it's not my place.

"I'm sorry, Scarlett." Lexi's soulful eyes lock onto her daughter's. "Jared and I are going through a little bit of a rough patch right now . . . if I don't go with him, it'll probably be the end of the road for us. And he's letting me crash with him, so that's a whole thing."

My jaw falls.

"Mama . . ." Scarlett's voice breaks. "Don't do this . . ."

Taking a step closer, I start to interject before stopping myself, lips pressed together so tight they burn with all the things I want to say to this woman.

"Maybe we can get breakfast tomorrow?" Lexi asks. "Jared goes to work tonight, and I'm picking him up in the morning when he gets off. I could meet you guys somewhere before that?"

"Since when do you get up before noon on a Saturday?" Scarlett teases her.

"Jared's been good for me," Lexi says with a girlish chuckle as she tosses a smirk his way. Releasing her daughter's hand, she fusses with her thin blonde hair, sweeping it into a messy bun and securing it with a leopard-print scrunchie.

"Our time here is limited," I say.

Jared revs his engine before cranking his classic-rock radio station so loud we have to shout to hear one another.

"I'm sorry, Scar." Lexi cups her daughter's face in her hands before leaning in and kissing her forehead. "Tomorrow at seven. Let's meet at Joe's Café on the square. You can tell me all about New York and everything then, okay?"

With that, Lexi climbs back into Jared's mustard-yellow El Camino, leaving us in a trail of exhaust.

"I'm so sorry, Scarlett," I say.

She sniffs before grabbing her suitcase. "For what?"

I try to find the right response, only it escapes me. I can't relate to her situation—not even close. My mother is the opposite of hers in every aspect of the word.

We check into the hotel a few minutes later, settling into our two-queen room. When Scarlett heads to the bathroom to change for the pool, I take a second to text West.

If anyone can salvage this, it's Superman.

CHAPTER TWENTY-SEVEN

WEST

"Mr. Maxwell." Stanford, the gray-eyed bartender at the Winslow Hotel, places a linen cocktail napkin before me. "Long time no see. Will we be having the usual tonight?"

I glance around the half-filled room, giving him a tight nod. It's been months since I've set foot into civilization on a Friday night.

He drops a rounded ice cube into a crystal tumbler before pouring two fingers of Macallan single malt.

"Thank you." I take a sip and settle in, trying not to think about what's currently taking place thousands of miles from here. While I trust Elle to have Scarlett's best interests at heart and to keep a close watch on her, there's no guarantee Scarlett won't see her mother and suddenly grow a wild hair.

Granted, she's been on her best behavior all week, and I've been making an effort to use positive reinforcement over verbal lashings.

But anything could happen.

I'm halfway finished with my drink when my phone buzzes in my jacket. Sliding it from the interior pocket, I'm met with a text from Elle that makes my heart stop short for a second.

ELLE: You weren't wrong about Lexi.

A longer text follows.

ELLE: She wasn't home when we got there, but we ran into her on the way to the hotel. She ditched Scarlett for her boyfriend, but told her she'd meet up with her in the morning for breakfast. Our girl is crushed.

Our girl.

ELLE: She's wanting to catch up with her friends, but she doesn't have anyone's numbers since they're in her old phone . . . any chance you might still have that somewhere?

I drag a hard breath into my tight chest, rapping my fingers against the wood bar top. I have her old phone in a drawer in my home office somewhere. The battery is surely dead by now.

ELLE: I told her we could get pizza and watch a movie at the hotel, but I know she's absolutely crushed. She was so looking forward to this . . .

Elle's right.

When I sprang the surprise trip on Scarlett this morning, I'd never seen her blue eyes so lit. Every part of her came to life, and she hugged me.

She's never hugged me.

While I'm not thrilled with the idea of Scarlett meeting up with her ragtag group of Whitebridge friends, this was part of the deal. And as long as Elle is there to supervise, I'll allow it. Besides, she deserves a distraction from the pain of being ditched by her own mother.

ME: I'll be home in an hour. I'll see what I can dig up.

ELLE: Thank you so much, West. I knew you'd come through.

I finish my drink and return home to an empty, quiet apartment to follow through with my promise. There isn't a fiber of my soul that longs to be in Whitebridge, Nebraska—but the smallest part of me can't help but wonder if I'm missing out.

CHAPTER TWENTY-EIGHT

ELLE

The hotel room is filled with the scent of delivery pizza and the sound of giggling teenage girls. Earlier tonight, West came through for Scarlett, sending me a handful of phone numbers he found in her old phone. She managed to get ahold of two friends—Katie and Mackenzie—and we invited them over for a girls' night.

Settled in with a book on the balcony, I'm doing my best to give them space while also leaving the sliding door cracked enough to hear what's going on.

So far they've discussed a pregnant classmate, a beloved gym teacher who passed in a car accident last month, and Katie's psychotic stepmom (among other things). While Katie wears far too much makeup for a girl her age and Mackenzie's wardrobe choices leave little to the imagination, they don't seem nearly as awful as West made them out to be.

"Hey, I just got a text from Clay Briggs," one of the girls says.

I glance up from my book, ears perked.

"He says we should come over after ten. His mom goes to work then, and he'll have the whole house to himself," she adds. "And his older brother said he'd get some . . . *stuff.*"

Ugh.

"Oh my God. Let's do it. My parents think I'm staying at your place tonight. Just tell them you're staying at mine," the other girl says. "Scarlett, you're *so* coming with us!"

I brace myself for Scarlett's answer.

"Yes, you have to!" the first girl says.

I steal a glimpse from the corner of my eye, watching the girls bounce on the bed in premature excitement as they close in on Scarlett. One of the worst things you can do to a teenager is make them feel like they'll miss out on something epic, and it's been months since she's been truly included by anyone her age.

"Scarlett, come *onnnnn,*" the girls whine in near unison.

Closing my book, I head on in to intervene. If Scarlett tells them no, she'll incinerate into a pile of humiliated ash and forever be labeled "lame" by her peers.

"Hey, girls." I offer a soothing smile. "It's getting a little late, and Scarlett and I have a breakfast date with her mom in the morning."

Katie and Mackenzie exchange looks before sliding off the bed.

"Maybe you can see each other again tomorrow for a bit?" I walk them to the door and wait as they shuffle and slide into their respective flip-flops and sandals. "We'll be in town until Sunday afternoon."

"Yeah, we should hang out again before I go," Scarlett pipes up.

Katie shrugs.

Mackenzie checks her phone before nudging Katie and whispering something under her breath—probably related to that party.

"Bye, Scarlett," Katie says as she gets the door.

Mackenzie gives a parting wave.

Neither seems enthused about hanging out with her again. Girls that age can be so fickle and opportunistic. I get the sense that perhaps

Scarlett's return has already lost its novelty and they'd rather keep their Saturday-night options open.

"Thanks for coming, girls," I say when I show them out. Biting my tongue, I resist the urge to tell them to make good choices. I don't need to embarrass Scarlett any further.

The heavy door shuts with a slam just as the hotel AC kicks on.

"I know it feels like you're missing out on—" I begin to say to Scarlett. But before I can finish my words of wisdom, she flicks the bedside lamp off, climbs under the covers, and rolls over.

All right, then.

Grabbing my pajamas, I wash up for bed before doing the same, taking a moment to send a photo of a sleeping Scarlett to her uncle. Something tells me it'll help him rest a little easier tonight.

———

My stomach is clenched as we walk through the door of Joe's Café Saturday morning. I'm almost afraid to scan the little diner for Lexi's face, because every part of me expects her to be MIA. Only my fears are squashed the instant Scarlett squeals and dashes toward a corner booth where Lexi is waiting, bright eyed and grinning. Hopping up, Lexi greets her daughter with a bear hug before motioning for me to join them.

Sliding into the booth, I slip my purse down my shoulder and marvel at the way the two of them act like nothing happened last night. Lexi's hair is still shower damp, her clothes smell like they're fresh out of a dryer, and her lips shine with a coat of lip balm.

"I just can't get over how grown you look." Lexi fawns over Scarlett, playing with her hair.

Scarlett pretends to be annoyed, rolling her eyes despite the beaming smile overtaking her mouth.

"Whatever, Mama," she says. "It's only been four months. You act like it's been years."

"Are you hungry?" Lexi changes the subject before reaching for a couple of menus from behind the napkin rack. She hands one to Scarlett and the other to me. "They've got the best blueberry pancakes. Remember those, baby? They were your favorite."

"Actually, it was the chocolate chip," Scarlett says.

Lexi chuckles, splaying a hand over her thin décolletage. "Oh my goodness. You're right. How could I have mixed those up?"

"It's okay, Mama." Scarlett rests her head on Lexi's shoulder for a moment. Side by side, it'd be easy to mistake these two for sisters. Same big blue eyes, same pointed chin, same expressive eyebrows.

A purple-haired waitress with a stained smock ambles up to our table, pulling a pen from behind her ear as she mutters a half-hearted "Good morning, ladies."

Scarlett orders an orange juice, I request a carafe of coffee, and Lexi gets a Diet Mountain Dew—no ice.

"So how do you know West?" Lexi directs her attention to me. "I don't think I asked."

"I used to work for him," I say.

"Ah. Makes sense." She chuckles. "I thought maybe you were a girlfriend or something, but you definitely don't seem like his type."

I get the impression she's more honest than catty, that she doesn't mean any offense. But once a journalist, always a journalist, so I can't help but use the opportunity to ask a few questions.

"The feeling's more than mutual," I say with a wink. West would totally be my type—if my type were the beastly prince from "Beauty and the Beast." "What is his type anyway? I don't think I've ever actually seen him with anyone."

Lexi rolls her eyes, waving her wrist. "Oh, you know. Exotic super-models. Socialites. Heiresses. The kind of women he doesn't actually have to have a conversation with because they're content just to dangle from his arm like an overpriced accessory. The man's got insane standards.

Nothing's ever good enough. Hell, no one's ever good enough. It's why he can't keep anyone around more than a few months at a time."

Our waitress delivers our drinks, grabs our orders, and shuffles over to the table behind us.

"Just be glad you're too normal for him." Lexi pinches her straw between her thumb and forefinger before taking a generous sip. "God forbid he subjects himself to a real relationship with a real person. Would just about kill him, I bet." She takes another sip. "But it's ironic, isn't it? West desperately needs someone to bring him back down to earth. He's forgotten his roots. That's his problem."

I soak in Lexi's words, taking mental notes and rearranging everything in my mind to fit the context.

"You seem pretty passionate about West's dating life." I rip a packet of sugar and dump it into my coffee before reaching for a creamer pod.

"He's family." Lexi shrugs. "Family always has a lot of opinions about family."

I sniff a laugh, thinking of my mother and sisters. "Amen."

"It's just been interesting, watching this small-town nobody become . . ." Squinting, Lexi pauses. "You know, he wasn't always like this."

"What was he like before?" I stir in my creamer until my coffee turns a milky-cappuccino shade.

"West was always a little different than the rest of us," Lexi says. "Quiet but observant. Big dreams. God complex. Was always wanting more and better for himself. And for Will, too, but that's a whole 'nother story. Guess it's nice that West made it out of here. But it'd be nice if he wouldn't pretend we didn't exist."

"Mama, that's not true," Scarlett pipes up. "He bought us a house and a car."

Lexi huffs. "Yeah. But would it have killed him to pick up the phone once in a while? To visit when he wasn't here for a funeral? Maybe things would've been different. I dunno."

She takes another pull of Diet Mountain Dew.

"Just seems like he abandoned us," Lexi says, voice low. "Kind of seems like it's the Maxwell way. All the men in that family just . . . sooner or later . . . poof . . . gone."

Scarlett's hands rest folded in her lap, her gaze fixed on her untouched orange juice. I don't know anything about West's father, but I don't think it's fair to say Will abandoned them just because he died. West, on the other hand . . . I'm sure there's more to it than any of us realize. He's nothing if not a complicated and layered man.

"It's never too late," I say, "to change things. I recently quit my job. I know it's not the same thing, but sometimes you have to do something drastic in order to be the person you were always meant to become."

"I guess . . ." Lexi perks up when our food arrives, elbowing Scarlett as they eye her chocolate-chip pancakes.

As soon as we finish our breakfast, I excuse myself to call my mother, whose call I missed a few minutes ago. Leaning against an exterior window, I fill my mom in on the latest before listening to her vent about the caterer for a hot minute. Peeking in, I watch Lexi and Scarlett; I never realized how much joy and sadness a person could hold on their face at the same time.

Deep down, I'm sure Lexi wishes she could be the mother Scarlett needs.

And deeper beyond that, I know Scarlett's love for her mother is unconditional.

It's a tragic, beautiful bond.

I finish up with Mom and shoot West a text before heading in.

ME: Finishing breakfast with Lexi.

WEST: Glad she showed up.

ME: Same.

ME: Our girl needed this. So much.

I settle back into the booth just as Lexi is sliding her purse over her shoulder.

"Taking off already?" I ask.

Scarlett pouts.

"I have to pick Jared up from work. He's on nights." Lexi pouts back to her daughter before slipping her arm around her shoulders. "Cheer up, kid. I'll come out and see you next time, okay? I've always wanted to see New York City."

I smile at the empty promise, praying Scarlett doesn't hold her breath.

"That'd be wonderful," I say. "You should definitely come visit. We'll give you the grand tour. Scarlett's quickly learning her way around the city. I'm sure she'd love to show you some of her favorite places."

I paint an enjoyable picture for Lexi in hopes that it makes a trip out east that much more appealing. It should be enough to want to visit her daughter's new home, but Lexi isn't a typical mother. I suspect there has to be something else in it for her—like a grand tour as a guest of honor. Either way, I have no problem pushing Lexi to visit. I'll be as relentless as I need to be to make this happen for Scarlett.

Climbing out of the booth, Lexi reaches for her daughter's hand, giving it a parting squeeze.

"We don't leave until tomorrow afternoon," Scarlett says, brows lifted in hope. "Maybe we can see you again before then?"

Lexi winces. "I'm dancing tonight, baby girl. Otherwise I'd be all yours."

"You said you weren't going to work there anymore." Scarlett's voice is low and laced with disappointment. "After that guy followed you home. And you said the younger girls were getting all the tips. And you—"

"Sh, sh, sh." Lexi silences her with an apologetic wince of a smile. "It's better now, baby girl. They even started featuring me once a week."

I had no idea Lexi was an exotic dancer . . .

Dipping down, Lexi deposits a kiss on the top of Scarlett's head before strutting out, and I let Scarlett have a moment of silence to digest the heaviness of this morning. Shoving uneaten pieces of pancake around her plate, she sighs.

"All right. Let's go," she says. Though I'm not sure where we're going, seeing how her friends and her mother have blown her off in the past twelve hours.

I place enough bills on the table to cover all three of our meals, seeing how Lexi conveniently forgot to pay her tab, and we head out. Taking our time, we stroll the narrow, cracked, and pitted sidewalks of Whitebridge. Past sagging houses with scuffed paint. Leaning fences barely containing barking dogs. Barefoot children running through overgrown yards. An apartment building with a foreclosure notice on the front door. A hair salon with a weedy parking lot and a **PERMANENTLY CLOSED** sign in the window. A rusted Hyundai motors along, rolling through a four-way intersection without stopping, its muffler dragging on the road as it leaves a trail of sparks and exhaust.

There's a sad, forgotten sort of heaviness to this town.

I don't blame West for wanting more for himself.

This place is too small for big dreams.

My mental puzzle of West is far from complete, but I'd say it's coming together nicely. For the first time, I can appreciate how far that tyrant of a man has come from his humble roots. Only one question remains unanswered: Why the obsession with burying them?

CHAPTER
TWENTY-NINE
WEST

"Scarlett," I say when the ladies get home Sunday evening, half past eight. "How was your flight?"

I don't ask about her trip, only her flight. Elle kept me abreast all weekend, and I'm well aware of the fact that their time in Nebraska was disappointing at best.

Scarlett wheels her bag across the foyer before pressing the elevator call button. "Fine. But I'm really tired, Uncle West. If you don't mind . . ."

"Good night, Scarlett," Elle calls after her from the front door. "I'll get ahold of you Tuesday, okay? We'll check out that performance art exhibit Indie was telling us about last week."

"Sounds good," Scarlett says before stepping inside the cart.

"Good night, Scarlett. We'll talk over breakfast," I add before she disappears.

My gaze travels to Elle on the other side of the room. She drags in a long breath, a bittersweet, exhausted smile painting her cherry blossom lips.

"I think she has a lot to process from this weekend," Elle says. "A lot of closure. A lot of disappointment. A lot of realizing that the grass isn't as green as she remembers . . ."

Stepping toward her, I close the space between us. "I appreciate everything you did for her, Elle. I'm sure it wasn't an ideal weekend for you, but—"

She lifts a hand, stopping me. "Don't."

"Don't what?"

"Don't make me into some kind of martyr. I went because I wanted to go," she says. "My heart breaks for her every time we're together."

Same. Though I don't share that.

"You want to stay for a drink?" I offer before I think better of it. The weekend was quiet. Too quiet. And dare I say borderline lonely—a word that hasn't been a part of my vocabulary since a lifetime ago. I could use a little company. "Unless you have somewhere else you need to be."

Her brows lift as her eyes broaden. "Oh? Um, yeah . . . no . . . sure."

"Which is it?"

"Yes," she says. "I can stay for a drink . . . but only if you let me pick your brain a little."

"About Scarlett?"

Her mouth twists. "No. About you. Now that I've seen your hometown, I have some more questions."

I roll my eyes and head to the elevator, slipping one hand casually in my pocket. "Always with the questions."

She sidles up to me as I press the call button and we step inside.

Three minutes later, we're in my study, and I'm fixing her a gin and tonic while she browses my collection of first-edition novels.

"Have you always been a reader?" she asks.

"For as long as I can remember," I say. "I was an insatiably curious boy, reading everything I could get my hands on. Old issues of *Reader's Digest* and *National Geographic* at my grandparents' house. Stereo instructions my father shoved in the bottom of a junk drawer. Paperback mysteries I'd get for a quarter at neighborhood garage sales. Boxes of old magazines people would set out with the trash. We didn't have a library in Whitebridge. Closest one was the next town over. I took what I could get."

"What else did you do as a kid?" she asks, sliding a copy of *The Scarlett Letter* from the shelf. "Besides read anything and everything?"

"Kept my brother out of trouble." I huff as I deliver her drink. "I lost track of how many times I had to bail him out of fights or cover for him. My father—when he was around—tended to use Will as his own personal whipping post."

She takes the drink, eyes holding mine. "That's . . . awful."

"That's how it was." I return to my bar cart and pour myself a drink. "Will was a talker. He liked to run his mouth. He was always getting himself into some sort of situation."

"Good thing he had you, then."

I sip my drink. "I don't know about that."

"Scarlett showed me where you grew up—the house, I mean. She gave me a walking tour of Whitebridge Saturday night."

"I'm surprised that place is still standing." The house was a blink-and-you'll-miss-it two-bedroom postwar ranch that perpetually stank of cigarette smoke, spilled beer, cat piss, and general filth.

Home sweet home.

"Whoever lives there now seems to be taking great care of it," Elle says. "They planted a bunch of marigolds out front. The lawn is lush and green. And Scarlett said it used to be a dingy tan color, but it looked like it'd recently been painted a bright white."

"Well, isn't that heartwarming." I take another drink before return-ing to her side to slide a copy of *Moby-Dick* off the shelf. "This one is signed by Herman Melville himself."

"It's crazy how far you've come." She doesn't buy into my attempt to change the subject. "You're truly one of those rags-to-riches, American dream stories."

"Me and a million others." I don't mean to undermine my life story. It's a hell of a story, and I'm damn proud of how far I've come. It's just not what I want to be talking about at this exact moment in time.

"I just . . ." She turns to me, studying me as if she's peering into the recesses of my cold, black soul. "You went from that . . . to becom-ing some internet overnight social media sensation . . . to building a print-media empire. But what drove you from point A to point B?"

"Wouldn't you like to know?" I offer a playful wink.

"Yes," she says, exasperated. "That's why I'm asking."

"Does it matter?"

"I told you, after seeing your hometown, I have questions," she says, angling herself to face me head on. "There are a lot of blanks that need filling in."

I stifle a chuckle at the serious expression blanketing her pretty face. "I can assure you it's not as exciting as you're probably making it out to be in your mind."

"Then why keep everything buried? It's like before you struck it big, you didn't exist."

"Isn't that how it is for everyone who 'strikes it big'? You're a no one until you're a someone."

"Of course," she says. "But aside from your very curated, very trimmed wiki page, the only readily available information about you is that you graduated from the University of Nebraska before growing your influencer following and founding your magazine. It doesn't men-tion your family or your brother or even your hometown."

"I told you before: privacy is priceless." I take a drink, focusing on the vibrant blue gaze piercing back at me. "Besides, none of my followers give a damn where I came from or where I've been. All they care about is how they can get to where I'm going."

"Fair enough." She lifts a shoulder. "But I'm not one of your followers."

"Clearly."

"And I *do* give a damn where you came from and where you've been," she adds. "Because I'm sort of fascinated by you . . ."

"Only sort of?"

She wrestles a smirk. "All right. Utterly. *Utterly fascinated.* Is that better?"

"No. Because it's irrelevant either way. And a complete waste of your time."

"Unfortunately, that's not for you to decide." Elle narrows the distance between us, though I'm not sure if she realizes it. "You're a walking contradiction. Hard yet soft. Closed yet open. Shallow yet deep. The world's most likable jerk."

"Now that's a compliment." I toss back the rest of my scotch, but I'm so enthralled by the gutsy woman before me that I don't taste a single drop.

"I'm barely scratching your surface." Her head tilts as she examines me.

"You've scratched deeper than most ever have," I say. "And I can't be that complicated if you already figured me out."

"What are you talking about?"

"Your article," I say. "Your swan song. You captured me pretty well in those four hundred words."

She squints, as though she doesn't quite follow.

"I believe you used the words *ambitious . . . attractive . . . intelligent . . . wealthy,*" I say. "Really hit the nail on the head."

Laughing, she moves to swat at my chest, only to let her hand linger over my thundering heart. I can't remember the last time I felt this unencumbered in someone else's presence. Every time I'm around Elle, it's like the rest of the world melts away. My outside problems cease to exist. I'm simply present. With her.

Strangely, wonderfully, woefully disarmed.

Her infectious smile wanes as our gazes hold.

I'm an unfeeling bastard, but tonight I'm feeling *something*—which means she's got to be feeling it too.

"What?" I ask. "You have that look on your face—the one you get when you're about to say something profound."

I'm teasing, but I'm not.

I take in her half-squinted stare and the way she toys with the inner corner of her lip and adjusts her shoulders ever so slightly, like she's editing her words before she even speaks them.

Typical writer.

"What are you thinking about, Elle?" I attempt to coax her thoughts out of her.

Swallowing, she clears her throat. "Just trying to wrap my head around all of this. It's weird, right? I mean, a few weeks ago, the mere mention of you would send the entire office into a tailspin. And the way you called me out in that meeting . . . *infuriating*. I couldn't stand you. And now here I am, in your home, touching you, standing so close to you I can smell the traces of your morning shower, and the only thing I can't stop thinking about . . . is if you're going to kiss me or not. And it's all really confusing for me . . ."

My entire adult life, I've always been the one to make the first move. And traditionally, a true gentleman should. But seeing how this woman has stolen my niece's affections, my attention, and my late-night thoughts, why not add another thing to the list?

I cup the side of her cheek, running my thumb along her lower lip. "Do you *want* me to kiss you?"

"Honestly?" She winces in a sexually tortured sort of way. "I don't know if I want you to kiss me . . . or if I just want you to want to kiss me."

Leaning in, I graze her soft mouth with mine. "I want to kiss you—if that helps you make up your mind. So I'll ask again, Elle: Do you want me to kiss you?"

She exhales, her breath sweet and hot like cinnamon yet as smooth as the top-shelf gin on her tongue.

"Maybe you should just do it," she says, eyes clenched.

Removing my hand from her face, I pinch the bridge of my nose and step back.

"What?" She unclenches, though she's still very much braced for a kiss that hasn't happened—yet.

"I can't tell you how many times I've thought about kissing you," I say, dragging her perfume into my lungs before letting it go. "But not like this. Not with you squinting and wincing like you're about to kiss a damn frog."

"Wait." Her expression softens. "You've thought about kissing me before?"

"Don't act so surprised."

"Up until the day I quit, I didn't even know you knew my name until you dragged me through the mud in your meeting. And then, when you came to my house and told me you were a fan of all of my articles . . ." She lifts a hand to her head, mimicking an explosion. "And now. Now. You tell me you've thought about kissing me so many times you've lost track?"

I roll my eyes. "So you've never thought about kissing me? Not once?"

"Until tonight, I hadn't allowed the thought to cross my mind," she says, enunciating each word. "I don't know if you know this, but you and me? We don't travel in the same circles. We're not in the same orbit. I don't even know that we're on the same planet . . ."

"And yet here we are. Having a drink. Ruining a perfectly kissable moment with a ridiculous debate."

"Ridiculous debate? You realize if we kiss, it's going to change everything."

"Only if we let it."

She tucks her chin, lips moving like she's about to say something. "West . . ."

"For the record—and for what it's worth—I think you're stunning. Kind. Generous. And wildly talented." I close the distance between us. "I also think you're a grown woman who's perfectly capable of kissing a man and dealing with whatever consequences may befall you afterward."

Her eyes flash.

"So I'll ask you one last time, Elle," I say. "Do you want me to kiss you?"

As she sucks in a hard breath, her chest rises and falls, and she lifts a hand to her chest as if to steady her heartbeat.

"For someone who preaches about truth and fearlessness . . . I don't understand the hesitation," I say.

Her shoulders fall, and she nods. "No, you're right. You're absolutely right."

"So what are you so afraid of?" I hook my hands on her hips, steering her closer.

"I've seen what you've done to people's careers . . . I can only imagine what you're capable of doing to someone's heart."

She's not wrong.

I've been known to obliterate a myriad of things in my life—but they were always out of necessity. But I can't imagine destroying a single piece of the beautiful soul standing before me.

I cup her cheek once more, lacing my fingers around the back of her neck while tipping her chin upward, until our mouths are angled in the perfect position.

I've never had to beg for a kiss.

"'Perspective is everything.'" I quote her article about first times. "And life is just a series of first times. Remember?"

Her lips angle at one side, flashing a hint of a dimple. "You can't use my lines on me."

I sweep a strand of hair from her temple. "The first time I saw you, you were wearing this tight little sweaterdress. Navy blue. And you had this confident sway in your hips when you walked. You'd give everyone this little finger wave, eliciting a smile every time you walked by anyone."

"I forgot all about that dress," she says, her voice distant.

"Well, I for one could never." I tease my mouth against hers, noting the way her body doesn't brace for impact as I pull her into my arms. "I've waited five years for this moment. I'll wait five more if I have to. Fair warning, though: I'm terribly impatient and awfully persuasive."

"Tell me something I don't know."

I'm fully prepared to be a perfect gentleman tonight despite the uncomfortable bulge that's been growing in my pants for the past hour and the solid case of blue balls I'll be dealing with tonight—when Elle once again does the unexpected . . . and kisses me first.

Her lips melt against mine, silken and warm. Pillow soft and sugar sweet. I circle her waist with my hands, gripping her soft flesh as I hold her tighter against me. Parting her lips with my tongue, I taste her cinnamon mouth and the sharp tang of gin.

It's only when we come up for air that I realize I've backed her against a bookshelf. Wild eyed and in a daze, she gives me a breathless stare, as if she's seeing me for the first time all over again. But I've seen this moment before—I've lived it a hundred times in my head. Only this is a million times better. To feel her, to taste her, to breathe her in.

Burying my mouth against the bend of her neck, I bite a kiss into her creamy skin before returning to silence the moan on her swollen lips. Pressed against me, she writhes at my touch before gathering a fistful of my hair.

Without a second thought, I gather her into my arms. Wrapping her legs around my hips, I carry her to the elevator. Punching the call button with a clenched fist, I can't get her to my room fast enough.

Wherever this leads, whatever happens tonight, the last thing I want is for Scarlett to walk in. Not only that, but Elle deserves more than a quick ravaging in my study, where countless women before her have fallen to their knees to suck my cock without an ounce of self-respect.

The elevator deposits us on my suite floor, and we stumble through the darkened hallway, mouths crashing and hands exploring.

"You have no idea how badly I want you, Elle," I growl into her ear as I pull her into my room and shut the door. "How badly I've *wanted* you."

A break in the curtain on the far wall paints her body in just enough light to highlight her impeccable curves. Pulling her into my arms, I sample her mouth once more before tugging her shirt over her head and tossing it into the black void behind me.

A shiver runs through her, and I trace a trail of gooseflesh along her arm.

Gliding a satin bra strap down her left shoulder, I press another kiss against her hot flesh before unhooking the clasp. She lets it fall to the floor before reaching for my fly and sliding her hand inside my boxers. Pumping my length, she presses her naked torso against me, her wanton mouth silently begging to be claimed.

"You're sure this is what you want?" I need to hear her say it. If she's stroking my cock, she might as well stroke my ego too. There's nothing hotter than knowing the sexiest woman I've ever known wants me deep inside of her.

Besides, I've never heard her so quiet before.

A million thoughts must be running through that pretty little head of hers.

Slipping her fingers through my hair, she bites her lip and nods. This woman wants me.

She doesn't want my money. She has no interest in my power. She doesn't care about the doors I could open for her, the places I could fly her, or the luxuries I could gift her.

She doesn't want a damn thing.

Just me.

"Yes," she says. "You've got me so worked up; I couldn't walk out of here even if I tried."

She pumps me faster, rising on her toes to steal another kiss.

Guiding her to the center of my bed, I lay her down before tugging her leggings and panties down her thighs. Undressing, I examine her in the sliver of moonlight that trickles across my bed.

"You're so damn sexy," I say under my breath. "You know that?"

Climbing over her, I run a finger down her wet slit before sliding it inside of her, my thumb circling her swollen clit. Her hips buck, a silent urge for more. And as if my body has known hers a hundred times before, I glide another finger inside, stretching her wetness before lowering my mouth between her thighs to taste her arousal, to consume every damn ounce of her.

Digging her fingers into my back as I devour her, she writhes and sighs until she utters the hottest dirty truth I've ever heard: "I want you inside of me."

Reaching over her, I tug a nightstand drawer open and retrieve a gold foil packet, ripping it with my teeth before sheathing my swollen cock. A second later, her thighs are wrapped around my hips, and I'm pressed against her slick entrance.

Our eyes hold for an eternity. We've come too far to turn back— not that I'd ever dream of that. But what comes next is anyone's guess.

"What are you waiting for?" she whispers, slipping her arms around my neck. "Having second thoughts?"

"Never."

Plunging deep inside of her, I bury my face in the warmth of her neck as she rocks against me, accepting every inch of my need for her until our mutual satisfaction leaves me drained and her breathless in a way that transcends the physical.

Elle Napier isn't just some woman, and this wasn't just sex.

Collapsing beside her, I'm washed in a warm euphoria like nothing I've ever felt before, and I steal a glimpse of her perfect peach-shaped ass as she saunters to the en suite to clean up—a quiet parting gift to fill the emptiness on the bed. And that's exactly what it is when she isn't with me—a void. One that only she can fill with her radiant warmth and that unapologetic illumination in her eyes when she looks at me.

"Top drawer on the left." I point to the dresser in the corner when she emerges from the bathroom. "Grab a T-shirt. You're sleeping in my bed tonight."

I don't normally extend overnight invitations, but in Elle's case, I'm willing to make an exception.

This entire woman is one giant exception.

And I'm here for it.

CHAPTER THIRTY

ELLE

"Hey, stranger," Indie greets me in our apartment Monday morning. "Wondered when you'd be rolling in here. Sex hair is on point, by the way."

After ten years of best friendship, I should know by now that nothing gets past her.

Nothing.

I wheel my bag inside and lock the door behind me, casually dragging my fingers through my bedhead.

"So?" She pours an overflowing bowl of apple-cinnamon Cheerios. "Was it worth it?"

I haven't even had a chance to ask myself that, let alone prepare an answer for someone else. Everything happened so fast last night. The tension was ripe, palpable almost, and suddenly the wicked glint in his familiar blue-green irises was sending shock waves through my body.

It's the strangest thing—swinging from one extreme to another. While West is unnervingly gorgeous and a powerhouse of a man, I'd never let myself so much as consider him as a romantic option. But as he stood there, telling me he'd thought about kissing me before, that he wanted to kiss me, that he thought the world of me—it changed something inside of me.

"Why are you so quiet?" she asks before I have a chance to gather my thoughts. "This is weird. You're weirding me out. Say something."

West was gone when I woke this morning, but he'd left a note on his pillow telling me to dial three on his bedside phone and Bettina would bring me breakfast in bed. He also asked that I wait until eight to leave so I wouldn't run into Scarlett. My mind instantly flashed to my suitcase, since I'd left it in the foyer before he'd invited me up for a drink. But when I sat up in bed, I noticed it resting beside the door, as if he were one step ahead of me.

"We got caught up," I say. "It just sort of . . . happened."

"Mm-hmm."

"It doesn't mean anything." The second the words leave my lips, they burn like lies. So much for living my truth. I, Elle Napier, am officially a certified hypocrite. I don't know what it meant last night—just that it meant something.

"Would you hook up with him again?"

"I don't want to complicate things. With Scarlett being in such a fragile state right now . . ."

"Is that how you really feel, or is that what you're telling yourself?" She points her spoon at me, giving me side-eye.

"It doesn't matter how I feel—all that matters is how it should be. We got carried away, and it can't happen again; that's all."

"Okay, wait, wait, wait." Indie plunks her spoon against her bowl, shoving herself up from the kitchen table before diving for a stack of magazines on the living room coffee table. A moment later, she fans through an old issue of *Made Man* I didn't know was there. "I literally just read this one the other day. Yes! Here it is. 'The Dirty Truth about One-Night Stands.'"

Carrying it back, she places it in my hands.

"Convenient," I say.

"Poignant." Indie shrugs. "Anyway, read it."

"I wrote it; I don't need to read it."

Looking me up and down, she sniffs. "Yeah, no. I think you do."

THE DIRTY TRUTH ABOUT ONE-NIGHT STANDS

by Elle Napier

That girl you took home the other night? The one with the witty comebacks and stunning hazel eyes? The one who flirted with you for two straight hours at the bar while somehow playing hard to get? The one who tossed back a shot of liquid cocaine before debating whether or not to bite the bullet and have a good time with you? The girl whose kisses made your head spin and whose body got you harder than you've ever been? The girl who casually cleaned up and let herself out when it was all over because God forbid a woman in this day and age suggest seeing you again after the two of you shared an intensely intimate night together?

Yeah, her.

You felt it too, didn't you?

You felt the sparks.

You thought about asking for her number—until you realized you'd forgotten her name.

Or maybe you never asked for it in the first place.

So instead, you watched her go. You thought about all the humblebrags you were going to share with your buddies the next time you saw them—about the hot chick who couldn't take her hands off you. You proudly added another tally mark to your "number." And then you promptly tucked her into the back of your mind with the intention of telling yourself she was nothing special.

But the truth is, one-night stands are overrated.

And if you ignored a spark, you're an idiot. (I say that with love, by the way. You guys know I love you.)

The thing about sparks is that if you don't blow on them, if you don't keep them lit and kindled, they extinguish. And once they're snuffed out, maybe you can light them again someday, but it's never the same. That's why I've never been a believer in second-chance romances: because they never hold a candle (pun definitely intended) to the first time around.

That girl who made you feel alive that night? Chances are you made her feel alive too. And while she slipped out in the early-morning hours, odds are she thought about you on the walk home. She probably thought about you again when she grabbed a coffee, washed you out of her hair, and folded a load of laundry that night. Maybe she thought about you the next day, wondering what you were up to or if you were thinking about her too. I bet she thought about you a week later, completely out of the blue. Maybe she was reading a clever line in a book, and a word reminded her of something you said that night, and she paused, looked up, and pictured your face.

And then there's that question.

That glaring, never-to-be-answered question.

"What if?"

She'll think about you again someday. A week, a month, even a year or so later. Maybe when she's on the phone with a chatty aunt or watching a sappy movie on a quiet Sunday afternoon.

And you'll think about her too, when you pass the bar where you first spotted her chatting up some stranger about her love for the Mets—the very thing that caught your attention long before you lost yourself in her captivating whiskey-hued gaze.

You'll think about her again, when you take someone else home—someone who lacks the blazing-hot connection you first felt with the girl whose name you'll never know and whose number you'll never have, all because she was a one-night stand.

Yours in truth—

Elle Napier

I fold the magazine and toss it on the counter.

"So tell me, Elle—is there a spark?" she asks before adding, "And don't lie to me. I'll know if you're lying."

A tickling flutter spreads through my chest before settling in my middle at the mere thought of seeing West again.

"Unfortunately, yes," I say. "I wish there wasn't."

"How much of that article was supposed bullshit, and how much of it was you?" Indie asks.

Twisting my mouth to the side, I slink onto a barstool and rest my elbows on the counter.

"That one was . . . pretty solid," I say. I wrote it before meeting Matt, after I'd gone through a phase of embracing my young, single, city-girl persona and convincing myself everyone else enjoyed one-night stands, so why shouldn't I?

But at the end of the night, I'd always feel empty.

And I'd be haunted by those what-if guys. The ones I sparked with, the ones I could close my eyes and picture something more with. Those guys were rare, but when it happened, it would always be like a punch to the gut. Nothing stings like wasted potential of the amorous variety.

"So West makes you feel alive?" she asks.

"He makes me feel a lot of things."

"Good things?"

"Confusing things."

Indie chews a mouthful of cereal, nodding as if in silent agreement with her own thoughts. "I can't tell you what to do, but I think it'd be weird if you didn't take your own advice."

Gripping the handle of my suitcase, I wheel it down the hall. "Going to grab a shower."

As I strip out of last night's clothes and step into the streaming hot water, I think of West.

I think of him again when I'm warming a bowl of soup for lunch. And later, when I'm washing my sheets. I think of him that afternoon as I take a stroll around the block. And at night, when I mindlessly page through a chapter of the new book I started over the weekend, I stop to think about West then.

I think about him in a whole new light.

And I ask myself that million-dollar question: What if?

CHAPTER
THIRTY-ONE
WEST

"HR lined up a few interviews to fill Elle Napier's position," Miranda says over speakerphone Wednesday afternoon. "I'll add them to your iCal if you want to listen in. I think there are a few promising candidates we're absorbing from the *City Gent* merger, though. Tom's been speaking with a couple of them. One in particular captures a lot of Elle's conversational, approachable style. I think you might like her."

Elle.

It's been a hellish week so far, and despite the fact that I haven't taken my mind off that woman since I left her in my bed Monday morning, I've yet to reach out to her.

It isn't that I haven't thought about it a hundred times.

It's just that there's no need to rush any of this.

And there's nothing more repellent than a man coming on too strong.

"Thank you, Miranda. Send the writing samples my way, and I'll give them a look," I say before ending the call and heading to the foyer. Any minute now, Elle will be ringing the doorbell to take Scarlett to some art exhibit in Tribeca, and I'd be remiss to waste an opportunity to see her, even in passing.

A minute later, I step off the elevator just in time to catch Elle trotting up the front steps, a floral sundress flouncing behind her as fresh curls bounce over her bare shoulders.

"Elle." I get the door, showing her in.

She checks her watch. "A little early for you to be off work, isn't it?"

It's half past four, and she isn't wrong.

"Taking a break," I say. "I wanted to see you."

Tucking her pointed chin, she says, "Really? Because my phone's been pretty silent the last few days."

"I've been absolutely swamped with this merger."

She blows a puff of air through her cherry blossom lips. "Come on, West. You don't have to do this."

"Do what?"

"Make excuses." She shrugs like this is no big deal, but the disappointment laced through her tone begs to differ. "It was just a hookup. We don't have to make it into a whole thing."

"What makes you think it was 'just a hookup'?"

She lifts a hand before letting it clap against her side. "Oh gosh. I don't know. You said all the right things and used all the right moves, and then I didn't hear from you . . ."

"Right—because I've been swamped." I emphasize each syllable in case she missed it the first time around.

I didn't take Elle for the type to need extra reassurance, but obviously something's gotten under her skin. Stepping toward her, I begin to say more until Scarlett steps off the elevator.

"You ready?" Elle changes her tune, perking up for my niece's sake.

"Yep!" Scarlett flicks her hair over her shoulder before shooting me a quizzical look. "What are you doing here? Aren't you supposed to be working or something?"

Elle's gaze drifts to mine, as if she has the same question.

"We should get going if we're going to beat the crowd," Elle says before I have a chance to answer.

Just like that, the conversation is over.

But only for now.

CHAPTER THIRTY-TWO

ELLE

"So now no one wants to talk to Piper." Scarlett is filling me in on the latest high school drama on the way home from the exhibit. "And one of her old friends invited me to hang out this weekend. Can you believe that?"

"Crazy," I say, half listening. I can't stop thinking about West—particularly his propensity for being hot, cold, or confusingly luke-warm at his convenience. I'd have expected a true one-night stand to seduce me and go radio silent. Our situation is different. Or so I thought.

"Maybe you could put in a good word for me with Uncle West?" she asks.

For the last two days, my thoughts have been a dizzying roller coaster of emotion. One minute I'm analyzing my night with West, and the next minute I'm convincing myself I had it all wrong, that I misinterpreted all the kind things he said, the tenderness in his touch, and the unapologetic hunger in his kiss.

Anyone can pretend they like someone else.

People do it every day.

I lost track of how many times I checked my text messages yesterday, hoping for a smart-mouthed, flirty quip from West to magically appear . . . only to get nothing. By the time today rolled around, my hope had deflated faster than a dollar store helium balloon.

Sunday night, I felt special.

Today I feel like a fool.

I should've known better than to fall for a single word out of his mouth. He's a skilled salesman. A professional liar. That's how he made his millions—by selling the illusion of hope.

"Yeah," I say to Scarlett. "I'll put in a good word for you."

But that's all I'm saying.

From now on, we're getting back on track and making Scarlett our main focus.

Our *only* focus.

No more detours.

CHAPTER THIRTY-THREE

WEST

"Hey, I'm back." Scarlett raps on the door of my study at a quarter past seven.

"You're home early. Where's Elle?" I glance up from my book—an advance copy of some inspirational self-help tome I'm thinking of pushing in July's issue.

Scarlett squints. "Walking home . . . why?"

I imagine her halfway down the block by now.

"No reason." I play it off with a shrug, given the fact that chasing after her isn't an option. It would only beg questions from my niece that I'm not prepared to answer, and given the fact that Elle is currently upset with me, I don't know that there's an answer to give at the moment.

I should have called her.

But I'm not used to having to do that, nor am I used to sleeping with women who represent more than a means to a sexual end.

"Don't you have some homework to do?" I ask Scarlett after she cooks me with the heat of her stare.

"You're acting weird."

"It's been a long week, Scarlett."

"It's only Wednesday . . ."

I close my book. "Thank you for that news flash, but I'm aware."

She rolls her eyes, turning to leave.

I deserve that (for once).

Reaching for my phone, I compose a quick text to Elle.

ME: Was planning on inviting you up for a drink.

ELLE: If that's code for hooking up, I'm good.

ME: It's not code for anything. Just wanted to see you. Come back. You're, what, three blocks from here by now?

ELLE: I don't think that's a good idea.

ME: It's a brilliant idea.

We need to finish our conversation. I despise how we left off on opposite pages of the same book. A single kiss could clear up that misunderstanding; I'm certain of it.

ELLE: And how would you explain that to Scarlett? Me randomly showing back up to have a nightcap with you?

Fair question.

I've been so buried this week with *City Gent* miscellany that I haven't had time to think about what I'd say to Scarlett if she caught on to any of this.

ME: Then let me take you on a real date. What are you doing tomorrow night?

ELLE: Not going on a date with you . . .

ME: Pick you up at eight.

ELLE: West . . .

ME: Eight o'clock sharp. And wear that blue sweaterdress . . .

She leaves me on read, which I interpret as a begrudging yes. But a yes, nonetheless.

CHAPTER THIRTY-FOUR

ELLE

I run my hand down the front of my navy sweaterdress, plucking the skintight fabric that suffocates my curves—and then I promptly rip it off and toss it on my bed. I didn't want to go on this date in the first place, but he blew my phone up all day today until I gave him a solid yes. Wearing the dress would only reward his stubborn persistence.

Not only that, but it's ninety degrees out.

I change into a creamy linen dress with buttons down the front—a number that skews more cute than sexy. And then I finger comb my curls back into place before digging a pair of heels out from under my bed. Only in my quest for shoes, I manage to find a wayward, wrapped Dove white chocolate.

Peeling the foil off, I pop the faux chocolate into my mouth and read the message: *You are exactly where you're supposed to be.*

I laugh through my nose. Am I?

Is this *exactly* where I'm supposed to be? Running around my room like a crazy woman, getting ready for a date I have no business going on?

But it's too late to cancel.

I wiggle into my heels, tuck my phone in my bag, and head out of my room to wait for Prince Charming to roll up on his chauffeured steed.

"I knew you'd go," Indie says from the sofa, her computer perched on her lap as she grabs the remote to pause the TV. "You nervous?"

"I'm a little bit of everything."

Peeking out our living room window, I watch car after car roll past our building. My stomach somersaults when I spot his shiny black car in the distance. Gathering a lungful of stale apartment air, I head down to meet him.

Stepping out of his car, he greets me under my building's entry awning, pausing to drink me in with his enchanting aqua gaze before leaning in to steal a kiss.

But at the last minute, I turn my head, offering my cheek instead.

"Fair enough," he says into my ear after his warm lips graze my skin. "Just know you won't be doing that by the end of tonight."

CHAPTER THIRTY-FIVE

WEST

"Where do you think we go when we die?" Elle asks, peering into the starry sky from the rooftop bar of the Belmond Hotel. A quick phone call to the owner yesterday—a longtime business associate of mine—and he had no qualms about clearing the place out for a few hours. I wanted to take her somewhere special for our first date, somewhere with a view—and privacy. This is perfect.

At ninety floors in the air, with glimmering stars overhead and a glowing metropolis below, it's like we have the whole city to ourselves.

Our own little world.

"I was hoping we could start our evening with a toast." I fill our champagne flutes from a bottle of uncorked Cristal. "Not an existential crisis."

Her glossy lips twist at the side as she peels her pretty eyes from the heavens back down to earth.

"But do you ever think about that?" she asks anyway.

"Not if I can help it." For the first twenty-odd years of my life, death was the quiet theme song playing on a loop in the background. I intend to spend the rest of my years running in the opposite direction, and someday when my number is called, I don't plan on going down without a fight. Lifting my flute, I nod toward hers until she does the same. "To another first."

She clinks her glass against mine, takes a sip, and drags in a temperate, early-June breath as the flickering candle between us turns her eyes an incandescent shade of blue.

"You're getting that look again," I say when she squares her shoulders. "Like you have something profound to say."

"I died a few months ago," she blurts.

Nearly coughing on my Cristal, I place the flute aside. "Excuse me?" If that isn't profound, I don't know what is.

"When I had my aneurysm. I was clinically dead for three minutes," she continues. "And you know what I saw?"

"What . . . ?"

She shrugs. "Nothing. Absolutely nothing."

"Maybe you weren't actually dead. Doctors have been known to be wrong once in a while . . ."

Elle shakes her head in disagreement.

"You read all of these stories about near-death experiences and people seeing bright lights and loved ones and feeling pure peace and seeing colors that don't exist on this earth—but no one ever talks about the black void." She reaches for her flute, swirling the golden liquid but not taking a sip. "It makes me think that this could be all there is, you know? This one life. I mean, no one knows anything for sure, but what if this is all we get? One chance at this."

"If that's all we get, then that's all we get. Nothing we can do about that."

The wind tousles her hair, and she sweeps a wayward curl from the side of her face before her pretty gaze is replaced with a far-off look.

"I made a promise to myself last month," she says. "To engage only in the things that give my life meaning and joy and purpose. So if I'm here with you now, it's because this means something to me." With a slight chuckle, she adds, "I don't know *what* it means, but it means *something*."

"Likewise."

"I don't want superficial, West." She tilts her head. "Five-dollar champagne on your rooftop would've been just as lovely as all of this. Not that this isn't wonderful. But you don't have to impress me with things like this."

"Isn't that the entire point of dating? To impress each other?"

"On some level, yes," she says. "But I just mean, your life is so curated and filtered and perfect. And if you want to date me, you're going to have to let your guard down."

"I've let my guard down with you more than you realize."

"You let your guard down only when it's convenient for you," she says. "Only when you feel like it."

I toss back a mouthful of champagne, swallowing the resentment I harbor at that statement.

"So for the sake of meaningful conversation and getting to know each other a little better . . . tell me, West: Where do you think we go when we die?" She sits straighter, studying me, waiting patiently for my response.

I contemplate my answer before offering a simple "I think we become stardust."

"That's it? Poof—stardust?"

"Poof. Stardust."

While the idea of my brother looking down on us from some paradise in the sky sounds awfully reassuring, I can't bring myself to subscribe to such an idealistic notion. If he does exist in some other dimension, I only hope he's far away from my parents—who are likely bickering from here to eternity.

"Interesting." She rests her chin on top of her hand, leaning in. "And what drew you to that conclusion?"

"Science." I take a drink. "We're made of stardust—and when our bodies die, what do we become? Dust. Only *stardust* has a nicer ring to it, I think."

"Doesn't it scare you? The idea that one day the lights just . . . go out?" she asks.

I shake my head. "Fear is a wasted emotion."

"I agree, but everyone's afraid of something. So tell me . . . What are you afraid of?"

Disappointing the memory of my brother.

Something unspeakable happening to Scarlett.

Dying with regret.

"The same things everyone else is afraid of," I say. "What about you?"

She sits back, wringing the napkin in her lap. "This is exactly what I'm talking about—your guardedness. You only open up when you want to."

My jaw sets, and I force a breath through my nostrils. "For years, I learned how to answer questions without having to fully answer them, and now it's become second nature. I can't shut it off."

"You're going to have to try."

"I know."

Sliding off her chair, she slips her fingers around her champagne flute and saunters to the railing edge of the rooftop bar. The wind rakes her dark curls behind her shoulders as she leans against the metal banister.

"Why do you want to date me?" she asks when I join her. "When I was in Nebraska, Lexi told me I wasn't your type. That you only dated supermodels and women you didn't have to hold an intelligent conversation with."

I smirk. "Sounds like something she'd say."

But she's not wrong.

"I think it's fair to say I had a type in the past," I add. "Elle, I've admired you from afar for years. And after getting to know you these last several weeks, my only regret is that I didn't do it sooner. You're not like anyone I've dated in the past, and that's one of the best things about you."

Turning, she gives me a dubious look. "I don't know how you can say so much without saying anything at all."

"Ah, so you're wanting specifics."

"I'm a details girl."

"All right." I align my shoulders with hers, leaning against the railing. "You're brave. Outspoken. With a single email, you put me in my place in a way no one ever has. You have an unparalleled sense of purpose and the kind of free-spirited determination most people only dream of. You put others before yourself in a world where most people seem to have lost that ability. And you're a deep thinker in a world where everyone else keeps their thoughts at the surface level so they don't drown in their own feelings. You're genuine, Elle. As real as they come. And my God, are you beautiful. The crazy thing is, I don't think you realize how gorgeous you are—which is another reason I'm utterly entranced by you. Inside and out, you're the entire package."

The city lights flicker in her moonlit eyes, and she fights a pleased smile.

"Was that comprehensive enough for you?" I ask.

She brushes a strand of hair from her cheek and nods. "It'll do."

Cupping her cheek, I drag my thumb along her lower lip before lowering my mouth to hers, taking the kiss she justly withheld from me earlier tonight. The sweetness of champagne on her tongue clashes with mine a second later, and I pull her into my arms, where she belongs.

"You're coming home with me tonight," I say. It isn't a question. "And I promise you, Elle, I'll call you the second you leave in the morning if that's what you want."

"I just want to know this is as real to you as it is to me. I don't want to have to question anything every time you pull back." She peers up at me through a fringe of dark lashes, her gaze melting into mine. "All you have to do is let me in."

She's already there.

Her soft perfume invades my lungs—even when she's not there. Thoughts of her play on a loop in my head every waking minute of every hour. Pieces of Elle occupy the stardust of my soul.

Claiming her cherry-sweet lips once more, I quell her concerns without a single word, because talk is cheap.

And what we have is priceless.

CHAPTER THIRTY-SIX

ELLE

"Why did you reject my article?" I saunter out of his en suite Friday morning, a sweet soreness between my legs, and help myself to a T-shirt from his dresser drawer. Tugging it over my head, I fluff my hair over my shoulders before climbing back in bed with him. Propped on an elbow, I flash a playful smile. "What's the real reason?"

Trailing my fingertips up his chiseled abs, I stop short at the dimple in his chin before leaning in to steal a kiss.

After our date last night—in which I tortured him for hours with meaningful conversation—I feel like I'm making bigger strides with him. Connecting new puzzle pieces. Getting a glimpse of the bigger picture, though there's still a gaping hole in the middle.

"Because I didn't like it." He tucks his hands behind his head, staring at the ceiling fan overhead.

"Obviously," I say. "But why?"

"Because it didn't fit the narrative I wanted."

I could push this. I could push it so hard. I could call him out on his ambiguity until I squeeze an answer from his perfect mouth—but we had such a magical night last night, and I'm still coming down from this morning's orgasmic high, and I'm not about to ruin any of that.

Another time, maybe.

But not now.

"I'm going to hit the shower." He leans up, flinging the covers from his lower body, and makes his way to the bathroom. I take a moment to admire the view.

The clock on his nightstand reads 6:00 a.m., and I debate whether I can sneak down to the kitchen to grab a glass of water without being caught by Scarlett. She doesn't leave for school until seven thirty, so I should be safe . . .

With all of this being so new and unexpected, West mentioned he didn't want to say anything to her yet until he had time to sit down and explain it.

Sliding out of bed, I slide my feet into a pair of his oversize house slippers before tiptoeing down the hall and taking the elevator to the kitchen level. The hallway is enveloped in early-morning darkness when I step off, but I make it to my destination without a sound.

Tugging on the fridge door, I feast my eyes on an illuminated, professionally organized assortment of beverages and produce. Selecting a bottle of Evian from the top shelf, I let the door glide closed before turning to leave—only the second I spin on my heel, I come face to face with a wild-eyed Scarlett.

She screams.

I scream.

My heart free-falls to the floor. "Good Lord, Scarlett. You scared the hell out of me."

"What are you doing here?" Her lips are twisted in disbelief as her pale gaze drags the length of me. The mental and physical breeze

I've been floating on since last night comes to a screeching halt before swiftly evaporating into thin air.

Tugging the hem of West's T-shirt, I take a step back.

"Did you sleep with my uncle?" Her jaw sets, and her arms fold across her chest. "Oh my God. You did. You slept with Uncle West."

"Scarlett, I'm so sorry," I say. "I'm sorry you had to find out like this."

"I knew it. I knew you were on his side."

"This isn't about sides . . ."

"You were probably telling him every single thing we talked about, every single thing I did, everything I told you in confidence," she says.

"Not at all, Scarlett. It wasn't like that—"

"Then what? Were you using me to get to him?" She spits her words in a heated frenzy, dragging her hand through her hair before grabbing a fistful. "Was the whole mentor thing just a way to—"

"God, no." I splay my hand over my chest. "Scarlett, on my life, none of that is true. Your uncle and I . . . it just sort of happened."

She rolls her eyes, refusing to look at me. "How long have you two been hooking up behind my back?"

Her entitlement to this information bewilders me, but I restrain a reaction. She's in shock. She feels betrayed and kept out of the loop.

"Not long," I say. I begin to elaborate until a tall figure fills the kitchen doorway and flicks on the lights.

Not only is the dark room suddenly illuminated—but so is the clenched expression on West's face when he sees what's going on.

"I'm so sorry," I say. "I was just grabbing a water . . . I didn't know she'd be up."

"You're such a liar, Uncle West," Scarlett says to him, eyes brimming with tears. "You didn't hire her to mentor me; you hired her to spy on me. She's not here for my benefit—she's here for yours. Mama was right about you. You only care about yourself."

"I told you that's not true," I say to her, before turning to West. "West, I told her that wasn't true; I—"

He lifts a hand to silence me.

The dark countenance on his face is one I've seen before in the boardroom: disappointment. The jovial mood he was in earlier this morning has deserted him, replaced with a furious glint in his eye and a heavy, unnerving silence that suffocates the room.

But this isn't a staff meeting. I won't be muzzled. Or afraid of his wrath.

"I know this isn't how we wanted her to find out, but she was going to find out sooner or later," I interject in an attempt to quell his mood. "Scarlett, why don't you have a seat, sweetheart, and we can talk about this?"

She swipes at a tear, her pointed glare tracking to West and then me and back again. It's going to take a fair amount of talking to convince her none of this was intentional, nor were we going behind her back in any kind of nefarious way. And I can see her point—she viewed me as a friend, a trusted confidante. Now that trust is in question because I'm sleeping with her uncle unbeknownst to her. It's weird, it's sticky, and I get it.

"Scarlett, please?" I ask, batting my lashes and injecting hope into my tone. "I know this is probably really uncomfortable for you, but let's talk about it."

"That won't be necessary." West's words slice through mine. "Scarlett and I will have a talk later. *Privately.*"

Just like that, he cuts me out of an equation that I'm a part of whether he likes it or not.

West's terrible track record in communicating with his teenage niece was sort of the whole reason I was brought on, but I silently digress. He's clearly not in an amenable mood.

"I was just trying to help," I say. My mouth is dry, but I don't dare uncap the bottled water in my hands. Nothing about this moment is casual.

West directs his attention to me. "It's not your place. Need I remind you, you're not her parent; you're just her mentor."

Just . . . her . . . mentor.

The words land with a sharpened, heavy thud, and even Scarlett gasps.

Maybe I am "just her mentor," but the curtness of his voice reduces me to a rung far lower.

Pinching the bridge of his nose, West exhales. "Fuck. Elle. I didn't mean it like that."

"I should go." I turn to Scarlett. "Again, I'm so sorry."

"Elle," West calls after me as I head for the elevator, but I don't stop.

I grab my things from his room, change into last night's clothes, and leave.

CHAPTER THIRTY-SEVEN

WEST

I check my phone for the hundredth time today.

Elle has been ignoring me for days—deservedly so, if I'm being truthful with myself. I didn't mean to snap at her in the kitchen Friday morning, but Scarlett's blatant disrespect and accusations were getting the best of me. I found myself in a position that I hadn't been anticipating, and I did what I do best—command the situation like the epic asshole I am.

"You going to eat, or are you just going to push your food around your plate?" I point to Scarlett with my fork. "Bettina worked hard on this meal."

I leave out any mention of starving children in third-world countries. The comment would surely fall upon deaf ears.

Scarlett has been a girl of few words lately as well. Only speaking when spoken to and only offering a handful of sullen words. It's impossible to know if she's upset with me for getting romantically involved with Elle—or for not telling her I was romantically involved with Elle. Either way, she feels betrayed, and the foundation of trust we've been building these last few months has been shaken.

Still, it's a minor setback, and I'm confident we'll get through it with a little bit of time and effort.

"I know you think the world of Elle." I slice into my filet as Scarlett's goes cold and untouched. "And I do too. Which is why we need to get past what happened the other day. Once I talk to Elle, I intend to make things right again."

Scarlett sits unmoving, unresponsive.

"Elle is going to be a part of our lives regardless of how you feel about what took place this past week," I say. She may be ignoring me now, but she won't ignore me forever. She's upset with me—and she has every reason to be. But she would never ghost Scarlett. "Your support would make it easier on all of us. Yourself included."

Shoving her plate aside, she slumps back into her seat. "It's your life. Do what you want."

I swallow my bite. "So you're not upset about Elle and me?"

She lifts a shoulder. "What's it matter? You're just going to screw it up."

"Not this time."

Scarlett chuffs. "If you say so."

I take another bite, contemplating her mood, though it's a futile effort. Every time I think I have an idea what she's thinking, she throws me for a loop.

"Are you worried you'll never see her again if things don't work out between us?" I ask.

Releasing a breath that sinks her shoulders, she says, "I guess."

"I take it you're not upset with Elle anymore?"

She rolls her eyes. "I don't know. This whole thing is weird, and I really don't want to talk about it. Can I please be excused?"

My gaze flicks to her untouched meal. "Yes."

Wasting no time, she shoves herself out from the table and trots off, arms crossed. I finish my dinner alone, and in the deafening silence my thoughts veer toward tomorrow—the thirteenth anniversary of Will's passing. While I'm not a man of tradition, I've always taken that day each year to reflect and do something in his memory—always alone, always watching *The Karate Kid* (Will's favorite) and ordering Thai take-out (also Will's favorite). One of these days—when Scarlett and I are on more affable terms—I intend to include her in that tradition. Until then, if I could spend the day with Elle and Scarlett, it'd be a symbolic gesture, a step in the right direction. Will would've loved Elle. He'd have given her shit to see if she could roll with the punches, and I imagine she'd go head to head with his one-liners without missing a beat.

"Scarlett," I call out, hoping to catch her before she boards the elevator.

"Yeah?" She pokes her head in the doorway a second later, her tone making no bones about the inconvenience.

"Have you texted Elle lately?" I ask. "In the last few days?"

Hesitating, she nods. "I did . . . this morning, actually. Why?"

"Did she respond?"

"Nope." She folds her arms. "She's probably done with us . . . I don't blame her. We were so cruel to her on Friday, and all she's ever been is kind to us."

It's the most Scarlett's said in days—and she isn't wrong.

Dragging my hand along my tight jaw, I contemplate my next move. It's one thing for Elle to ignore me, but she would never abandon Scarlett this way.

I owe her an apology . . . in person.

"Can I go now?" Scarlett asks.

Folding my napkin over my plate, I nod. "Yes, Scarlett. Good night."

And then I call my driver, arrange for Bettina to stay a little longer, and make my way to Elle's apartment to grovel like my life depends on it. Because in a way it does. A life without Elle is no life for me.

227

———

"If you're looking for Elle, she's not here." A curly-haired blonde stops me outside Elle's building. "She's at Lenox Hill."

"What?"

Skipping to the curb, she lifts her arm to hail a taxi.

"I'm Indie, by the way," she says, waving at a cab that passes—and ignores her.

"West."

"Yeah." She smirks. "Trust me, I know exactly who you are."

Another cab speeds past without so much as slowing down.

"Why is she at Lenox Hill?" I ask. "What happened?"

"She was having blurred vision . . . a severe headache . . . good Lord." She stamps her foot when a third cab passes. "Am I invisible or what?"

"I'll take you." I usher her to my car, grabbing the passenger door for her.

Indie slides across the back seat, watching me through a side-eyed glance. "You're just dropping me off, right? You're not actually thinking about going in . . ."

"Of course I'm going in." Leaning forward, I tell my driver to take us to Lenox Hill immediately.

"I don't know if that's a good idea." Indie winces. "She hasn't exactly been singing your praises the last few days."

I can only imagine the colorful opinions she's been sharing, but I'll be damned if I leave her in some hospital like a heartless bastard.

"I'll sit in the waiting room if I have to," I say. "But I'm staying. And I'm not leaving until she does."

CHAPTER
THIRTY-EIGHT

ELLE

"Hey." Indie's voice fills my ear, and her soft hand slips over mine. "Sorry I couldn't get here sooner. They said they admitted you. Any updates?"

I leave my eyes closed despite knowing the room is as dark as they could make it. Any hint of light sets the pain in my head ablaze tenfold.

"They did some scans," I say. "Just waiting on the doctor to read them."

"I called your mom."

"Did she freak out?" I'd laugh, but it would hurt too badly.

"Of course. She said she's going to book the next flight here, but your dad talked her into waiting until we know what's going on."

"I bet that didn't go over well."

Indie chuckles. "Yeah, I had the privilege of listening to them argue for about five solid minutes. Solid entertainment."

I'll never forget the first time I met Indie's parents during our early college days. I'd gone home with her for fall break, and by the end of the weekend, I commented on how perfect her parents seemed. They were like the Cleavers—proper and sweet and wholesome. She told me it wasn't an act. That she'd never seen or heard them fight in her entire life. It was one of those weird little life moments that has always stuck with me.

"So . . . don't be mad." Indie draws her words out. "But there's someone here who wants to see you. Any wild guesses?"

I groan. Now's not the time for his legendary tenacity.

"I ran into him on my way out. He was at our apartment looking for you," she says.

My head pulses. I've been dodging West's calls and texts ever since his outburst the other morning. At first, I wanted some space. A little bit of time to separate myself from all the things I wanted to say in that moment. I knew if I fed into his messages, I'd get roped back in by his charming ways.

All I wanted was a little more time to figure things out.

And I wanted him to know I'm not a doormat—that he can't speak to me the way he speaks to everyone else in his life and have me come crawling back the instant he apologizes.

As of last night, I was undecided about moving forward or pulling the plug on whatever this is—but then I woke up with a massive head-ache and blurred vision this morning, and now here I am.

"He said he'd hang out in the waiting room if you didn't want to see him," Indie says. "But he's not leaving. He made that clear."

I'd expect nothing less . . .

With eyes squeezed tight, I exhale a hard breath. "Send him in."

The soft tap of Indie's sneakers against the tile floor grows faint, replaced a few seconds later with the familiar steadfast pats of designer dress shoes.

Squinting, I peer at his dark shadow as he takes the chair beside my hospital bed. Without a word, he slides his hand over mine. The quiet beeping of the heart rate monitor kicks up a notch, much to my dismay.

"How are you feeling?" He keeps his voice soft and low.

"I've been better."

"Why didn't you tell me you were here?" There's a vein of concern running through his tone.

"You haven't exactly reached emergency-contact status in my phone," I tease, eyes drifting shut again.

"We'll be changing that the second you're out of here," he says as if his word is gospel. "What are the doctors saying?"

"Just waiting for a read from imaging. Worst case, there could be an unruptured aneurysm they'll have to clip."

"How long have you been waiting?"

"How's Scarlett?" I change the subject because I don't need him throwing his weight around here to get me special privileges. "I think she might have texted me earlier? I haven't been able to do much on my phone."

"She's fine," he says.

"Is she here with you?"

"She's at home."

"Alone?"

"Bettina's staying with her tonight," he says. "I'm not leaving your side until you're out of here."

"West, about the other day—"

"Get some rest." He cuts me off, leaving his hand with mine. "We'll talk when you're better."

I close my eyes, but it's difficult to relax when my mind won't stop spinning with a million what-if scenarios, the loudest of which revolves around the man sitting beside my bed in a rock-hard hospital chair, all but chained to my side. All the doubts, fears, and insecurities that have plagued me since the night West confessed how he feels suddenly seem small in comparison to this moment.

He can be an asshole.

And sometimes he is still the worst.

But other times, like now . . . he's the best.

CHAPTER THIRTY-NINE

WEST

"Elle, it's Dr. Breckenridge." A white-haired man in a lab coat leans over Elle's bed.

She stirs awake, her pretty face pinched as her eyes flutter open. Lifting a hand to her temple, she winces.

In the past two hours since I got here, I haven't left her side. I can't and I won't. It's been my experience that people leave when you least expect it. If I'm here, vigilant and watchful, she can't leave me.

And she can't leave Scarlett.

That girl has already experienced a lifetime of loss and disappointment in her fourteen years. The last thing she needs is more.

Indie wakes in the chair in the corner, quiet and blinking as we await the results.

"I have good news," he says, a genuine warmth enveloping his soft voice. "Your scans are clear. No aneurysm."

Elle tries to sit up, lines furrowing across her brow. "What?"

"No aneurysm." The doctor sniffs a chuckle. "I wanted to get a second opinion from a colleague, which is why it took so long, but I appreciate your patience. I know how unnerving it can be to wait."

I bite my tongue to keep from mentioning that an update would've been nice . . .

"We believe you're having an MBA—or a migraine with a brain stem aura," he continues. "It can mimic the signs of an aneurysm with the severe pain and the blurred vision, so you did the right thing by coming straight to the hospital."

"Are you sure?" Indie asks.

Dr. Breckenridge turns to her and nods. "Positive."

"That's wonderful." I squeeze Elle's hand.

"I'm going to order you some medication that should help with that migraine," the doctor says to Elle. "Might knock you out for the next twenty-four hours or so. Is there someone you can stay with, to help keep an eye on you?"

"Yes," Indie and I both answer at the same time.

Dr. Breckenridge snickers. "I'll let the three of you sort that out. Anyway, Elle, I'm glad you came in, and I'll see you at your next follow-up."

With that, he leaves, and a dark-haired nurse steps in to take Elle's vitals before disconnecting her monitors.

"I'm so sorry, you guys," Elle says to Indie and me. "I made you worry for nothing."

"*Stahp.*" Indie tsks and waves her hand. "You did the right thing. Your doctor even said so." Turning to the nurse, she says, "Ma'am, do you know when Elle's going to be discharged?"

"He'll have to put in the order," she says. "Could be an hour or two?"

"Go home, Indie," I say. "I'll take it from here."

Her jaw falls, and she sniffs. "Yeah, no, I'm good. I'll hang here until they let her go, and I'll take her home."

I'll be damned if she goes home in some filthy city cab.

"I insist," I say. "I can have my driver take you home if you'd like."

"She's going to want to sleep in her own bed, trust me," Indie says. "And I'm sorry, but you can't just waltz in here like you're her boyfriend after the way you talked to her the other day."

"You guys . . ." Elle lifts a hand, wincing. "Please . . ."

Silence blankets the room.

"I'm going to my home." Elle breaks the quiet. "To sleep in my own bed."

Tightness floods my chest. While I understand and respect her decision, it pains me to think about walking out of here tonight without her.

Settling into my chair, I plant myself without another word. If she won't be coming home with me, I'm at least staying until she's formally discharged, and then I'll see to it that she gets home.

"I'm going to call your mom," Indie says, disappearing into the hall with her phone in hand.

"You don't have to do this," Elle says to me after the nurse leaves and it's just the two of us.

"Of course I do."

She doesn't understand. And how could she?

"Go home. Be with Scarlett. I'll call you as soon as this stupid migraine goes away." She slides her hand away from mine. "I will. I'll call. And we can talk. But you should go."

I drag a sterile breath into my hollow chest before letting it go.

Shaking my head, I say, "I'm sorry, Elle, but no. I'm taking you home."

"You and your nonnegotiables . . ." Her lips twitch, as if she has more to add, but the nurse returns with a paper cup of water and a packet of pills.

Moving aside, I take a moment to text Scarlett to give her an update.

ME: I'm sure you're sleeping but just wanted to let you know Elle is okay. Just a migraine. Getting meds and going home soon.

SCARLETT: OMG! Thank god!!! I was so worried!!!

Despite the events of the past week, I knew deep down that Scarlett hadn't written Elle off. She was angry, yes. But it's moments like these that offer perspective.

If something had happened to Elle and the last words I'd spoken to her had cut through her kindhearted soul like a rusted knife, I'd never have forgiven myself.

She deserves better from me.

And that's exactly what I'm going to give her.

CHAPTER FORTY

ELLE

"You're awake." West is blurry from the other side of the room. I rub my eyes until he comes into focus. "Are you hungry?"

It's been a week since my aneurysm scare.

Six days since I let him back into my life.

Four days since I came home with West.

Twelve hours since he gifted me with the kind of earth-shattering, orgasmic romp people only read about in *Penthouse* magazine. These last several days have been nothing short of wonderful, with West doting on me and seeing to it that my every need is met. He's also apologized profusely for the way he spoke to me that morning in front of Scarlett.

I've forgiven him, but forgetting may take more time.

Rising from the work desk he set up in the corner of his master suite, West strides across the room before taking a seat on the edge of the bed. Brushing my hair from my forehead, he dips down to deposit a kiss.

"I'll have Bettina prepare your usual," he says.

While my migraine has long since left the building and my energy is on an upswing, I'd be lying if I said I didn't adore all this extra attention. Plus, I think it's good for West to devote his time and energy to someone other than himself.

Who knew he had a nurturing side?

"Thank you," I say before climbing out of his bed and heading for the shower. When I emerge smelling like his woodsy bodywash with my body wrapped in a fluffy towel, a tray of covered breakfast is waiting on the bedside table.

West drinks me in with his bedroom eyes, his phone pressed against his ear.

"Yes, that's what I said." West speaks into his receiver, though his gaze is wholly mine. "And if he won't agree, tell him we'll walk. We have options."

Last night Scarlett and I had a heart-to-heart about everything. We curled up under a blanket in the movie room while *Gilmore Girls* played muted in the background, and I told her everything from the beginning—about how much I hated working for her uncle, how he convinced me to help him with her, and how I've gotten to see a softer side of him I never knew existed. I assured her none of what has transpired was intentional, and I swore to her that whether or not things work out between West and me, I'll always be there for her.

Scarlett wrapped me in a long, tight hug, and in true teenager fashion, she pretended like everything was cool thirty seconds later.

Needless to say, we're all in a good place now.

I nibble a bite of toast, watching West work—a sight that would've sent me into a frenetic tizzy months ago. There's something undeniably sexy about a man who knows what he wants and isn't afraid to take it.

Contracts.

Deals.

Hearts.

There's no refuting that West has a way of making everyone fold to his whims sooner or later.

"He has until the end of business today," West says before hanging up.

I perch on the edge of the bed, legs crossed and towel slipping loose.

His mouth pulls into a sideways grin as he watches me. "You're making it impossible for a man to get any work done around here."

"I'd be happy to take my breakfast elsewhere, Mr. Maxwell," I tease in a terrible mid-Atlantic accent.

Abandoning his chair, he strides across the room, all but pouncing on me like a lion about to make a meal out of a gazelle. In an instant, the warmth of the damp towel around my body disappears, replaced with cool air and the heat of his mouth against my goosefleshed skin.

Slipping his fingers between my legs, he drags them down my seam before sliding two inside of me. My hips rock against him as his lips crush down onto mine. Without wasting another second, I work his belt and fly, freeing his throbbing cock and guiding it to my slickened sex.

"I have a conference call in a few minutes," he groans against my ear.

"Then you're going to have to be quick," I whisper back, taking a nibble.

Shoving his veined hardness deep inside, he drives himself into me again and again, deeper, harder, faster.

"For the record," he says, breathless after collapsing over me after a mere three minutes, "*that* was a record."

His phone rings, and he slides himself out of me, tucks his still-engorged member into his pants, and makes his way to the other side of the room.

"Let me know when you can pencil me in for another meeting," I say before wrapping my towel around my body and returning to my half-cooled breakfast. "We didn't really get to touch on everything I wanted to touch on . . ."

West shoots me a wink before pressing the green button on his cell phone. "West Maxwell speaking."

West Maxwell. I say his name silently in my head, noting that it no longer sends a nauseating tightness to the pit of my stomach. A radiating heat floods through the entirety of my body as I watch him work, appreciating the way his muscles strain against his white dress shirt and the deep tenor of his voice as he commands the conversation.

Funny how I used to loathe this man—and now all I can think of is how easy it would be to love him.

———

"About damn time," West teases me the following night when I get back from taking Scarlett to an evening production of *Hamilton.*

Settled in his favorite chair, swirling a glass of bourbon and looking every bit the part of a sexy, refined gentleman, he gifts me a wink before closing the magazine in his lap.

We were halfway through the intermission when a uniformed theater staffer pulled us aside and said to stick around after the show because they had a surprise for us.

"I'd have been here sooner, but a certain someone phoned in a favor to another certain someone and managed to get us a backstage meet and greet." I place his drink aside before climbing into his lap.

His fingers lace around the back of my neck as he guides me in for a kiss. A smooth hint of bourbon dances from his tongue to mine.

"What were you reading?" I ask when I come up for air.

"The column you wrote two Septembers ago," he says. "'The Dirty Truth about Open Relationships.'"

"Ah yes," I say, recalling that interesting little rabbit hole of research I jumped into for that write-up. It turns out open relationships aren't as prevalent as people think. And most of those who engage in them are doing so on the down low for fear of judgment. It took me two straight months of asking everyone I knew to ask everyone they knew if they were aware of anyone who was in an open relationship *and* willing to be interviewed about it. "Interesting choice. Any particular reason you're reading that one?"

He shakes his head. "Just grabbed a random issue off the shelf. Felt like being surprised tonight."

"Really?" I lift my brows. "That's not like you to *want* to be surprised . . ."

"A wise woman once told me to take something I normally do and then do it in a different way, and it would change my life," he says.

A smile spreads across my lips. "She sounds like a genius, this wise woman."

"Some could argue that," he says. "Some could also argue she's kind of in her own little world with her own little rules."

"And are you visiting that little world, or are you just passing through?"

His hands settle at my straddling hips.

"I hope to be here a very long time," he teases with a playful sniff in his tone. "Until I outstay my welcome."

Glancing at the magazine on his side table, I say, "Just so you know, I don't do open relationships."

"Good." He presses my hips into his. "I wouldn't dream of sharing you with anyone else."

"Glad we're on the same page." I roll my eyes at my silly pun. "By the way, you still haven't told me why you didn't like my last article."

I cross my fingers that his jovial mood means he'll finally answer my plaguing question.

"You won't let it go, will you?" he asks, once again deflecting the question and turning it around.

"It's important to me," I say.

"The article coincided with the thirteenth anniversary of my brother's death."

241

"I don't understand the connection?"

"It's complicated."

I lift my hands and let them clap on my sides. "So explain it. I've got nothing but time on my hands, seeing how I'm currently unemployed . . ."

"Another time."

Just like that, the man who's been opening up to me for the past week withdraws, tightening up like a crocus in the night.

I climb off him, the lightheartedness of the evening withering on the vine.

"Where are you going?" he asks.

"You say you want to be with me, West. And I want to be with you. I'm giving you all of me, but you're still picking and choosing which parts of you I get," I say. "Your brother is a sore subject for you, and I get that. But that sore subject is a huge part of what makes you . . . *you*. If you keep that locked up, you're keeping the biggest part of you locked up as well."

"I'm *trying*." His shoulders are rigid, and he stares off to the side. "I'm giving you more than I've given anyone before . . ."

"And yet sometimes I look at you, and it's like looking at a stranger," I say. "Like, who *is* this man? You want me to let you into my heart, but you can't even tell me why you rejected my column."

"Does it matter at this point?"

"Of course not," I say. "The reason doesn't matter. But the fact that you won't tell why? That's what matters. Every time I ask, you sideline the question or change the subject or come up with some clever way to not have to answer it."

He drags in a breath that lifts his tight chest. "I'll tell you someday, Elle."

"When? When it's convenient for you?" I throw my hands in the air. "Everything can't be your way or the highway all of the time. That's not how relationships work. If there's no foundation of trust and transparency, we have nothing to build on."

"So you don't trust me?"

"I want to trust that if I ask you a question, I'm going to get a straight answer." I continue, "I want to trust that the West Maxwell I'm getting is the real West Maxwell—not the one from the glossy pages of some bullshit magazine."

I clasp my hands over my mouth when I realize I've taken it too far. I should've chosen my words better instead of flinging them out in the heat of the moment without thinking of how they'd land.

Before I have a chance to apologize, West shoves himself up from his chair, storms out of the room, and disappears into the darkened hall.

His silence is deafening—but it speaks volumes.

CHAPTER FORTY-ONE

WEST

Blazing through the doors of my home office, I march toward my desk
and yank the bottom left drawer so hard it nearly comes off its hinges.
Buried beneath a mountain of miscellany is Will's tenth-grade wood-
shop box. Tracing my fingers along his crooked, soldered monogram,
I think back to the day he brought it home from school. At the time,
it was nothing but a class project he'd turned in for a solid B-minus,
and the teak-oil stain has long since faded, but the pride on his face
when he showed me what he'd made is something that has stuck with
me twenty years later.

Flipping the lid, I take visual inventory of the contents before sort-
ing through them. A stack of baseball cards. A wallet-size senior portrait. His beloved Saint Louis Cardinals key chain. A matchbox version
of his dream car: a Gotham-black McLaren Elva. A copy of his death
certificate tucked into its original envelope.

Digging into the bottom of the box, I retrieve the first letter he sent me after being stationed overseas.

I haven't read it in years.

And I've never shared it with another human being before.

But if Elle wants to know the real me . . . the parts that I keep locked and hidden . . . if she wants to know all my whys . . .

Unfolding the letter, I pore over Will's shitty handwriting with a gnawing burn in my chest, soaking in his words privately one last time. And when I'm finished, I pleat the letter into fourths, tuck it into my pocket, and return to the study where I left Elle.

Only when I get there—she's gone.

CHAPTER
FORTY-TWO

ELLE

I'm almost home when West calls. I thought about leaving a note when I left his study—or even sending a text. But I couldn't find the right words, and all I could think about was that scene in *Sex and the City* when Carrie gets dumped via a Post-it. It all felt strange and surreal and unfitting, because that was fiction and this is real life.

"Hey," I answer.

"Why did you leave?"

"You left first . . ."

The line goes silent.

"And I assumed you had nothing more to say and the conversation was over," I add. "Did I assume wrong?"

A city bus whirs past, leaving a warm trail of exhaust fumes.

"Absolutely you assumed wrong." His words are curt and biting and 100 percent him.

An image of West comes to my mind—specifically the cocktailed flicker of hurt and anger in his eyes when I insulted his magazine, the way he stormed off without a word. He was upset with me. And I was upset with him. With Scarlett being down the hall, our only options were to take our spat to another floor . . . or go our separate ways.

"There was something I wanted to show you," he finally answers.

I almost spit back a brusque *Then you should have communicated that,* which would've been followed up with a tangent about his lack of communication skills. But I stop myself. The whole reason I left was that I didn't want to fight with him anymore.

"I don't think this is a good idea, West." I gather in a lungful of night air and let it go.

"You don't think *what* is a good idea?"

"This," I say. "Us."

"Because of a fight?"

"No." I switch my phone to the opposite ear, gathering my words and editing them in real time. "You're a mesmeric man, West. On your best days you're charming and wonderful and all the things that make a girl all rainbows and butterflies. But on your worst days, you're a padlocked safe of a man. And it's exhausting trying to pick your lock."

He says nothing—whether that's a good sign or bad, it's impossible to know.

"Relationships only work when both people get what they need," I say. "I want all of you, West. Not just fragments."

"Not everyone is an open book." His words are laced with heat and frustration. "But my God, Elle, I was trying for you."

"I'm almost home," I say. As soon as I walk in that door, I'm pouring myself a glass of wine and running a hot bath—in that order.

I don't know what I'll do after that, but chances are I'll lie in bed, staring at the ceiling fan and wondering if I'm making the right decision.

"We'll talk tomorrow, yeah?" I ask.

"What are you afraid of, Elle?" He ignores my attempt to pause our conversation. "You waltzed into my life preaching about being fearless and living your truth and being your authentic self—but you can't even be honest with yourself right now. You're terrified. You're falling for me, and you're scared that this is real and you're going to get hurt."

My gait slows as I approach the awning outside my building, and I let the sting of his words wash over me.

He isn't wrong.

In fact, he couldn't be closer to the truth.

"You're right, West." I stop before going inside. "I'm terrified of falling for you without ever fully getting to know you."

"I shouldn't have walked away," he says. "But at least I came back. You kept walking. Remember that next time you're concerned about me breaking your heart."

"West—"

"Good night, Elle," he says. "We'll continue this conversation in the morning."

The line goes dead.

And I head inside with a hollowness in my chest that wasn't there before and a fullness in my middle from eating all my words.

I pushed him away.

And I did it because I—the fearless crusader blazing through her second chance at life—was terrified of falling in love with the one man who didn't walk when things got hard.

Curling onto my bed a few minutes later, I roll to my side only to come face to face with a stack of books I purchased months ago—*Near Death: A Collection of Essays*, *What Comes Next*, and *To Live and Die among the Stars*.

Each of their spines is flawless and uncracked, their hundreds of pages pristine and untouched.

Ever since my world collided with West's, I've been so busy living that I stopped obsessing about dying.

The irony of this is not lost on me.

———

I'm washing my face the following morning when the door buzzer goes off in the next room. Trotting to the kitchen, I press the answer button.

"Yes?" I ask, fully expecting the FedEx guy. Indie's constantly ordering things online, and she always pays extra for the signature-required option when she can because she's had far too many packages stolen over the years.

"It's me." West's voice plays over the intercom.

When I told him we'd talk in the morning . . . I meant over the phone.

"Come on up." With my heart hammering in my ears, I press the button to let him in, and then I pace the confines of our little kitchen, waiting for that knock at the door.

A minute later, he's standing at my door in a midnight-black three-piece suit, looking like a billion bucks, and my pride is somewhere between my belly button and spine.

Brushing my hair off my face, I zip my posture straight, throw my shoulders back, and offer him a cool and casual "Hey."

"Was on my way to the main office." He holds a folded slip of paper between his fingers, flicking it toward me. "This is what I wanted to show you last night."

Waving for him to come in, I usher him to my room. Indie had a late-night muse-chasing session, and she's still sleeping.

I close the door behind him.

The last time he was here was after my last hospital stay, when he insisted on having his driver take me home so I wouldn't have to ride in a dirty NYC taxi. And while in the car, he also insisted on his driver taking the smoothest streets so I wouldn't be jerked around in the back seat.

"What is it?" I take the creased notebook paper from West, unfolding it before settling on the foot of my bed to give it a read. The date on the upper right-hand corner tells me it's over thirteen years old, and the scribbled handwriting has a hurried, masculine slant to it.

West—

Hey! It's your annoying kid brother writing you from a sandbox in the Middle East. Okay, not literally, but I can't tell you exactly where I am. Just know it's hot as hell, Grandma Iris's inflatable pool sounds like paradise right now, and I will never complain about a Nebraska summer heat wave ever again.

Anyway, how's Lexi? She stopped sending me her weekly emails. Maybe she's running out of things to say. I'm sure Scarlett's keeping her busy. Every time I have a rough day here, I think about Lexi holding down the fort back home and it keeps me sane. Miss them like hell though. I think about them a hundred times a day and I can't stop staring at Scarlett's pictures. I bet she'll look so different by the time I get home. She's got my shit-eating grin though, doesn't she? Ha! I can't wait to see if she grows up to be a stubborn ass like us or a free spirit like her mom. Probably a little of both . . .

My tour is ending in less than three months, so it's got me thinking about all the things I want to do when I get home:

Go to New York City. I've always wanted to see it and I think we should go together. (Would have to be a guys' trip because Lexi hates big cities—they make her feel claustrophobic.)

I want to drive a McLaren Elva—Gotham black, preferably, though I'll settle for magna violet. A buddy of mine said there's some place in Vegas where you can rent one for a few hours. Don't know how much it costs, but my birthday is in October so that should give you plenty of time to save if you catch my drift . . .

I want to climb a mountain. Preferably the Swiss Alps, though I won't be picky. All this sand, sun, and heat is really messing with my brain. Last night I dreamt we were having a snowball fight in Mom's backyard. Then I woke up covered in sweat. It was weird.

I also want to take you to the Pyramids of Giza. Remember when we were kids and you went through that phase where you were obsessed with ancient Egypt and you went as a mummy for Halloween three years in a row? I know it's random, but I think we should go (after I cool off, of course). Preferably in January.

Anyway, the list is longer than that, but my hand is cramping up so I'll save more for the next letter.

Also, I wanted to apologize for what I said to you before I left last time—that I'd never forgive you if I didn't make it back alive to take care of my girls. I know you only want what's best for us, and if I'd have stayed in Whitebridge, I know I'd still be kicking tires and pulling parts at the salvage yard for thirteen bucks an hour. You did the right thing talking me into enlisting. For the first time, I feel like I've got something to look forward to—like my whole life is ahead of me. Might sound silly, but I feel like doing something big.

I just don't know what yet. Call it a gut feeling, but someday we're going to have it made, man.

Your favorite (and only) brother,

Will

PS—Seriously though, if I don't make it home for some reason, take care of my girls. That's all I ask.

Tears cloud my vision as I fold the letter and hand it back.

"Not a day goes by that I don't blame myself for his death," West says.

"You couldn't have known . . ."

"You want to know why I rejected your article?" he asks. "I didn't like how it made light of dating in the military. It made me think of Lexi and Scarlett and all the people like them who have a loved one overseas, who have lost husbands and wives and mothers—meanwhile *Made Man* is peddling active-duty dating apps."

"West, I never would have . . ."

"You didn't know," he says. "And you couldn't have. It wasn't intentional on your part, and I get that. But I didn't feel like explaining it to you that day outside the boardroom. And I didn't feel like explaining it to you the other night, either, because being with you, Elle . . . is the only time I don't feel that gnawing void inside of me that nothing seems to fill—except you. We were having such a good time together, and I didn't want to lose that; I didn't feel like excavating an old wound."

For a sliver of a second, I don't see a boardroom tyrant, a multimillionaire titan of industry, or an infuriating playboy. I see a man. Nothing more, nothing less.

Rising from the bed, I slide my hands up his chest before resting my eyes on his glassy teal gaze.

"Everything you've ever done was for him, wasn't it?" I cup his chiseled cheek as I study him.

"Everything."

I was wrong about him.

He's not a human Fyre Festival. He's just a man struggling to forgive himself, trying to live the life his brother never got to. He's not fake perfect. He's not fake chocolate. He's not fake anything.

He's 100 percent genuine West Maxwell.

CHAPTER
FORTY-THREE

WEST

One Week Later

The Napier house is abuzz with prewedding festivities. Mona is flitting about, calling out orders in her sweet drawl and making sure everyone is fed and on task. Elle's father, Bob, is on a ladder, cleaning the gutters, while two of her sisters make wedding mints and the bride-to-be is chatting Scarlett up in the next room.

It's like a scene out of that movie with Julia Roberts—minus the diabetes.

Settled on the living room sofa, feeling like a bum despite the fact that I was ordered to "relax and make myself at home," I check my phone and handle a few work emails before heading over to the family photo above the fireplace.

Four daughters is no small feat.

I can hardly raise one young woman, and these two managed to raise four of them without issue. Once the wedding dust settles, I'll have to pull Bob aside and ask him for pointers. I only have Scarlett a few more years, but I'll be damned if I screw those years up.

"Bob!" Mona yells from another room. "Has anyone seen Bob?"

"He's outside, Mom," one of the sisters yells back. "Cleaning the gutters like you told him to, remember?"

"Why on earth is he doing that? I told him to clean those days ago. I thought he was waxing the car? We've got to be at the rehearsal dinner in less than an hour, and he still needs to get showered . . ." Mona's voice trails into nothing as she disappears into one of the recesses of their old Victorian.

She returns within seconds, making a beeline for Elle this time.

"Sweetheart, can you please try your bridesmaid dress on again?" she asks with batting lashes. "I just want to be sure it fits."

"And what if it doesn't?" Elle asks, shooting me a teasing wink.

"You know I have my tailor on speed dial." Mona toys with her gold-and-diamond pendant, dragging it side to side on its fragile chain like a nervous tic.

"I can assure you it fits like a glove." Elle places her hands on the sides of her mother's shoulders before leaning in to deposit a kiss on her forehead. "Relax, okay? Everything's going to be perfect—just like you planned it to be."

Mona drags in a haggard breath and releases it with sagging shoulders. A moment later, she claps her hands together, paints a smile on her face, and marches into the next room, a woman on a mission.

"The one and only Mona Napier, ladies and gentlemen," one of Elle's sisters says once their mother is out of earshot.

"If you think this is nuts, you should see us at Christmastime." Elle sneaks up from behind me, slipping her arms around my waist as she hugs me from behind. "My mother puts up five trees. And my dad does a light display in the front yard that people drive from miles around to come see each year. Don't even get me started on the food either. You can't leave here without gaining a solid five pounds."

"Uncle West, Evie wants to know if I can run with her to town to pick up a few things for the centerpieces," Scarlett says from the doorway.

"Yeah, of course," I say.

From the second we arrived, Elle's sisters surrounded Scarlett, bathing her in attention like she was some kind of novelty, making her feel like the guest of honor, even going so far as to call her an "honorary Napier sister" for the week.

We weren't going to come to the wedding—at least *I* wasn't going to. Elle had planned on bringing Scarlett all along. But after a while, the thought of sitting this out while my best girls danced the macarena barefoot plagued me, and I didn't want to miss out on all the fun.

That and I couldn't help but remember Elle mentioning that her high school boyfriend was going to be in attendance.

I'm not a jealous man, nor am I insecure, but there's something about weddings and old flames that makes people nostalgic. Throw in an open bar, and it's a recipe for bad decisions. Not that I don't trust Elle. It's *him* I don't trust. Elijah with the Pacific-evergreen eyes. The one she wrote about in that column about first times.

He may have been her first everything.

But I fully intend to be her last everything.

At the very least, I should be there to serve as a buffer between the two of them should he choose to annoy her with his presence. She's a kind and gracious woman, but I'm a skilled conversationalist—and I'm fully prepared with an exit strategy for any and all encounters.

"You want to see my room?" Elle takes my hand, leading me up a polished staircase, past a wall of family portraits, down a hallway lined with vintage sconces, and into a bedroom anchored with a pink canopy bed covered in stuffed animals. "This is probably the least sexy room you'll ever be in in your entire life, but this is where I grew up."

The faint scent of strawberries and bubble gum fills the air, and I make my way toward a bulletin board hanging over a dresser on the far wall. It's pinned with track medals, prom pictures, and newspaper clippings, and I'm introduced to a version of Elle I've yet to meet.

"You were adorable, and I mean that in a noncreepy way," I tease, feasting my eyes on a picture of a freckle-faced girl with thick glasses and a mouth full of braces, silently imagining her image merged with mine. I was lucky in that I never went through that awkward teenage phase. By some stroke of good fortune, I was blessed with clear skin and straight teeth. "Is this Elijah?"

I point to an image of two awkward teenagers dressed in stuffy formal wear, standing in some mechanical pose in front of a balloon backdrop, her hand on the lapel of his rented tuxedo.

She laughs through her nose. "Yes. That's Elijah."

Maybe it's unfair to say this about a teenager, but the guy looks like a tool. Arrogant smile. Smug posture. Perfect hair. Dimples.

"Speaking of, you're going to meet him tonight, so don't say anything crazy." She turns me to face her, straightening the collar of my dress shirt.

"Elle." I tsk and tilt my head. "You should know me better than that by now."

"I'm serious. Be nice."

"I'll be more than nice. In fact, I want to shake his hand and thank him for sending you straight into the arms of someone who actually knows a good thing when he has it."

Rising on her toes, she presses her cherry blossom mouth onto mine, and I waste no time pulling her against me. I give her perfect ass a squeeze, and she swats me away.

"Later," she says. "We have to get ready for the rehearsal dinner. My mom will serve both our heads on a platter if we miss rehearsal."

I scan the restaurant for Elle's emerald-eyed ex the second we step inside the old barn turned winery turned rehearsal dinner venue.

I find him at the bar. At least I think it's him. He looks vaguely like the douche in the prom photo. Earlier I overheard one of Elle's sisters talking about how Elijah's a dentist in Saint Louis, and the guy at the bar is flashing a megawatt smile in an unnatural shade of ice white. It's so bright it's practically glowing from the other side of the room, like a beacon of light—or a bug zapper.

Placing my hand on the small of Elle's back, I navigate us through the crowded setting, watching to see if she's looking for him too.

"Aunt Candace!" Elle trots toward a woman in a floral jumpsuit. "I haven't seen you forever!" The two make small talk for a moment before she finally introduces me, which then leads to an introduction to her uncle Curt and her cousins Natalie and Natasha (twins), followed by another aunt-uncle-cousin set, as well as her grandparents on her father's side.

When her mother said the rehearsal dinner was for the wedding party and "close family" only, I wasn't expecting that to mean their entire family. Still, they seem like good people, and I'm living for the light in Elle's eyes and the smile that hasn't left her lips since we walked in tonight.

The clinking of silverware against stemware silences the space, and all eyes divert toward the head of the mile-long table, where Mona Napier has assumed her position. "If everyone could please have a seat, that'd be wonderful. I know normally rehearsal dinners follow the actual rehearsal, but in this family we're all a little nicer when our bellies are full."

Laughter drones through the room.

"Anyway, let's eat, drink, and be merry," she says. "And then we'll reconvene at Saint Mary's Church of Hope at seven o'clock sharp!"

I pull a chair out for Elle and another for Scarlett before taking the one between them. The room is filled with love and merriment, and I kick myself at the thought of missing out on this all because I'm not a wedding guy.

Three servers uncork champagne bottles at the foot of the table before filling flutes halfway and passing them out in quick order. In their haste, they place one in front of Scarlett, but I swipe it away before she notices.

"Elle, hi," a velvet voice coos from my left.

Turning, I find Elijah Green Eyes taking the empty seat next to my girlfriend.

"My God, it's been so long," he says, flashing his Day-Glo smile. "You look amazing."

"Thank you, so do you," she says, though I know her, and she's just being polite. No one with teeth so white you need sunglasses looks *good* except for news anchors and aging celebrities with Hollywood veneers.

"Your mom said you're in New York?" he asks, though he's clearly playing dumb. He's had to have googled her over the years, and any cursory search leads to her bio on my website—which I've yet to have IT remove because it makes me sentimental and I'm hopeful she'll write for me again someday.

"I am," she says.

"I'm actually speaking at a conference there next month. I should look you up when I'm in town," he says.

I roll my eyes at the fact that the idiot referred to Manhattan as a "town."

"Elijah, this is my boyfriend, West." Elle leans back, and I lean forward.

"Pleasure to meet you, Elijah." I extend a hand, which he meets with hesitancy. I give it a squeeze, though not too tight. I'd hate to destroy his ability to fill cavities.

He squints, smiling like an idiot as he studies my face. "You look familiar. Did you go to school here?"

"No," I say.

"Huh." He runs his hand along his lower lip, scrutinizing me harder. "I swear I've seen you before."

"Probably on the cover of *Forbes* magazine." I can't help myself. "Or *Made Man*."

Elle presses an elbow into my ribs.

Elijah's curious expression morphs into swallowed pride. "Wow. Yeah. Okay."

"All right, everyone, let's raise a toast to the bride and groom," Mona calls from the head of the table.

Elle lifts her glass, I lift mine, and Mona prattles on with some sappy story about the happy couple that leaves everyone teary eyed and grinning ear to ear. Elijah steals a glance our way, and I slip my arm around Elle.

For the rest of tonight and for the entirety of the wedding weekend, I'm not letting her out of my sight. I'll be that guy for her. I'll hold her purse while she does the bridesmaid thing, I'll chat up all her cousins, and I'll dance the macarena with her nieces and nephews like a drunken fool.

I'll show her that if she only gets one shot at this life, she should spend it with me.

CHAPTER FORTY-FOUR

ELLE

"How cute were you last night?" I say Sunday morning, cozying up to West in our hotel room bed, my sex pulsing from the tongued orgasm he just gifted me.

Evie's wedding ran until 2:00 a.m. last night, but we soaked up every minute of it. When West first declared that he wanted to come with me last week, I was secretly worried he'd be one of those dates who spends the whole night sulking in the corner and checking their watch every five minutes. But I'm thrilled to have been wrong.

"Cute wasn't exactly what I was going for," he says, pulling me on top of him. "But I'll take it."

He drags his hands along the outsides of my thighs, sending a tingling thrill along my bare flesh.

"My parents adore you, by the way," I say. "My dad said he loves that you don't talk too much." My father has always said people who talk for the sake of talking are the worst kind of people. They're trying to distract you from their ineptitudes. "And my mom is smitten with you. She loved that you danced the Electric Slide with her grandbabies." I pat his chest. "How did you know how to dance that, anyway?"

"The lyrics are literally the instructions."

I laugh, dipping down to kiss his smart mouth.

"Mom thinks you're way better looking than Elijah," I add. "So bonus points there, because I'm sure she's dying to brag to all her friends at her book club about what a catch her last unmarried daughter is dating."

"Good," he says. "Because I really fucking hate that guy. Glad to know I'd beat him in a beauty pageant."

"Let's be real—you'd beat every man alive in a beauty pageant," I say. "And a lot of women too. But don't let that get to your head. We don't need it exploding."

"Are you saying I have a big head?" His hands encircle my waist.

"I'm saying you have a healthy amount of confidence and self-esteem."

Before West has a chance to respond, two knocks at the door interrupt him.

"Did you order room service?" I ask. I don't know who else it could be at 7:00 a.m. Certainly not Scarlett—she went home with my parents after my mother told her she could have my room.

"Did you see me order room service?" the smart-ass quips.

Hopping off the bed, I grab a hotel robe from the back of the bathroom door, slip it on, and head for the door. Only when I answer, no one's there. It's nothing but a Sunday paper and the July issue of *Made Man*, complete with a smirking Bradley Cooper on the cover.

"West? Did you . . ." I stop when I hear the spray of the shower coming from the en suite bath.

Plopping down on the bed, I flick through the glossy pages of his magazine, skipping to the section that once housed my column to see who's writing for me now—or if he scrapped the feature entirely.

Only, to my surprise, The Dirty Truth isn't scrapped at all.

Centered on the right-hand page, where my professional headshot once was, is a different image of . . . *me*. One that wasn't taken in a well-lit studio by a professional photographer. One that hasn't been retouched or filtered. One of me standing by the east window of his bedroom in nothing but one of his white T-shirts, my back toward him as I sip coffee and take in the sunrise.

And below it is a headline I never thought would see the light of day.

THE DIRTY TRUTH ABOUT WEST MAXWELL

by Elle Napier

What image comes to mind when you think of West Maxwell?

It's okay if you need time. I'll wait . . .

I know there are thousands of them in existence.

Maybe you thought of that Instagram picture from four years ago where he's riding on the back of a camel, pyramids in the distance and an orangesicle sunset coloring the background? What about the one where he's geared up and rappelling down some snowcapped mountain in Switzerland? Or better yet, maybe it's the January 2019 cover of *Made Man*—the one in which West appeared shirtless, leaning against a gleaming Gotham-black McLaren Elva and looking like he'd just won the lottery, his dream woman, and a one-way ticket to paradise all at the same time, all while push-ing his "Ultimate Guide to Your Best Year Ever."

But who's the man behind the filtered image? Who's the man writing the inspirational captions that make you want to set your alarm for 4:30 a.m. so you're not late for tomorrow's grueling CrossFit session? Who's the man that inspires both professional and interper-sonal greatness with a single square-shaped, likable, shareable photo?

I bet you think you know who he is.

Or maybe you have a general idea.

Ambitious? Yes.

Attractive? Undeniably.

Intelligent? I'd say so.

Wealthy? Does Saturn have rings?

But what lies beyond that? What drives him? What keeps him going day after day? But more importantly, does it matter?

Spoiler alert—no. It does not matter.

I'm about to drop a dirty little truth bomb—you are not West Maxwell and you never will be.

The West Maxwell you see is a marketing machine's carefully crafted version of the ideal man.

Let me drop another bomb on you while I'm at it: the average woman is not looking for her own personal Made Man. Not even close. She simply wants a partner who listens, who shares her interests, values, and life goals—and bonus points if they're not a jerk and happen to be in close geographic proximity.

I'm oversimplifying, but you get the point.

You want the secret to having it all? You're not going to find it in the pages of this magazine.

Save your money.

Save your time.

And simply be yourself.

There may be a million men trying to knock off West Maxwell, but there is only one you—and that, my friend, is what makes you a genuine catch.

Yours in truth—

Elle Napier

The shower water from the next room ceases, and I sit in stunned silence for an endless moment. A second later, West appears in the doorway, a white towel cinched low on his hips.

"You . . . published . . . my article," I manage to say despite the confusion and bewilderment funneling through me.

"I'm thinking about taking the magazine in a new direction. The new *Made Man* is all about authenticity." He strides to the bed. "Which means I'm going to need a killer co–editor in chief. Fair warning, I'm extremely particular about whom I work with, and I have ridiculously high standards. Also, I'm not the easiest jerk to work for, so this person has to be able to hold their own around me. Looking for someone who is fearless, outspoken, forward thinking, and brutally honest. Know of anyone?"

My lips twitch to the side. "Sounds like you already have someone in mind for the job."

Never mind the fact that Connie Marsden with Winlock Media Group called me yesterday to offer me the position I'd interviewed for last month. She caught me off guard, and in the midst of all the wedding day hustle and bustle, I stammered a quick response letting her know I'd get back to her by Monday. We've been so busy I forgot to mention it to West. And to be honest, I haven't had a spare second to give it much thought.

"I do," he says before digging into his suitcase and producing a stack of papers.

I promised myself I'd never work for West Maxwell again—nor would I exchange my priceless time for meaningless work.

"I'm not sure what to say . . ." I press my lips flat, studying his chiseled face and the hopeful yet confident glint in his penetrating gaze.

"I expected some reservations from your end, so I came prepared should you need some convincing."

When he hands the pages over, I feast my eyes on what appear to be printed emails upon printed emails, some of which date back years, others of which date back to as recent as a few months ago.

To: letterstotheeditor@mademan.com
From: Jake Trotman (jaket3399@mailmail.com)
Subject: Dirty truths

Just wanted to take a minute and tell you how big of a fan I am of your magazine. It has truly changed my life. Specifically the dating advice column. I always thought it'd be cheesy, getting advice from a magazine. But your Dirty Truths column is different. The advice is legit and useable. I'm happy to say that because of the August 2018 article, THE DIRTY TRUTH ABOUT BLIND DATES, I finally let my sister set me up on a blind date with one of her coworkers—who is now my wife. We are currently expecting our first kid and couldn't be happier. I never would've gone on that date if it weren't for that article. So thank you, Elle Napier and thank you Made Man.

———

To: letterstotheeditor@mademan.com
From: Chandler P. (thislimehasnojuice@redmail.com)
Subject: on ghosting

Just wanted to say how much I liked the December article—THE DIRTY TRUTH ABOUT GHOSTING. I've suffered with chronic low self-esteem my entire life. Being perpetually single and in my thirties, it has only gotten worse. After a while, it takes a toll on a person to go on a sling of "successful" dates only to be ghosted when you least expect it. I spent far too much time analyzing what I could've said or done differently. I can't tell you how much money I've wasted on gym memberships and self-help books and seminars. But then I read Elle Napier's article and it changed everything. I now know not to take it personally when someone ghosts me because it's almost never about me or something I did—it's almost always about them. And taking it a step further, why would I want to build a relationship with someone who is that flippant about other people's feelings anyway? Elle's two-pronged perspective was exactly what I needed to hear. In fact, I've gone so far as to laminate her article so I can read it any time I need a reminder.

———

To: letterstotheeditor@mademan.com
From: Derrick Pollastrini (dpol73dpol@gotmail.com)
Subject: Doing God's work

Hey, just wanted to say I'm a huge fan of Elle Napier. Wanted to let her know if she's ever in Philly to look me up. Would love to take her out for dinner— as a friend (because I'm sure she's got a man plus her article on long-distance relationships was legit eye-opening). Just want to pick that big beautiful brain of hers. Every month I read her column and I think she can't possibly do better than the month before. And every month she hits it out of the park AGAIN. If dating is my religion, Elle's column is my church. Anyway, offer stands. Dinner in Philly!!!

"This . . . this is all fan mail?" I ask, fanning the endless pages of the thick stack.

"Every last one." He narrows the distance between us, gathering the letters from my grip and placing them aside. "Your work at the magazine was never meaningless. You changed a lot of lives for the better. Maybe not the way you'd always imagined, but your work inspired people to change. You've made a difference in people's lives, Elle. You always have."

Pulling me off the bed, he gathers me into his arms. Inhaling his damp, clean scent, I bask in his warmth, and I lose myself in the very same aquamarine gaze that once unnerved me to my core. Only this time, I'm disarmed. I'm malleable. I'm smitten. And I'm utterly his.

"I love you, Elle," he says.

"I love you too."

It turns out West Maxwell isn't the worst after all . . .

He's the best.

EPILOGUE

WEST

Five Years Later

"I don't know why I'm crying. It's like I can't shut these tears off." My very pregnant, very hormonal wife dabs a tear with the back of her hand for the dozenth time today as we walk from Scarlett's dormitory building to our rental car. "I'm not sad—I'm happy."

I slip my hand over hers and pull her close as we stroll among young adults clad in Dartmouth gear, emotional parents, and a handful of movers hauling TVs, plastic totes, and oversize boxes.

A tearful mother snaps a picture of her young son in front of the entrance to Woodward Hall, stopping to straighten his forest-green baseball cap. He waves her off in annoyance as a group of pretty blondes walks past, eyeing his situation.

"She'll be fine," I assure Elle. "Remember last year? She made a new friend before we even pulled out of the parking lot. I bet she's up there right now giving her new roommate an earful."

Elle chuckles, resting her cheek against my arm as we head to the car.

"I still think of her as that lost, lonely little fourteen-year-old," she sighs.

"Me too."

It took a solid year or so of living in the city before Scarlett truly grew into her skin and started accepting that Manhattan was her home, that *I* was her home. Of course, Elle played a significant part in that transition. But watching her bloom into the Maxwell woman she was always meant to be has been one of the most fulfilling journeys I've ever had the privilege to witness.

But she wasn't the only one who "bloomed" during that period. Elle likes to remind me of this as often as possible. I changed just as much as Scarlett—growing into a man who accepts that controlling every single person in his life is no way to live. Together, the two of them showed me the difference between pushing someone to do the right thing and simply giving them advice and guidance.

"She sent me her schedule," Elle says. "Eight a.m. classes every day. Can you imagine? When I was a sophomore, I was doing everything I could to avoid those."

"She's become quite the go-getter, hasn't she?"

Nudging me, Elle chuffs. "Can't imagine where she gets it from . . ."

Scarlett was halfway through her senior year at Highland Prep when she announced she wanted to major in social psychology at Dartmouth with a minor in human development. Marching around my office with a college-admissions booklet in her hand, she told me all about her big plans, and I sat back, listening in awe and marveling at the driven young woman she'd become.

Last year, during winter break, Elle and I shared the news that we were expecting our first child together, praying Scarlett wouldn't feel displaced in any weird sort of way, only she blew both our minds when she squealed with joy and said she couldn't wait . . . to help us raise the child. Teasing that we were two of the most intense people she'd ever met (in our own special ways), she quoted some professor and declared that it was paramount that we not "mess this child up."

As soon as she's finished with her undergrad, Scarlett intends to pursue a graduate degree in clinical counseling. She hopes to specialize in adolescents and teens who struggle with abandonment issues or major life changes, much like she did.

Something tells me she'll make one hell of a therapist. She never used to miss a thing—and she still doesn't.

Approaching our rental car, I trot ahead to get the door for my wife, getting her settled before skipping to the driver's side and cranking the air the second the engine roars to life. Should she melt in this ninety-degree heat, I'll hear all about it from here to the airport. She claims being pregnant in the summertime is like having someone bump your personal thermostat up ten degrees every time you step outside.

I'll take her word for it.

"Think we have time to stop at that Thai place off Main Street?" she asks as we pull away from the dorm parking lot and head toward the heart of Hanover. When she rubs her swollen belly, her diamond glints in the midday sun. "Little guy's extra hungry today."

Warmth blankets me as I reach for her hand, giving it a squeeze.

"What kind of man would I be if I deprived my beautiful wife of her favorite som tum?" I wink, flicking on my turn signal.

Our scheduled departure isn't for a few more hours, and even then, I have half a mind to cancel it and stick around here for a few more days. Something about going home to an empty town house devoid of Scarlett's blaring pop music, shuffling sneakers, and toast crumbs in the kitchen makes me want to linger in this place a little longer. Besides, the hectic schedule that awaits us back in the city isn't going anywhere. Work will be there when we get back.

"What do you think about naming him William?" Elle asks, turning to me. "We could call him Liam for short. It'd be a way to honor your brother while also letting him be his own person and blaze his own trail."

I contemplate her suggestion in silence.

For months, we've been mulling over a mile-long list of monikers, researching meanings and scribbling the ones that go well with our last name. We've come close to settling on a few, but ultimately we end up with reservations and go back to the drawing board. The names never feel right. They're never special enough. They never give us that spark of contented perfection we're looking for.

I thought about suggesting it to her before, but I know this woman's heart, and she'd have said yes for the sole purpose of making me happy. This child is just as much hers as it is mine, and his name should be a reflection of that.

"It's brilliant," I say, settling into the idea. "Liam it is."

Bringing her hand to my lips, I deposit a kiss.

"I love you," she says.

"I love you more."

"It's not a competition . . . ," she teases.

"You're right," I say. "It's not a competition. It's simply the truth."

ACKNOWLEDGMENTS

Many thanks to my editor at Montlake, Lauren Plude, for her contagious enthusiasm and unwavering love of shaping ideas into the best versions of themselves. And to my developmental editor, Lindsey Faber. Your knack for finding little details to bring full circle is unparalleled, and this has truly been an enjoyable developmental-editing experience. The two of you together are an editorial dream team, and I am so excited to do this all over again soon!

To my incredible agent, Jill Marsal, thank you for your tireless efforts and for making this happen. I can't wait to see where we go from here!

To my readers, who have supported me from day one and have stayed with me through this whirlwind journey I've been on since 2015, thank you, thank you, thank you! I could not do this without any of you. I read all your reviews, all your messages, and all your emails. I'm beyond grateful that you make time in your life and space in your head for my stories.

To Neda Amini of Ardent Prose and to the bloggers and bookstagrammers, librarians, and reviewers who help spread the word about my work, thank you! You are such a vital part of the book community, and your efforts do not go unnoticed.

To my parents, friends, and family, and to my husband and our three kids—your support gives me life. I love you.

Lastly, to you, dear reader. Thank you for making room in your life for *The Dirty Truth*. I hope you enjoyed my book from the minute you cracked the spine to the second you read the final word.

ABOUT THE AUTHOR

Photo © 2017 Jill Austin

Wall Street Journal and #1 Amazon bestselling author Winter Renshaw is a bona fide daydream believer. She lives somewhere in the middle of the USA and can rarely be seen without her notebook and laptop. When she's not writing, she's thinking about writing. And when she's not thinking about writing, she's living the American dream with her husband, three kids, the laziest puggle this side of the Mississippi, and a busy pug pup that officially owes her three pairs of shoes, one lamp cord, and an office chair.

Winter also writes psychological and domestic suspense under her Minka Kent pseudonym. Her first book, *The Memory Watcher*, hit #9 in the Kindle Store, and her follow-up, *The Thinnest Air*, hit

#1 in the Kindle Store and spent five weeks as a *Washington Post* bestseller.

She is represented by Jill Marsal at Marsal Lyon Literary Agency.

Visit her website at www.winterrenshaw.com, or connect with her on Facebook at www.facebook.com/authorwinterrenshaw or on Instagram (@winterrenshaw).